GODDESS OF WAR

AN ILLUMINATI NOVEL

SLMN

Kingston Imperial

Goddess of War Copyright © 2020 by Kingston Imperial 2, LLC

Printed in the United States of America

Rights Department, 144 North 7th Street, #255 Brooklyn N.Y. 11249

First Edition:

Book and Jacket Design: Damion Scott

Cataloging in Publication data is on file with the library of Congress

ISBN 9780998767437 (Trade Paperback)

1

The enveloping rush of the freezing water was brutal. The current tossed her body about like a rag doll, filling her lungs and stealing her breath. She opened her eyes. The water was clouded with blood. Everything was tainted crimson.

She was dying.

It ought to have hurt more, but the only pain she felt was existential; a deep, stabbing in her heart; the pain of betrayal.

A hand reached through the crimson darkness and seized her wrist.

She woke up, gasping and flailing her arms.

"Baby, baby, I'm here. Relax, I got you," Hector, her husband, said. His voice was calm, soothing. He wrapped her in an embrace. Faith clung to him like she was still drowning. The dream was *so* real; her body prickled with goosebumps. She shivered uncontrollably.

"The same one?"

She nodded.

He sighed and kissed her on the forehead.

"It's okay. We'll get through this."

"What if we don't? The dreams... They're getting worse every night. I'm going out of my mind."

"I'll get your meds."

She bristled, pulling out of his arms.

"No. I don't want them." But Hector was already out of bed and heading for the bathroom.

He paused in the doorway.

"They'll help," he promised.

Faith sank back down into the damp sheets, running her hand through her hair. Her fingers lingered on the scarred indentation around her right temple.

"What's wrong with me?" The question wasn't meant to be answered. It was pitched so low the words were barely vocalized.

Hector came back and handed her a small glass of water along with her pill. She took it, chasing the foul tasting pharmaceutical with lukewarm water and handed back the glass.

He sat down on the edge of the mattress. "You want to tell me about it?"

"Not really," she admitted, "I was drowning again... It's so vivid, Bry, and getting worse. This time... I swear... a hand came up from below and *grabbed* me. Like it wanted to keep me under."

"A hand? Whose? Did you see anyone down there?"

Faith shook her head. "The water's so cloudy... filled with blood, it's impossible..."

Hector pulled her close, then lay down, her head on his chest, and gentled her fears with soft, soothing strokes across her hair.

"Let it go."

He began to sing softly. It was something that had always worked before, but not this time.

The dreams were so much worse.

Nothing was going to be the same again.

It couldn't be.

After a few minutes, she felt Hector's breathing change, shallow against her skin, and knew he was asleep.

She put her hand to her mouth and spit the pill into her palm.

She didn't need anything to make her sleep.

She never wanted to sleep again.

Her daily routine had become mind-numbingly monotonous, but Faith never complained. There was a certain kind of security to the repetition; knowing her place in the world and knowing what to expect was a far cry from the turmoil inside of her.

"Jada, honey, wake up. Time for school," she called through, same as every day, same pitch, same time. Her timbre was etched in the walls in the hallway. I the wind blew just right, you could hear a soft echoing of her words, like a needle stuck in a groove crackling and popping with dust.

Jada slowly peeled herself from her small bed as Faith watched her, smiling. At four years old, she was her mother's miniature—except Jada's long black hair fell down to her waist, a gift from Hector's side of the family. Faith had an Egyptian gold skin tone that glazed her 5'9" svelte frame; her button nose and catlike eyes lent an uncanny resemblance to a certain pop star. Or at least she liked to think so.

Her eyes were barely open before Jada was asking the same question she'd asked last night, lights out. "Can I get my ears pierced? Jamie has hers pierced and she said it didn't hurt," Jada's voice was still groggy from sleep. No doubt the question had been dancing through her little head all night.

"Brush your teeth, sweetheart. We'll talk about it later."

"Which isn't a no," the little girl grinned.

"And isn't a yes, either," Faith grinned right back at her.

Faith padded back to her bedroom in her bra and panties as Hector passed her in the hallway, same as he did every morning, heading for the kitchen. Life was all about these little habits. Every time she saw her husband, her heart hummed like the soulful beginning of a Motown love song. He was what every woman looked for in a man. Strong, confident, caring, and a provider.

Whoever said white boys weren't holding was a hater, she mused to herself, bringing a mischievous smile to her face. Seemingly, reading her mind, he matched her smile with one of his own and kissed her softly.

"We've got a little monster to get to preschool," which was Daddy Speak for don't start anything we can't finish, and slapped her juicy ass on his way through to the kitchen.

He looked good. Rugged. Stubbled and chiseled, with deep soulful eyes, and moved with a swagger that made people take notice when he entered a room. Some people had it. Hector was one of them.

Breakfast, as usual, was pancakes and eggs before Faith put Jada into her Lexus Coupe and Hector headed in the opposite direction in his Chevy Silverado. The pair of them owned their own small businesses on opposite sides of town. The benefit being while mornings may've been hurried, they were never rushed.

"Bye baby, love you," Faith sang as she kissed Jada on her cheek then launched her like a heat seeker from the front seat and into schoolyard.

Jada never failed to hit the ground running, and never stopped all the way to the front door.

"All legs and giggles," Faith mused to herself, hoping her only child would keep that trait all her life.

She slid onto Highway 76, which would take her from the suburbs of Upper Darby on the outskirts of Philly to the King of Prussia Mall, where she had her shoe boutique. The traffic was unusually treacle thick, slowing everybody to a creeping crawl.

Must be an accident, she thought to herself.

The radio had been playing the Russ Parr morning show the whole time, but she hadn't been paying attention until she heard a riff from a song she hadn't heard in a *long* time. It was a song that she'd forgotten, but it hadn't forgotten her.

"If God one day struck me blind, your beauty I'd still see / Love's too weak to define just what you mean to me..."

Dolce & Gabbana for Men. The soft touch of silk against goosebumped skin. Dancing? No, just swaying. Prelude. Foreplay. A strong hand with a gentle touch at the small of her back.

"From the first moment I saw you, I knew you were the one / That night I had to call ya, I was rappin' til the sun came up..."

Her back against the wall, between a rock and his hard place. His tongue on her neck, licking, tasting, kissing lower and lower and...

Faith jumped back into reality as the balding man in the late model Chevy behind her leaned heavily on his horn. Her heart hammered a mile a minute because of the daydream, because of the sudden bray of the horn, but the wetness was only because of a dream.

2

"Oh wait, *shhhhhittt* ma, goddamn," Spook grunted, fighting to keep from crashing his brand-new droptop Bentley.

It took every ounce of concentration and every firing reflex to swerve out of the path of truck as the redbone in his passenger seat sucked him damn near cross-eyed.

She devoured him like it was her last meal.

"You gonna make me crash," he groaned, gripping the back of her head.

"Mmmmm, it'd be worth it," she cooed, looking up at him, lips cherry red as she began slowly jacking him with her hand while she concentrated her action on his dickhead, swirling her tongue around and around until Spook got dizzy trying to follow it. She had a killer smile. A real dame to die for thing going on as she looked up at him. He lost control. She swallowed every drop.

"Damn," was the sum of his world, every word boiled down to that long drawn out syllable.

At the stoplight he rested his head against the seat.

The redbone sat up, making sure to get every last fluid ounce before she popped down the passenger mirror and reapplied her cherry red lipstick, smacking her lips as she dabbed them down.

"Welcome to Philly."

He hadn't been in town an hour and it was already worth the trip. He had met her when his strip club in Brooklyn hosted an all-Philly night, featuring girls from the City of Brotherly love. She was by far the thickest, with lips like a Hollywood B-Lister all up on Botox. He had to have her, plain and simple, and once he had, like he was mainlining her, he had to have her again, and again, even if it meant going all the way to Philly.

"Shit, if I knew it was like this, I would've been moved to this bitch ass place years ago," Spook joked.

She laughed despite the fact it wasn't particularly funny.

Spook checked his diamonded-jeweled Jacob watch.

"So where y'all keep the malls around this shithole? I'ma show you how Daddy treats a good girl."

She thought she had hit the jackpot. The way Spook was spending money on her, she knew she'd hooked him. It wouldn't take much more to lure him to wife her. But he had different ideas, very much in line with setting her up to be his out-of-town hoe; a chick no one knew about, who would take the weight off if shit hit the fan.

"Baby, you make me feel so special," she cooed, as they came out of Yves Saint Laurent loaded with bags straining to contain all the damage they'd done to his plastic.

"You *are* special, sweetness," he winked, thinking *special like a retarded bitch*, then added, "That's two wishes. You rubbed the lamp, you always get three, so what's your final wish?"

"Uhm, there's this little shoe boutique upstairs, got shoes in there to die for," she replied.

"Your wish is my command; your command is my wish. Let's go."

The boutique was branded with the name *Fetish* and offered wall-to-wall designer shoes.

Just as they crossed the threshold, Spook's phone rang.

It was his Baltimore jump off.

"Ma, go 'head and do your thing. I gotta take this," he said, handing her his black card.

Just the feel of the card in her hand made her feel like she had died and gone to consumer heaven.

"I love you," she blurted out before she knew it, then stammered, "I–I mean..."

Spook just chuckled and turned his back on her. There was never going to be any I love you back. Spook didn't do love.

"What's good, baby? You miss Daddy?" He crooned into the phone as he crossed the walkway to lean against the glass railing. Down below more shoppers worshipped their gods of Visa, Mastercard and Amex.

"You know I do, but that ain't why I called. Your boy took care of that."

"Beautiful. Tell him I said—"

Meanwhile, Redbone was inside the designer boutique, ravishing the scrumptious display with her eyes. It was barely a six inch heel from sexual assault.

Kareema walked over.

"How are you doing today?"

"Better than good," Redbone said, smiling, hands full of bags. "Could I see these, these, and those in a size eight?"

"Of course. It'll just take a minute."

As Kareema walked toward the back, Spook stepped inside, all smiles. His eyes fell on Redbone, but didn't linger. The second person he saw damn near blew his mind.

Faith.

"What the *fuck*?" he said, louder than he realized, thinking he was only screaming in his mind.

The tone startled everyone in the store.

Faith looked up.

Redbone instantly got him stuck. Faith looked at him, wondering what he was staring at. Spook couldn't believe his eyes. He felt the blood in his veins turn to ice.

Faith looked away.

Spook found his feet and backed out of the store, shaking his head.

This went beyond ghosts.

"Ain't no fuckin' *way*," he thundered under his breath as he paced the marbled floor of the gallery, careful to keep out of eyesight of the boutique. He was raging. A fire inside. He couldn't help himself, he had to go back and check he wasn't seeing shit. Faith's back was turned, but she was facing a mirror. He wasn't wrong. He knew he wasn't. But...

"Ain't no way *what*?" Redbone questioned, coming out of the shoe shop to see what had him thundering.

"Yo, I need you to go back in there and ask the chick behind the counter if her name is Achilleía."

Redbone cocked a hip full of attitude.

He seethed, the bulging vein in his neck letting her know he was maybe a second off her ass.

She sucked her teeth, nodded and went back in, huffing all the way.

"Umm, excuse me," Redbone said, approaching the woman at the counter.

Faith looked up with a polite smile.

"Yes?"

"This is going to sound strange, but is your name Achilleía?"

Taken aback, Faith chuckled nervously.

"Achilleía?" She shook her head. "No, no it's not."

"Good," Redbone said, more nods before she strutted off, queen of his world again, simple as that, one word, no. A big word. Powerful.

Kareema and Faith exchanged a glance, the silent exchange: *where did that come from?*

Redbone returned to still-pacing Spook, offering him a smile that promised it was all good. "Not her," she said.

"That bitch lyin'. I *know* it's her. Fuck it, let's go."

As he walked by the boutique he held his phone low but aimed it Faith's way, hoping to catch her face.

Faith saw when he walked by, and could tell by the way he held his phone, the camera lens aimed at her, that he was taking her picture. Creep was probably going to post it on the Internet for God-knows-what. She rounded the counter and headed for the door, but by the time she was out on the walkway the mall traffic had swallowed the pair of them without a trace.

"Crazy," she mumbled, heading back inside.

3

Paris stood in front of the floor-to-ceiling window of his multi-million dollar studio in the heart of New York's SoHo district. His calm exterior was an absolute lie. His mind raged. But then that was Paris. Even his tailor-made Armani was an absolute deception. He looked smooth, sophisticated. He was a savage killer.

"Achilleía?" he said, feeling the syllables on his lips again, still not believing what Spook had said. His man Spook was a lot of things, but a liar? He didn't have him down as one. A fool? Not the last time they interacted. So what did that leave?

"Yo God, you ain't gonna believe this shit," Spook said down the long-distance line.

Paris had been having lunch on the terrace with the female pastor of one of the larger Brooklyn churches.

"Believe me, Mr. Butler, your donation will go a long way in helping the children of the parish," Pastor Randolph smiled.

"Well Pastor Ran—" he began, but she smoothly cut him off.

"Patricia, please."

Paris smirked, because he knew how to read between the lines. She may've been in her late fifties, but her smooth cocoa skin and long hair made her look more like 30. She had a real Mrs. Cosby thing going on. Of course, that little fantasy had all these fucked up connotations now.

"Patricia it is then."

She sipped her wine, eyeing him over the rim of the glass. Paris was the type of man who rarely heard no from a woman, even a woman of God. He had that rugged handsomeness that could have opened doors into an entirely different career if he hadn't made certain life choices way back when. His phone rang before he could continue. He glanced at the screen and saw it was Spook.

"Excuse me," he said politely.

Out of earshot, he grunted, "Yeah?"

Spook's message made him cut the lunch short, not exactly rudely, but with less charm than she'd have liked, he was sure. Once Patricia was gone, he went into the apartment.

"Are you *sure*?" he growled, holding the phone like a grudge.

"See for yourself."

Spook killed the call and sent the picture through.

It wasn't a good picture. Not the kind of thing that left you haunted when you looked at it like the kid crying and running from the napalm or the black guy carrying the wounded white supremacist through the angry crowd to safety. It didn't need to be. As soon as Paris laid eyes on her, he knew Achilleía was alive. And he knew what that meant.

"They lied," he muttered, watching his own reflection in the window.

He called Spook back.

"Yo."

Paris spoke calmly, struggling to control the fury he felt building within him. It started as a single spark, ignited by that familiar forgotten face, and smoldered, rising into a heat, that heat combusting, an inferno.

"Don't let her out of your sight. Wait. Snatch her up and bring her home. You feel me?"

Spook hesitated because he knew the measure of the order wasn't to be taken lightly.

"This is Achilleía. Not being funny, but what if we can't?"

"Then kill her, she already died once, it shouldn't be too difficult to make it stick this time," Paris replied, before hanging up.

"You want me to help you with that?" Kareema offered, watching Faith give herself her insulin shot.

"No, thanks. I've got it."

"It's no trouble, my mother is a diabetic."

"It's okay, I've done it a million times. Runs in my family," Faith explained as she tossed the needle in the trash and stood up. When she got to her feet, she wobbled slightly. Kareema reached out to brace her.

"Are you okay?"

"Huh? Yeah, I'm good. I just stood up too fast, you know, head rush," Faith smiled.

"Well don't worry about closing, boss," Kareema winked, "I've got it. You look exhausted."

Which, of course, was because she'd hardly been sleeping. Every time she closed her eyes she dreaded the dreams returning.

"Thanks, really would be appreciated," Faith chimed.

"No problem. Go on home and get you some rest."

"She's leaving the store now," one fat goon reported, speaking clearly into his phone.

About time, Spook thought. He'd been sitting outside the store for over four hours, his ass was number than his brain. He was more than ready to get the shit over with.

"Alright. Remember who this is. Don't fuck up," Spook warned.

He was parked in the same spot, though it had been hours

since he sent Redbone home in a cab. On another day she might have been a fun distraction, but not today. His mind was on something much more urgent than a piece of pussy.

Faith's heels clipped along the polished floor of the mall as she headed for the front door. Several men gave her smiles. There were flirtatious words. There always were. Her presence was like the sun, leaving light and warmth in its wake.

"I see her," the driver of the van confirmed.

Dred, the dreaded goon in the back, pulled a ski mask over his tribal scars, and gripped the caliber tightly. "Let's do this!" he growled, psyching himself up. One look at Faith's long shapely legs and Coke bottle figure, and he knew he was going to enjoy the trip to New York.

Fats, the obese goon, was so close behind Faith, he could reach past her to hold the door for her. She looked over her shoulder and blessed him with a smile.

"Thank you."

"No problem, pretty lady."

She stepped out into the cool night air, oblivious.

The parking lot was far from empty, but very few people were out there. Most of the stores were already closed for the night.

Spook, six rows over, had a bird's-eye view of the whole scene.

He picked up the desert eagle 9mm and cocked it back. If all else failed, he would be the one to kill her, not one of the others. He wanted the honor, even if he didn't want to catch a body so blatantly in public, and the alternative, failing, was much worse.

"I'ma empty the fuckin' clip on her ass this time!" he growled as they made their move.

The van screeched up in front of Faith, blocking her path.

Shocked by the abruptness, she tried to backpedal as the van door slid open on the ski-masked Dred, sitting in the door, pistol in hand.

"Oh my—" she gasped then she felt a pair of hands shove her

forward, hard. She couldn't help herself. She stumbled into the reach of the dreaded goon who spat, "Come here, bitch!" at her.

The action was so quick that even if they saw it, few would've realized what was happening if it wasn't for what happened next. Because when Dred snatched her in, he hit her mouth on the floor of the van, the jarring impact causing her to bite into her tongue. The taste of blood quickly filled her mouth.

Faith's body went rigid. The taste of her own blood jolted her whole being like she'd been hit with a thousand volts. Her mind went into overdrive, like a computer being loaded with too much information, images, sounds, tastes, and smells at the speed of light, firing through her in a crazy rush. She lost herself in them and instinct took over.

The fat goon scrambled into the van behind her.

She kicked out, driving her foot into his gut and knocking the wind out of him. He tumbled backwards, spilling out of the van, and grunted as he hit the pavement, hard.

"What the—" Dred spat, when he realized the docile woman he thought he'd snared turned into a lioness in the blink of an eye.

He tried to raise the gun, but Faith grabbed his wrist.

He tightened his grip, but her intentions weren't to take the gun; she used his weight to angle the muzzle toward him, and forced his trigger finger down.

Boc!

Dred squealed like a pig in agony as the bullet tore through his thigh.

"You shot me, you bitch."

"No, *you* shot you, Tupac!" Faith quipped as she wrangled the gun from his hand.

Just as she was gaining control, the fat goon found his feet and aimed his own piece at her back. Something, some deep-buried instinct warned her a couple of seconds before the bullets came and by the time the fat man had squeezed off a shot, Faith had Dred wrapped up in a chokehold and yanked his body in front of hers to use as a human shield.

Boc! Boc!

Both were head shots, blowing Dred's brains all over the van in a gory arterial spray, and splattering Faith's face with his last thoughts.

Still using the dead man as a shield, she returned fire, hitting the fat goon in the chest four times.

Boc! Boc! Boc! Boc!

Each shot blew him back another yard until weight and gravity took over and he spun, dropping like a hot sack of shit bursting through a wet bag.

"Oh shit," the driver wailed.

Reactions were going to get him killed. He knew it. As soon as the first shot had went off, he'd panicked, foot on the brake, and stopped the van. They'd barely travelled a few feet. He tried to hide, crouching beside the seat. But then Faith shot Fats and instead of cowering he saw his chance and took it, diving on her back and grabbing for her gun hand as he tried to put her in a chokehold. It was a mess of a move. He should have stayed hidden. He might have seen tomorrow if he had, instead of waking up dead.

She sank her teeth into his arm as it snaked around her neck, and threw her head back, driving it into his face and busting his nose in an explosion of blood and pain.

"Fuck!" he grumbled flailing over Dred's dead body as he fell.

Boc! Boc!

Two shots ended his life, making a pretty mess of dripping spaghetti on the roof of the van.

Spook knew something was wrong the second the first gunshot rang out. It was an unmistakeable sound. Nothing like it in the world. He thought they had shot her on the spot. He couldn't blame them, really, but he was pissed he hadn't got to put the slug in her pretty face. He expected to see her body get tossed into the street, but it was the fat goon who fell from the van, taking four to the chest. She had turned the tables.

Again.

He cursed as he threw the car in gear and slammed the gas pedal to the floor.

Spook skidded up on the driver's side of the van and jumped out, running around to the open sliding door, Desert Eagle leading the way. He came around the door, gun aimed and waving, trigger finger itchy, nerves as tight as a piano string.

She wasn't there. All he saw were the dead goons and most of the blood that should have been inside their bodies.

"Where the *fuck* did she go?"

Faith listened to every word.

When she'd heard a car suddenly accelerate then skid up besides the van, she transitioned into defensive mode. Again, it was all instinct. She didn't know what the threat was beyond the sound of the engine, or how many there were. It didn't matter. She knew she couldn't take off running for the mall. It would make her a sitting duck for whoever was in the approaching car. She did the next best thing. She rolled out and slipped under the van like a cobra slithering into its hole; hood flared, prepared to strike.

A second later, Spook came around the corner.

She felt his weight shift the van over her.

Just watching the way the van rocked told her *exactly* where he was.

So, when he came back to the door and started to step down, she slid from under the van, stolen pistol gripped in both hands.

He knew he was caught slipping.

"Achilleía!"

"I'm back," she sang and these last words became his lullabye.

Boc! Boc! Boc!

Two shots hit him in the throat, a third blew through his eye socket, exploding out the back of his head and taking his last thought with it. Spook slumped over and fell, landing on the metal flatbed floor right above her. Faith looked into his dead eyes in that heartbeat a name flared across her waking mind.

"Spook," she spat, as though the name tasted like mucus.

She came out fully from beneath the van and jumped up, looking around. She saw the mall sign.

King of Prussia.

"What the fuck am I doing in Philly?" She scowled, looking around for her motorcycle. It was nowhere to be found. She couldn't hang around with four dead bodies. That way lay Rikers. Thinking on her feet, she rushed over to Spook's Bentley. The key was still in the ignition. She clamberd in behind the wheel and skidded off in a shriek of rubber.

As she drove, she pulled out her phone—though she didn't recognize the model—and thumbed through the contacts.

Hector (work).

Hector (cell).

Camille.

Deidre.

Kareema.

Jada's school.

She didn't recognize a single one of them.

Her first thought was that she'd snagged somebody else's phone by mistake. She tried to think, her thoughts going everywhere at once and nowhere fast, as her attention was stolen by the needle on the gas resting on the E over the gas.

She spotted a gas station across the way and pulled up to the pump.

What the fuck is going on?

She pumped her gas then went inside to settle up, where the young Mexican cashier eyed her up like she was a hot tamale.

She handed him her credit card.

"Fifty on pump six."

He swiped her card, then put a small iPad-looking screen in front of her and held out a stylus.

"Please sign," he requested.

"Where? On the screen? Okay."

She took the stylus and scribbled her signature.

The screen flashed red.

The Mexican looked at her suspiciously.

She scowled.

"What?"

"Please try again," he said.

Again, she signed. Again, it flashed red again. Again, she scowled.

"This shit must be broke."

"No. No. No broke, work fine," the Mexican assured her.

She was getting impatient.

"Look, do I look like a broke bitch that would scam for gas?! I'm pushin' a fuckin' Bentley!"

The Mexican didn't look impressed. She pulled out her license and pointed at her name.

"See? Achilleía Black! Ain't but one me," she boasted.

He looked. Squinted. Scowled. Then eyed her.

"This say Faith Newkirk."

"Faith Newkirk? Bullshit," she exploded.

She hadn't even bothered to look at it when she pulled it out, so sure of herself. But when she looked at it herself, she was shocked to see the strange name next to her picture.

"Who the hell is Faith?" she blurted. She had many aliases, dozens, but none of them were a Faith Newkirk. Something was definitely off. Her head was splitting, like a migraine was coming on.

She put her hands on the counter to steady her buzzing nerves.

"Look, amigo, some bugged out shit is goin' on, but I ain't try and jack you, okay?"

She went through her pockets but only found a few dollars.

She glanced at her hands.

"This ain't even my wedding ring, this little ass shit," she felt her neck; she was wearing a small necklace.

She took it off and laid it on the counter.

"Take that. The diamond looks like a chip but it's gotta be more than fifty bucks," she said dismissively, wondering what the hell she was doing with something so plain.

"How I know it real?"

Now she was pissed.

She put the gun on the counter.

His eyes got big as plates.

"I'm tired of playin' with you, plata o plomo," she said, using the Spanish for "silver or lead."

He threw up his hands, dropping the necklace.

"Take! Take!"

She handed it back to him.

"No, *you* take. Fair's fair. I'm not robbing you, okay? I'm buying the gas with this," she explained, waving the gun at the necklace on the counter top between them.

He nodded like a bobble head on a bumpy road.

"Put your hands down. Relax. Forget you saw me here, okay?"

"Okay."

With that, she was out of there, moving like a fire had been lit under her ass. She jumped in the car and skidded off.

Achilleía sat in the car on a dark block.

She flipped through the pictures in her phone.

There were several of her holding a little girl. She instantly fell in love with her. Of course she did. The kid looked just like her. Exactly. Like a clone.

What the hell is going on? she stressed, feeling the heat of confused tears coming on. None of this made a damned lick of sense. The tears leaked down her check, warm and salty, stinging her bruised lip and reminding her of her injuries.

"Who the fuck is this Faith woman?" she asked the empty car knowing there wouldn't be any answers.

She laid her head back and closed her eyes, just to clear her mind, but before she knew it, she was out cold.

The rays of the rising sun warmed Faith's cheek like a lover's kiss waking her up.

She had to shield her face from the sun; her head throbbed with a real bastard of a migraine. She felt like she was going to puke with it. Her whole body felt like it had a migraine.

She looked around but didn't recognize the neighborhood.

Then she noticed the car, which wasn't hers.

But what *really* threw her was the gun in her hand.

She dropped it on the passenger seat and got out of the Bentley.

What the hell is happening to me?

Million dollar question.

She backed away, looking around, trying to wrap her mind around the weirdness all around her and not understanding what was going on. Her phone rang. She leaned back in the car, careful not to touch anything and grabbed it.

Hector's picture filled the screen.

"Hello?"

"Oh my God! Baby, where are you? I've been calling and calling all night. Are you okay?" His voice was full of concern.

"I don't know. Hector, I'm scared," she admitted, the strength in his voice allowing her to feel vulnerable. She wanted to curl up on the backseat and just wait for him to come and get her and bring her home.

"Where are you?"

"I'm," she looked around and spotted a street sign, "on Gerald Avenue. 54th and Gerald."

"I'm on my way."

Hector sat on the edge of the bed watching his wife sleep.

She'd crashed after he gave her a pill. After everything she'd told him, he knew she needed it.

"I-I-I remember someone trying to push me into a van," she had explained. "And then..." a shrug that spoke volumes. "That's it. Then I woke up in that car with a gun."

When he'd first seen her face, freckled with dried blood, he'd checked her out for injuries, fearing the worst. But it wasn't her blood. He didn't know if that was better. Hector's mind was going a million miles a minute.

"Spook. Spook. It was... Spook," Faith mumbled in her sleep.

"Did what, baby?" Hector asked softly.

"Spook... tried to kill me."

His entire body tensed up.

He had heard that name before.

4

P aris sat on his leather couch, legs crossed, his drink resting
on his knee as Medea walked through the front door.

He couldn't help but smirk to himself as he watched her strut
across the floor.

He adored confidence in a woman. From head to toe, she was
a bad bitch and she knew it. Her half-Egyptian half-Brazilian
heritage was an exotic combination that made her look a golden-
hued goddess. Her silk dress clung smoothly to her as she
strutted across the hard wood floor.

"Hey baby," she cooed; her voice soft and angelic. Sexy
enough to turn a saint into a sinner.

Paris stood as she approached.

She opened her arms for an embrace.

Smack!

He backhanded her so hard that if it wasn't for the couch, she
would have slid back to the door.

"Baby!" she gasped, holding a hand to her purple cheek.

Paris stood over her, his fists balled so tight, his wrist muscles
twitched.

"Achilleía is *alive!*" he thundered.

Medea couldn't do anything but stare, shaking her head, mouth agape. Her expression angered Paris. He snatched her up by the throat and slammed her against the plated glass window so hard that regular glass would have shattered and left her learning to fly twenty-four stories above the New York streets.

Instead, he pinned her there, eyes inches from her face, breath sour, and it looked as though she was suspended in mid-air.

"I can't breathe," Medea gurgled.

"Do you think I *care*?" he seethed in her face. "I explicitly told you to kill her. No room for mistakes. No fucking resurrection miracles. You assured me she was dead. I should break your goddamn neck for lying to me!"

The whole time he spoke, he dug his fingers deeper into her throat, choking her.

Medea's golden skin began to turn a ghostly pale, and just as she felt herself going out, he released his grasp and let her oxygen-deprived body fall to the floor.

She writhed on the rug, coughing and gasping for air.

Her five-thousand dollar dress rode up around her waist.

When Medea finally found her voice, she stammered, "I-I... swear Paris, I didn't know..."

He squatted down beside her and lifted her head by the pony-tail forcing her to look into his eyes.

"Did you do what I told you? Did you shoot her in the head?"

"Yes!" she lied. "I shot her myself just like you told me. I swear to God."

"Then who the fuck is this?"

He held his phone, with the picture of Achilleía open, in her face.

When Medea saw her, all she could do is cry.

"Bitch, you better pray I get to her before..."

He let his voice trail off, battling down a mixture of anger and fear.

"...Because if I lose, then you lose everything. You get that? Everything. Including your life, do you understand?"

Medea nodded, his icy tone sending shockwaves down the ridges of her spine. And for the first time, she regretted selling her soul to the devil.

Quadir sat back in the passenger seat while Ox drove and Zay played the back, bobbing his head to the sounds of Raekwon's *Purple Tape* as it bumped through the speakers.

Quadir heard the music, but his focus was on the blue Toyota Corolla they were tailing.

"Don't lose her," Quadir warned calmly.

"Yo, chill, I know what the fuck I'm doin'," Ox shot back.

Quadir glanced over at Ox, but held his tongue. Although Ox looked like a linebacker and outweighed Quadir by at least 100 pounds, they both knew who the real killer was.

At first glance, the word 'schoolboy' came to mind because of the designer glasses Quadir always wore.

He kept his fade tight and waves spinning: a clean-cut look that made his baby face appear innocent, like he was the one to take home to momma. But under the surface, the truth; he was cold-blooded and sadistic enough to kill momma and the whole family.

A lot of women mistook him for some guy they'd seen in the background of loads of movies, but the only thing movie-esque about Quadir was his panty-wetting smile.

Under normal circumstances, he would've checked Ox but everyone in the car was feeling the weight of pressure bearing down from Paris. The boss had made it clear: *No. More. Mistakes!* Every man in the car took it to heart. The difference, for Quadir, was that he knew if shit went bad, he'd be the last man standing. Paris loved him like a little brother. That was his body armor. The Corolla pulled into a quiet neighborhood in West Philly and found an empty spot to park. Ox drove on by, eyes glued to the rearview.

"She goin' in," Ox announced, as he made a U-turn and parking up on the opposite side of the street. They all threw on dreaded wigs, cocked their pistols as they barreled out of the car, across the street in grim silence, heading for the house.

Kareema entered her house and kicked off her shoes.

She was exhausted.

Faith hadn't been to work in two days.

Not that she couldn't handle it, but if it kept up, she'd have to speak to her about hiring another sales clerk to take some of the burden.

She never heard them come in.

Zay was a master of locks. He'd never met one he couldn't pick, especially back doors. The three killers crept inside, moving as smooth as shadows on a wall. They heard the sound of water sloshing in a tub and headed for the bathroom.

As soon as Kareema's body hit the warm bubble bath, she felt like she was dissolving into a sea of bliss. After the day she'd had, that hot bath felt better than sex, as she laid back, relaxed, and quickly drifted off.

Something cold and metallic tapped her on the forehead.

She opened her eyes.

Her heart damn near escaped out of her throat.

She saw three black dreaded men with guns all around the tub. The one with glasses, who had tapped her on the forehead with the gun, was perched on the edge.

She opened her mouth to scream but never got to make a sound as he shoved the gun's barrel into her mouth.

"Scream and you won't live long enough to hear the sound," Quadir said, coldly but calmly. "We clear?"

Kareema nodded.

He slowly pulled the gun out of her mouth.

"Please, don't hurt me. I don't have any money," she begged, her tears hot and thick.

"Do you want to live?"

"Yes..."

"Tell me what I want to know and you will, understand?"

She nodded again, the hope in her heart momentarily outweighing the doomed feeling in her gut.

"What's her name?" Quadir asked, showing her the picture on his phone that Spook took.

"Faith... Faith Newkirk. She's my boss," she quickly replied.

Quadir shot her a smile that, despite the circumstances, made her feel better.

"Very good. Now tell me where she lives."

"Germantown. 109 East Chadwick," Kareema blurted out.

Quadir stoked her cheek.

"Good. Good. See that wasn't hard, was it? I want you to know that I really appreciate you helping me out like this. You really kept to your side of the bargain. Problem is, I lied, you don't get to leave that nice warm bath, sorry," Quadir replied, grabbing her by the throat and forcing her head under the suds into the water.

Kareema's legs and arms flailed, slapping at the sides of the tub, clawing at his hands. Water splashed everywhere. But Quadir wasn't about to let her wriggle out of his grasp. He held an iron grip on her, pinning her beneath the surface. He looked at his watch the whole time, counting off the seconds until she stopped fighting and the water was still.

"Damn near three minutes. Not bad," he chuckled. "Okay, off to Germantown we go."

"Are you sure, Faith? Really sure? I don't want to leave you right now," Hector protested.

"No Hector, I'll be okay. Jada's been looking forward to this recital for months. It's bad enough I can't go, but there's no way we cancel on her. This is the kind of thing kids remember forever. It's only for a couple of hours. I'll be okay," Faith smiled.

Hector took a deep breath, "I don't like leaving you, Faith."

She leaned up and kissed him sweetly. "And I love you for

that. But go, our little diva will have a hissy fit if she doesn't get to dance."

Hector chuckled.

"That she will. Okay, straight there and straight back."

"Have fun."

They smacked lips and then he walked out. Faith laid back, but couldn't sleep. Since the incident, it seemed she had a heightened sense of everything. Her hearing was clearer, her sight sharper. Even sex was better. Hector had always been a decent lover, but the afternoon after the incident, her body seemed to be extra sensitive. She closed her eyes, content to remember.

She heard a deep raspy voice in her ear, saying, *"You're the only woman I'll ever love."*

Faith's eyes popped open. She looked around, but she was alone, save for the haunting presence of an aura she couldn't name but knew.

Déjà vu.

Her mind even picked up a scent. A certain cologne.

"What is happening to me?" she mumbled, shaking her head.

Click!

Her heightened hearing picked up the small rasp of the lock being tripped and she knew the soft sigh that followed was a door opening.

She jumped out of bed and ran to the edge of the stairs.

She could distinctly make out three sets of heavy footsteps, all men.

"Shit," Faith cursed, trapped in her own home.

She ran to the closet and snatched Hector's .38 revolver from the shelf, cursing herself for making him keep it unloaded because of Jada. She grabbed the box of bullets, fumbling it and spilling the shells to the hardwood floor. She scooped up a handful and tried to make it to the draw door leading to the attic. But even as she grabbed the string to pull it down, she heard the men coming up the stairs.

Faith ran back in the bedroom.

She looked out of the window.

Her bedroom may've been on the second floor, but she could easily hang jump safely.

Except, there was no time.

They were coming down the hall.

She had an idea that made her wonder, *where the hell did that come from* even as it burst into her mind.

She backed into a corner, standing catty-corner to where the walls met. They were just far enough apart for her to wedge her way up the wall using her hands to brace herself and her legs to hoist her up. In the darkness, she was invisible, blending into the shadows she had become.

When Quadir had heard the sound of bullets hitting the floor, he looked up.

"Bullets... Those were bullets. Be careful," he warned the other two. He knew what he was up against; the others thought they were there to snatch up a broad. He trusted Achilleía wouldn't get the opportunity to disabuse them of that notion, but there was always going to be a risk factor with a bad bitch like her.

They came up the stairs, Ox in the lead, followed by Quadir and Zay.

Once they reached the top, Quadir pointed toward the bedroom. That was the direction the sound had come from.

Faith watched the door slowly open. One by one, the three killers entered the room. She took a deep breath like she was going under water and held it.

Quadir pointed at the closet.

Zay cautiously approached then threw open the door, waving his gun inside the closet. Ox hunkered down and looked under the bed, while Quadir stayed close to the door, scanning the room with his eyes.

With a bird's eye view, Faith watched.

Her heart was beating so hard and fast, she was convinced they'd hear it.

Quadir motioned with his head. They turned to leave. Ox was the last one out through the door.

He glanced in her direction.

She froze.

He squinted.

"She on the wall!" he exclaimed.

Faith didn't hesitate.

Boc! Boc! Boc!

All three headshots blew off watermelon chunks, pink brain debris misting the darkness as Ox collapsed to the floor, twitching.

She jumped down from her wall perch.

By the time the shots rang out, Quadir and Zay were over by the stairs.

"Fuck!" Quadir barked.

They turned to run back in the bedroom, Faith kicking the bedroom door just as Zay rushed into it head-on.

The door hit him dead in the face, breaking his nose on contact.

He fell back into Quadir, sending him sprawling in a heap.

Faith had no time to open the window. She ran straight for it, grabbed the curtain to protect her from the glass, and dove clean through it, headfirst in a shower of shards. She flipped her body in midair, twisting like a gymnast coming off the bars, so she could land on her feet, but miscalculated. It was down to the finest of margins, but even though she planted her feet solidly, she rolled her ankle so bad she knew it was broken.

Letting out a shriek of pain, she rolled in agony, clutching it as her mind screamed:

Get up!

Despite the pain, she forced herself into action, rising and hobbling for cover.

Boc! Boc!

Out of nowhere, a gunshot kicked up a tuft of grass at her feet and a second whizzed by her head so close she felt the kiss of displaced air.

She looked up and saw Quadir approaching, gun aimed, with Zay behind him.

Faith looked back and saw the pistol she had dropped.

He had her.

The two of them walked up to her.

"Hello, Achilleía. Long time no see," Quadir smiled.

"My name is Faith," she gritted.

Quadir shrugged.

"So I heard. But you're still Achilleía. Hey Zay?"

"Yeah Qua?"

"Hold this."

Boc! Boc!

Out of nowhere, Quadir put the gun in Zay's face, then blew his surprised look all over the grass. What was left of his face looked like chewed hamburger as his body dropped.

Faith looked at him, wide-eyed.

"Didn't expect that, huh?" Quadir smirked. "Just like I didn't expect to see you alive, so I guess we're both surprised."

"What do you want with me?" Faith demanded to know.

Quadir studied her face for a moment.

"You really don't know who I am?"

Faith just glared at him.

"Damn. What did they do to you? Look, I know it didn't seem like it at first, but I'm on your side."

"Get off my property," she spat, turning to limp off.

Quadir grabbed her arm.

"I need you to go with me."

"Fuck you!"

Quadir put the gun to her head.

"I'm not askin' you, I'm tellin' you."

She looked him in the eyes.

"I thought you said you were on my side?"

"I am. Don't mean I won't pull the trigger if you make me," he chuckled and then turned serious. "Now let's go."

Faith or Achileía, Quadir knew what she was capable of, and he was no fool, so zip-tied her hands behind her back. She shifted around, trying to get comfortable in the front seat.

Quadir glanced over at her.

"Put your palms down and sit on your hands."

"Where the fuck are you taking me?"

"Where you'll be safe. Now look, I need you to be very quiet. Don't say a word. If you want to live," he warned firmly.

He pulled out his cell phone and hit send, giving her one last hard scowl before someone picked up.

"Yo," Quadir spoke. "Yeah, shit is crazy, Unck... Zay and Ox both sleep and Achileía got away."

Faith could hear someone ranting and raving on the other end.

"Naw Unck, I got it. I'm not leaving until the bitch is dead..."

He hung up.

She looked at him.

"Who was that?"

He looked at her, then replied, "Your brother."

5

"What the hell are the Feds doing here?"

"First on the scene."

The two Philadelphia officers watched the swirling lights of the police radio cars and the ambulance in front of them. They lit the neighborhood up like the circus was in town.

Hector pulled up to his house, a sinking feeling in his gut that felt like rotten acid burning a sinkhole in his soul.

"Are those the police, Daddy?" Jada asked from the backseat.

"Yes baby," he said in a whisper, because he could hardly speak. Speaking made it real.

He looked at Jada and told her to, "Stay in the car."

"But Daddy—"

"Jada," he growled, harsher than he'd intended, frightened about what waited for him inside his house, and she fell silent.

He got out of the car, calling, "Where is my wife?" before he was halfway across the road to where the two federal agents, one black and male, the other white and female, looked at one another. The black man answered, "We don't know."

The answer came as a peculiar kind of relief because he'd

braced himself to hear 'Dead.' But now that the fear was gone, he was confused, and confused came across as pissed when he said, "What the hell do you mean you don't know? You were supposed to be keeping her safe."

The female agent took a deep breath. "Mr. Newkirk, I understand that you are anxious, but believe me when I tell you our officers responded as soon as they heard the shots inside."

"How the hell did a shooter get in without being seen? You were sat out here watching the door." Hector put his hands on his hips and shook his head. "What happened?"

The male officer pulled out his iPad, punched up the screen then handed it to Hector.

"The motion sensor camera picked up three black males, we believe the dreads are wigs designed to confuse any eye witness accounts."

"Faces?"

"Concealed at all times. The cameras never catch more than an angle, not a single usable image."

"They knew," Hector remarked.

"We have to assume so."

He watched as Quadir, Ox, and Zay approached the back door. Zay smoothly jigged the lock and they went inside.

"And all three are accounted for?" Hector questioned.

The female agent shook her head.

"No. Only two. The third assailant evaded capture and got away."

"With Faith," Hector retorted sourly.

"We assume so, yes, but that's not the whole picture we're beginning to see," she replied.

"What do you mean?"

She nodded at the other agent. He reached out and hit the iPad screen in Hector's hand. The mall parking lot came up.

"This is from two nights ago."

Hector watched as Faith came out of the mall. The angle was

strange, but he saw the fat goon hold the door for her. He saw the van skid up and the goon push her inside. The van rocked seconds before the fat goon pulled out and fired into the interior. A second later, shots returned, blowing Fats back to his maker. Hector watched in silent horror. A few moments later, the Bentley pulled up to the side of the van and he saw a dark figure slither over the edge of the van and slide underneath.

"What was that sliding under the van?"

"Not what, who," The female agent replied, "Your wife."

Hector shook his head. It made zero sense, even though he could see it happening right there in front of him. He couldn't trust his eyes. He watched Spook go in the van then as he got out, Faith slid half-out from under the van and blasted him. He fell dead on his face. Faith came from under the van and jumped in Spook's Bentley. She drove off screen. Hector handed the iPad back to the male agent.

"Why am I *just* seeing this?"

"Because this thing is bigger than us," she replied. "The mall wanted to keep it out of the media and the chief owed the mayor a favor."

Hector let out a frustrated sigh. "Absolute bullshit." He looked over towards the car to check on Jada. "Okay, okay. Listen, I know it's not your fault... come back in the morning, and I'll give you an official statement and answer any questions I can, but right now I'm tired and I need to put my daughter to bed without her worrying where her mother is."

"No problem. And Mr. Newkirk, I am truly sorry," she offered.

Hector nodded.

"Appreciated."

There was no way he was staying at the house when the law were going over every inch of the place with a forensic tooth-comb, even ignoring the fact there were a couple of corpses inside. Instead, he took Jada to a nearby hotel. She fell asleep on his shoulder going inside. As soon as he tucked her in for bed, he tried to call Faith's phone. It went straight to voice mail.

He didn't leave a message.

He dialed a second number.

"We may have a problem."

6

"Leave the door open," Quadir told her as soon as they got to the motel.

"Hell no. It's definitely not *that* type of party," Faith objected.

"Then no shower," Quadir said flatly.

Her ankle was killing her. The sequence of events had Faith feeling so dirty her skin itched. No shower was out of the question.

"Fucking pervert," she finally relented, then hobbled into the bathroom.

Quadir sat back, wide-legged in the chair, and tucked his pistol in his pants. He watched Faith, her long, shapely, bronze legs looking positively delicious as she stripped down, he could practically taste them.

She pulled the shower curtain, but not all the way, leaving a crack that Quadir could see through. Her skin glistened with water. It cascaded over her, every drop wanting to kiss up against her. When she turned to the side, Quadir caught a glimpse of her nipples against the teardrop curve of her breasts. His heart beat a mile a minute.

"Goddamn," he cursed under his breath as she dried off in the shower.

He couldn't take his eyes off her as she stepped out and pulled her T-shirt back on. She hung her panties over the towel rack to dry and hobbled back in and sat on the bed.

"If you were a half decent human being you'd get some ice for my ankle."

"You're a big girl. Shit, the Achilleía I know wouldn't need any ice."

"Which should tell you something then, shouldn't it? I'm not the Achilleía you know," she shot back.

He watched her for a moment.

"Then who *are* you?

"Faith Newkirk."

"Married? Kids?"

"Both."

Quadir leaned forward, resting his elbows on his knees with an amused expression on his face.

"Interesting. You really believe that, don't you?"

"Why wouldn't I? It's the truth."

"No it isn't."

She shook her head. "What makes you so sure I'm who you think I am?"

"Does the name Paris mean anything to you?"

She shook her head.

"Ray Butler?"

"No."

"Chiron Black?"

"Should they?" she asked.

"Your brother, father and husband? I'd think so."

She bristled.

"You're wrong. My husband's name is Hector."

He shook his head. "No it isn't. Shit ain't always what it seems," he said, reminding her.

"Fine. Whatever. I'm going to sleep," she replied, laying back.

Faith tried to act like she was so sure about everything in her world and herself, but deep down, knowing everything that had happened in the last couple of days, along with the certainty in his eyes, meant this little voice within her whispered... *Am I?*

She began thinking about how she'd reacted back in her bedroom.

She wasn't an athletic person, but instinctively used the angle of the wall like an expert climber. Then she'd killed a man without hesitation before throwing herself through a plate glass window.

She'd never done anything like that before.

But then again, no one had tried to kill her before, and, like they said, never does one know the force that is in them until it is tested.

And then there was the shower she had just taken.

She'd have to be blind to miss the effect her naked body had on Quadir. She needed to use that to her advantage. She had left the curtain cracked on purpose, putting on a show. It was all about gaining the upper hand. She knew full well the power of her sexuality.

Faith laid down and got comfortable.

Quadir watched her.

He couldn't take his eyes off her—and she knew it.

He watched her drift off. Her legs relaxed and gapped open, offering a tantalizing glimpse.

As wrong as he knew it would be, Faith had the kind of body made a man care less about right and focus on right now. He knew he was making a mistake even as he made it, but didn't care. He got up and stood over her. It wasn't about rape He wasn't that kind of man. But goddamn he'd kill to taste her.

He leaned down, moving closer. So close he could smell her.

Before he could pull back she'd wrapped her legs around his neck and flipped him over, contorting his body so he couldn't reach his gun, and ensuring that she could.

She gripped the handle and sat on his face, letting her lips lightly graze his lips.

That was the last thing on his mind; he was too focused on the gun between his eyes to be thinking with his dick.

"Whoa, whoa, whoa. Relax ma! We good, we all good."

"No we aren't. You're going to tell me what the fuck is going on," Faith told him, staring him down.

"Achilleía, I—"

"Faith, my fucking name is *Faith*! Call me that again and I'm pulling this goddamned trigger."

"Okay, okay, okay. *Faith*. I'm tellin' you, I'm on your side."

"Then why the fuck don't I believe you?" she spat, on the verge of blowing his brains out in hopes it would kill the confusion in her own.

Quadir looked her in the eyes.

"Hand me my phone. I'll prove everything I say is true."

Her finger rested on the trigger. It would take nothing to kill him. Not even an ounce of pressure.

"One call."

Long pause.

"If you're lying, it'll be your last."

"Fair enough."

She got off him, slowly, gun ready to bark, muzzle never leaving his center of mass. She didn't take her eyes off him as she crossed the floor to grab his phone off the dresser. She tossed it to him, landing square on his chest.

Quadir flipped through his contacts and dialed.

After a few rings, it was answered.

"Yo, you ain't gonna believe this, but I got somebody here you want to talk to. Hold on," Quadir said, holding out the phone. "It's for you."

"Who is it?"

He smiled.

"Your husband."

7

Medea laid her head on Paris's chest, panting to catch her breath, chest heaving, skin sheathed in sweat.

They laid in the afterglow until he finally broke the silence.

"This changes everything, you know that."

Medea nodded, because she knew exactly what he was talking about. It had nothing to do with sex.

"You think I'm a monster, don't you?" he questioned, staring up at the chandelier ceiling fan above his bed. When she didn't answer straight away he went on, "You think I'm heartless because I tried to have my own sister killed."

She lifted up so she could look him in the eye.

"You did what you had to do to keep the family together, like Ray would've wanted."

He winced subtly at the sound of his father's name.

"Yeah."

"And believe me, if anybody understands, it's me. Don't forget, she was my best friend," she reminded him. "Maybe it's ironic, but the one thing she taught me was to be loyal to the family. It's sacred. It isn't our fault she violated that. That was all her. She made a choice. She knew exactly what she was doing."

In the moments of silence that stretched out between them, both reflected on the nature of their regrets, until she kissed his nose, smiled, and said, "I'm going to take a shower, you coming?"

"Naw, I'm good," he replied, his mind a thousand miles away.

Medea got up and padded to the bathroom, enjoying the fact he was watching her. She ran the piping hot shower, and got in under the spray, luxuriating in the warm water as it cascaded all over her.

Achilleía...

Achilleía had quite literally saved her ass and Medea had paid her back by setting her up for what she thought was her murder. But in her mind, she still wasn't the snake Achilleía was. Achilleía and Chiron had been trying to take over the family knowing Paris became the boss after Ray's death. She'd worked hard to convince herself that Achilleía had been the one that violated tradition, not her. Still, she couldn't forget the look in her eyes when realized who her betrayer was.

"You too, 'Nique?" Achilleía had remarked, stone cold disbelief behind the words.

"There are consequences to every action, big sis. You taught me that."

"So, what's the consequence for Paris's?"

Medea didn't blink. The gun aimed steady.

"My loyalty."

Boc!

The memory of the gunshot was still so fresh in her mind.

The water had long gone cold, but Medea didn't feel it. She was lost in the past and the day that started it all.

As her memory had preserved so vividly, the smell of the club was beginning to make her sick. The heavy perfume mixed with various body odors reminded Medea that despite the expensive decor, the place was a flesh factory, pure and simple. And she was on sale. If it hadn't been for the Xanax and Codeine Paco plied her with, she would never have made it through a whole month.

Paco.

Just the sound of his name in her mind threatened to make her collapse in on herself. He'd started out as her manager, then ended up as her pimp. He started out loving on her and ended up beating on her. It was a pattern. A grim fucking pattern. And horribly predictable. Sometimes she'd had to plaster make-up all over her whole body to hide the bruises. She'd wanted out but had no idea how to take the first step.

Until Achilleía had become that first step.

Achilleía had just come back from a tour in Afghanistan; Medea had heard Spook, the manager of the club talking to someone else. Medea knew who Achilleía was. The daughter of Sugar Ray, one of the biggest heroin dealers on the East Coast. He was drug royalty, and practically the mayor, his other businesses were so close to legit they almost managed to drown the stink effectively enough the DEA couldn't sniff it out, tracker dogs and all. As she danced her set, she watched Achilleía watch her. She wondered why a beautiful woman who had the keys to the underworld and the city proper would join the army. It made zero sense unless Achilleía was a dyke. But that theory died on a hard dick when she realized the sexy ass Nelly-looking dude that Spook worked for was her husband.

Achilleía kept a crew of bad bitches around her. There was one they called Polyxena. She was Achilleía's shadow. Literally. Polyxena was from Guyana and glowed like black gold. Her eyes were sharp and blue as diamonds. They weren't contacts. Real and unnervingly hypnotic. Medea found herself sinking so deeply into them that she stumbled on the stage.

All four girls with Achilleía had their eyes glued to her.

She snaked through her routine, unemotional and detached, oblivious to the hands groping or the bills raining down on her.

At the end of her set, Achilleía held up a hundred-dollar bill.

Medea moved as though in a trance, leaving singles all over the stage like it was beneath her to pick them up.

Her eyes tangoed with Achilleía's until a rough hand snatched her back into reality.

"Bitch, what the fuck is you doin?" Paco snapped, spitting in her face. "You better go get my goddamn paper!"

He huffed so close to her face, she could smell the Patrón on his breath.

She stared at him, fearing his next move.

He looked like a scarred-face incarnation of a Pitbull made man.

"Now!" he barked, shoving her so hard she stumbled and fell, losing a shoe. As she scrambled for it one bodyguard began to move, but Achilleía caught his eye and shook her head. He relaxed and resumed his stance.

Medea put on her shoes, trying to maintain a shred of dignity, naked on her knees, as she gathered all the bills off the stage. She crushed them in her fists and handed them to Paco.

He slapped them down on floor.

"Is that how Daddy like his money, you dog ass bitch? Face 'em the same way," he demanded, relishing the attention dudes were giving him. It was all about putting his pimp power on full display. A dance.

"Yo Achilleía, let me rock this bitch ass nigguh to sleep," Polyxena hissed, fists balled as tight as rocks.

"Naw. If she want out, she gotta make the first move," Achilleía replied, sipping her drink.

Medea arranged the bills so they all faced the same way, dead presidents up, then held them out to Paco. This time, he took them.

"Now go make me some mo'," he spat, and slapped her on the ass.

"Yes, Daddy," her mouth said, but her eyes were talking an entirely different language.

If only...

Medea walked over to Achilleía, but her strut was gone. She looked defeated.

"You want a lap dance?" Medea questioned.

"Why you think I'm waving this?" Achilleía smirked, handing her the hundred-dollar bill.

Medea straddled Achilleía's lap and began to work her body like a snake.

"Medea, right?"

Medea was surprised Achilleía recognized her. It felt good to be known. Meant she'd asked around after her. That lifted her spirits a bit.

"Yeah."

"You know me?"

"Who don't?"

Achilleía laughed.

"Welcome home," Medea remarked.

"Thank you," Achilleía said. "Spook told me a lot about you. He says you could be a bad bitch if you just get off that shit and get that shit off you." Her eyes darted in Paco's direction.

"You know how it is. Paco 'bout that life."

Achilleía and her crew laughed like they were watching *Martin*.

"Who Paco? Man, if I had a dick, I'd make him suck it!" Achilleía laughed, shaking her head.

"Fuck that nigguh wit my double head," Polyxena added.

Paco was close enough to hear, but he wasn't crazy enough to respond. Instead, he flexed his jaw and acted like he was deaf.

The song changed. Medea stopped grinding.

"I have to go. Thank you," Medea said.

"You want to be on my team?"

"Yes," Medea replied, without hesitation.

Achilleía nodded. "I'll be in touch."

Achilleía sat on her green and black Triple 5 Ducati street bike.

Beside her was Polyxena on her cocaine white Suzuki 900. The other chicks in her clique had various colored bikes and models. They were settled in the parking lot of the strip club, watching Medea and Paco walk out. He said something to her and then backhanded her. The sound of the smack echoed off Achilleía's last nerve.

"Come on," she said, pulling her helmet down over her face as soon as Paco pulled off on his 2008 Mercedes C Class. They pulled out behind him, the roar of their motorcycles sounding like the roar of a hungry pack of lionesses.

"Who the fuck is that?" Paco spat angrily, pulling the gun from his waist and eyeing his rearview mirror as he rode the turn off Atlantic Avenue and onto a side street. The bikers seemed to transform, expanding their formation and enveloping him like a cloud of smoke. Two were behind him, one on either side, with two in the front of him. He was just about to let the window down and start squeezing when he noticed the license plate of Achilleía's bike.

Murder 1.

"Fuck she want?" he growled, but there was no gangsta bass in it.

He stopped the car.

They all got off their bikes and pulled out guns.

The white girl tapped his window with the barrel of her Desert Eagle.

"Get out of the car," she told him.

If it had been anybody but Sugar Ray's baby girl, he would've spazzed on the whole clique. But he wasn't ready for beef with Ray, so he got out.

"Ay yo, Achilleía, I hope you got a good reason for this bull-shit," he spat, as the white girl took his pistol.

Achilleía tipped her helmet onto the back of her head.

"I ain't got beef with you, Pac. I'm here to get Medea. You rollin' or what?" Achilleía called out.

Medea looked out the window at Paco glaring at her.

She knew if she got out of the car, there was no turning back.

She just didn't know how deep shit would get, but she was so tired of the abuse. Beyond tired. And maybe Achileía was right and there was a bad bitch trapped in a sad bitch's situation?

She knew it was now or never.

She chose now and stepped out.

"Bitch, get yo' ass back in the car," Paco growled.

Medea ignored him and walked to Achileía.

"Yeah I'm rollin'."

"Not yet," Achileía smirked.

Medea frowned in confusion. Achileía pulled her Glock out of her shoulder holster and handed it to her, handle first. Medea looked at the gun like it was a viper that might rise up and bite, then back at Achileía. The smirk was gone, replaced with stone.

"Handle your business."

Medea took the gun from her hand and turned to face Paco. Her mind played back the tape of their relationship; all the abuse, all the humiliation, all the disrespect. Every last fucking bit of it. Her blood began to boil inside.

"Ay yo, Medea, you ain't gotta do this. You wanna go, go. You'll never see me again," Paco pleaded with her, all the bass gone from his voice. He knew.

Medea looked him dead in the eye, the weight of her pain concentrated in her trigger finger, and replied, "You're right... I'm not."

Boc! Boc! Boc! Boc! Boc! Boc! Boc! Click.

She put all seven shots into his chest until the gun was empty and smoking, then walked back over to Achileía and handed her the gun.

"Now can we go?"

Achileía snickered.

"Hop on."

From that moment on, Achileía turned Medea into a beast,

teaching her everything she'd learned in the Special Forces. She taught her about guns until she could break them down and put them together again in the dark. She ran her until she threw up and then ran her some more. She taught her hand-to-hand combat until the black and blue bruises Paco put on her were nothing but love taps. But in the end, she made Medea into one of the baddest bitches in the crew.

And then she betrayed her, convincing herself that Achilleía had betrayed her first.

The water cascading down her face concealed her tears but the pain and the guilt couldn't be washed away.

"I'm so sorry," she sobbed to herself, knowing that she would have to face Achilleía one day soon.

8

Polyxena stepped out of her charcoal gray BMW 5-Series and put her Chanel shades on.

She pulled the strap of her pocketbook over her shoulder as her heels beat a steady rhythm across the parking lot. The heavily barbed wire fence slid open, allowing her to continue along the flower-lined walkway that lined the entrance to the Super-Max prison. Everything beyond that fence was about security gates. After walking through locked door after locked door and passing through three separate metal detectors, she finally made it into the prison.

As she walked along, she took every man's head with her—and not just because some of them hadn't seen a woman in months. Even the conservatively cut business skirt suit did little to hide the fact her body was built for crimes against mankind. Her eyes were mesmerizing.

"Good morning, Ms. Beauvoir," a young white woman, another case manager, chirped cheerily.

Polyxena flashed a smile.

"Good morning," she replied, before disappearing into her office.

She took a deep breath as she sat down.

She hated working in a prison, but it was all part of the plan, which meant she had no choice but to grin and bear it.

Before she could settle in, she heard a knock on the door.

She knew who it was before they even entered.

"Come in."

A tall, muscular black man came in. His hair was buzzed short so that none of the inmates could get a grip if things turned nasty. It made him look like a beautiful hooligan.

"Good morning, Captain Tillman," she greeted him.

He chuckled as he came over and sat down.

"Oh, it's *Captain* now, huh? What happened to Daddy?"

"We have to have some semblance of professionalism."

"If that means I get to bend you over this desk before we do our rounds, then I'm all for professionalism," he winked.

"Be careful what you wish for."

"I missed you."

"I'm sure."

"Long weekend. I tried to call you."

Polyxena shrugged. "I do have a life. Unlike you, I'm not married."

"Ouch."

"Exactly."

Polyxena could tell he was tightening. Tillman was the kind of dude who tried to control his women, and got sprung when he couldn't. It drove him crazy that she had the upper hand, and she knew it.

"As pretty as you are, and as much as I hate to throw you out, I do have a full slate today," Polyxena said.

"I just dropped by to see if I could take you to lunch?"

"Sounds good." As he stepped back to the door, Polyxena added, "Any word on that job?"

"I haven't forgotten, I promise you'll be the first to know," he blew her a kiss on his way out.

She knew he was trying to use the promotion to get what he wanted from her, dangling it in front of her like a carrot on a stick, but she had her own sticks and they didn't need any carrots.

She picked up the phone.

"Yes, this is Ms. Beauvoir," she said calmly. "Please send me Inmate D-319 from Green Unit. Thank you."

As soon as she hung up, her heart began to beat faster. She stood ,wriggling out of her thong, placing it in her drawer. Polyxena knew she had a good ten minutes before he made it through all the guards and detectors and she wanted to give him a taste, so she got herself ready for her visitor.

She had to catch herself before she cried out.

Several moments later, she got a knock on the door.

She cleared her throat to steady her voice.

"Come," she said, enjoying the double entendre.

Even in prison browns and a T-shirt, he was still a sexy motherfucker; especially since he had bulked up, even if it made him look like an action figure.

"Hey baby. Damn, I missed you," she purred as soon as he closed the door.

They hugged and she slipped her wet fingers in his mouth, but she could tell something else was on his mind.

"Baby, are you ok? I'm doing all I can to get you out of here. I—"

He mustered a smile and kissed her softly.

"It's not that, baby girl," he replied, walking over to the window.

He loved to gaze out her window because it looked out on the distant horizon of the city. From his cell, all he could see was the prison yard. And after five years in prison, he was tired of the view.

"Then what is it?" Polyxena questioned.

"I don't know how to say this."

She came over and made him look her in the eyes.

"Just say it," she replied, steeling herself for the worst. "It's always the easiest way. These things are usually bigger when they're locked up inside us, when we give voice to them we make them real, real is small."

"Not this time. It's Achilleía. She's alive," he said, still not believing it himself.

"What did you say, Chiron?" Polyxena questioned her own hearing, because she couldn't possibly have heard him right.

"Achilleía ain't dead, ma. I talked to her last night!"

Polyxena couldn't believe her ears.

She wanted to cry and jump for joy at the same time.

Part of her wanted to scream, *My girl is alive!*

But another part of her was lamenting the fact that the man she loved was still a married man, not a widower.

"Jesus," she gasped, walking around her desk and sitting down. "Last night?"

Chiron nodded.

"You sure? I mean—?"

"Yeah, yeah, no doubt," he began, trying to explain. "And, ma, listen. Believe me, I appreciate everything you've done all these years. You held it down for real and nothing can change how I feel about you. It's just... crazy right now, you know?"

Polyxena nodded. She wanted him out of there before the weakness she felt, the hurt at her core, made it out and she couldn't hold back the tears she was fighting.

"Go. I'm good."

"You sure?"

She couldn't look him in the eye.

"Just go. Please."

Chiron nodded and left.

As soon as he did, Polyxena broke down.

Her emotions were all mixed up.

Once Chiron got back to his cell, he picked up the picture he had of him, Achilleía and their two-year-old twin boys. It was a picture from the past of a stranger from the present. He couldn't grasp the implications of that call from last night beyond the first, most obvious one, Achilleía was alive.

"My husband?" Faith echoed, looking at the phone in Quadir's hand like it was a ticking time bomb.

"You said you wanted to know what's up, right? Take the phone, it's the only way you get the truth, and that's what you want, isn't it?"

Without lowering the gun, she took the phone with her free hand.

"Hello?" she said, tentatively. It felt as though she were entering a dark room, her hands outstretched, cautiously feeling her way.

On the other end, Chiron's heart seized up in his chest. The last thing he expected was to get a call from his dead wife. Nothing in the world could prepare you for that. And yet here she was, speaking to him from beyond the grave. He couldn't wrap his mind around that surreal feeling—it made no sense to him given the fact he was serving three consecutive life sentences for murdering her and their two-year-old twin boys.

He had been in the same cell for five years now, his soul slowly burning away. Pain and bitterness were constant companions. To hear her voice, to feel her presence after yearning for it for so long, to try to will himself into waking up from the hell his life had become... it was as though God had finally answered his only prayer.

"Achilleía? I... please tell me this is you, please," he urged, fighting to keep his voice low so he wouldn't be heard by the C.O. on the tier.

Quadir had told him that Spook thought he'd spotted her in a mall in Philly, but there were a dozen lookalikes out there, and two dozen nearly look-likes, and God alone knew how many almost but not quites up and down every mall in America. Chiron never expected it to be true.

"No. My name is Faith. Faith Newkirk. Not Achilleía," the voice spat back, sounding more firm than her own heart believed.

"Faith Newkirk? That's a pretty shitty alias, baby girl. It's me, Chiron, your fuckin' husband, no need to front with me," He promised, louder than he should've, but he didn't care.

"My husband's name is Hector."

Her words felt like a punch in the gut. He felt so sick, he had to sit down.

"You're... married?"

The anguish in his voice was so deep, Faith felt it in her soul.

"Look, I'm sorry I'm not who you think I am, okay? I—"

"Your favorite color is fuchsia, not purple, and you hate when people mix the two," he recited, like a mantra.

Faith stopped.

"That doesn't prove anything."

"You have a snake tattooed around your upper right thigh with a snake's mouth right by your second smile," he explained.

The words caught in her throat.

"How—"

"Because I'm your husband," he said, like it was the only answer that made any sense and surely she had to understand.

"No!" she shouted, dropping the phone and backing away as if the truth had burned straight through the phone.

Quadir picked it up and put it on speaker.

"Whenever you get a sweet tooth, you crave jelly and marshmallow fluff sandwiches," Chiron continued, losing himself in each memory as he spoke them aloud. "Your favorite movie is *Ghost*. Your favorite song is 'Adore'. When you cum, you laugh and cry at the same time."

"Stop!" she screamed, covering her ears and sobbing. "Just stop!"

Her whole body trembled.

Who was this person? How could they know so much about her?

Intimate things, things he couldn't know unless he was... Her mind wouldn't let her even think the rest.

"No... My name is Faith Newkirk and I'm married to Hector Newkirk. My daughter's name is Jada. She has her father's nose and my eyes. I own my own boutique ..." she tried to speak the reality she knew back into existence.

"I don't know what's happened to you, but you are my wife, Achilleía. Shit, I gotta go," Chiron blurted out, sensing that the police were coming to make their rounds.

Quadir put the phone down.

"I told you I was on your side."

Faith had forgotten about the gun in her hand.

It hung limply at her side.

Quadir walked over to her and slowly removed the piece, laying it carefully on the nightstand.

"I don't know what's happening to me."

Quadir embraced her and she let herself be hugged.

She cried on his shoulder.

When her emotions finally subsided, Quadir looked her in her eyes. "Ma, you may not know it, but you *are* Achilleía Black, daughter of one Ray Butler, who you may be aware is the biggest gangsta in New York," Quadir explained, walking her through her family tree patiently. "God bless the dead and wife of Chiron Black, the illest nigguh alive. You're the heir to the throne of an empire, but your bitch ass brother had you killed so he could keep it to himself."

Faith shook her head like she was trying to clear it, but the static wouldn't go away.

"I have to rest."

He helped her over to the bed and she laid down.

"That's fine. All good, ma. Just relax, okay," Quadir said, going over to check the window. "We good here, but in the morn—," he stopped short because when he turned back around, Faith was asleep. He looked at her, smiling. "Shit about to get real."

9

"Do you recognize this woman, Mr. Newkirk?" The black federal agent asked.

He and his white female partner had returned to show Hector a number of pictures. Hector gazed at the photograph of the woman on the agent's phone.

"Yes, I do," Hector replied. "She works for my wife. Her name is Kareema. I don't know her last name."

"Hannibal," the white agent informed him. "Kareema Hannibal. And, unfortunately, she doesn't work for your wife anymore. She's dead."

"Oh Jesus..." he said, solemnly. "And you think it has something to do with my wife's disappearance?"

"We're not sure," the black agent told him. "But there is a connection we intend to pursue."

"And what's that?" Hector probed.

He looked at his partner.

She nodded so he answered. "We have a car on one of the mall surveillance cameras following Miss Hannibal out of the parking lot," he said. "We picked up that car on multiple intersection cameras tailing her all the way home."

"We even have a picture of the men in the car," the female agent added, pulling up a picture of Ox on her iPad and handing it to Hector. "Michael 'Ox' Beasley. Brooklyn, New York. He just got out after doing four flat for drug charges. He was the driver."

Hector missed the past tense. "Do we know where to find him?" Hector questioned.

"We do," she replied. "He was one of the men killed at your home. Hence the connection."

"That's more than slight, I'd say."

"There's more," the black agent continued. "Though this is more tenuous, the vehicle your wife fled the scene in and the vehicle that Beasley drove are both registered in New York."

"You said, fled the scene," Hector noted. "That's a strange choice of words when we're talking about a victim."

"The Philadelphia police intend to charge Faith with murder once they bring her in," she answered.

"Murder? That's insane," Hector protested, shaking his head. "Jesus Christ, you've got it all on tape, you can see them attacking her!"

"That's one for the law courts, Mr. Newkirk, but as far as the police are concerned, when your wife crawled under the van to lie in ambush, then shot the driver of the Bentley, she was no longer the one being pursued," the black agent said, explaining how grave the situation had become.

Murder? The word echoed in Hector's mind like voices down a long, dark hall.

After they left, Hector tried Faith's phone for the umpteenth time. But this time it rang. His heart leaped until Jada's beautifully familiar voice answered.

"Daddy!"

"Baby! What are you doing with Mommy's phone?"

"I found it under the bed and I put it on the charger for her, because I wanted to call her," she replied. "I miss Mommy."

The whole time, her phone had been literally under his nose. Now he knew that he'd fucked up.

10

The taxi pulled into the parking lot of what looked like an abandoned hotel.

Looks can be deceptive.

But it wasn't abandoned; it was actually a welfare-slash-crackhead motel. The drug was so prevalent the pungent stench covered the building like cheap perfume.

The lamppost blinkered in and out, while shadowy figures scurried back and forth, and a rapid-fire exchange of words punctuated the darkness.

"$16.20," the cabbie said, eyeing his passenger in the rearview.

She was obviously out of place.

Dressed in a tight designer dress, she looked like a piece of fresh meat about to be tossed to the lions.

The cabbie sensed her hesitation.

"Ma'am, are you *sure* you're at the right place?"

"This is the Lincoln Motel, right?"

The cabbie guffawed, "Yeah, like thirty years ago. Now it's Crack Heaven in more ways than one."

She knew what Paris had said. The Lincoln Motel. She didn't want to disappoint him or herself.

"I'm supposed to go to room 131."

He squinted into the darkness.

"Second to the last door. Right there," he said, pointing.

She took a deep breath.

"Could you—"

"Of course. I won't pull off until you go in," he assured her.

She slid a fifty through the slot.

"Keep the change."

"God bless you," he replied.

She cringed at the irony.

She got out and headed to the room.

Eyes, bloodshot and cold, peeked at her through the darkness. In her mind, she thought she had heard a growl. She sped up her steps, licking her lips as she approached the door. She knocked.

No answer.

"Ay, pretty lady," a raspy voice called out. "Lemme hold somethin'."

She knocked harder.

No answer.

She tried the knob, sensing someone close and getting closer. It was unlocked.

She rushed through the door and slammed it behind her, her heart pounding in her chest. The room smelled moldy and stale, like beer gone flat and left alone since the seventies. The only lights were flashes of the red neon signs outside in the parking lot.

"You're late, Patricia."

The deep voice made her jump like a white bitch in a scary movie. She thought she was alone. Now she knew she wasn't.

Paris stood up from the chair in the corner, his sharp features accentuated by the stab of neon cutting across his eyes and nose as he approached her.

"I came as soon as I could get—" she started to say but Paris grabbed her by the throat.

"Wrong goddamn answer, I said, you're late," he growled.

"I'm sorry," she said, shaking, and not only from fear. There was a sweet tingle of anticipation.

Paris knew she was used to being put on a pedestal.

She was the pastor of the largest church in Brooklyn.

On top of that, her husband was a real estate developer and the president of the Brooklyn chapter of the NAACP.

But deep down, Paris knew what she wanted; she was simple like that. She wanted that thug shit in her life. He planned on dicking her down until she overdosed.

He flung on the bed and she landed with a solid bounce.

Her emotions gyrated between fear and pleasure, not knowing what to expect next.

"Paris, did I do—"

Smack!

He smacked her face hard enough to sting, but not hard enough to draw blood. She grabbed her cheek, but before she could protest, he'd snatched her dress so hard, the buttons popped to reveal her white Gucci bra: He pushed the cloth wider, like he was parting the Red Sea, until he saw her panties.

She tried to scoot away, but he grabbed her ankles and with surprising strength flipped her over on her stomach.

Then, standing over her, he slowly removed his alligator belt and wrapped it around his fist.

"Take off your panties," he told her.

Patricia looked over her shoulder. Her eyes got wide when she saw the belt.

"Wh-what are you—"

Sssssssswwwwappp!

The alligator bit into her ass with a loud swap.

"Oh Lord Jesus!" she cried, trying to scramble away.

But Paris wasn't about to let her go; he grabbed her ankle and snatched her back.

"I told you to take them off," he barked. "Don't make me tell you a third time."

"You nasty bitch!" he grunted. "You stand in that pulpit like you Miss Goody-Goody, but you ain't shit but a nasty bitch, ain't you?!"

"No don't—," she began to protest.

"Turn over on your back," he demanded.

She complied, while he grabbed her arms and dragged her to the edge of the bed until her head hung off the edge—it wasn't sex, it was more like sensory overload. Her body jerked like she was catching the Holy Ghost.

"Just ride with me, baby," he soothed, savoring the feel of her around him. "With your church and my money, we gonna take over this city," he vowed, from his lips, through her lips, all the way to God's ear.

11

Captain Tillman sat across from Polyxena in the dimly lit Italian restaurant, eyeing her like she was the finest dish on the menu.

She knew she was being admired, and played it off like she was looking around innocently and blissfully unaware, where in truth she was giving him the side eye and working her magic.

"I like this place. It really feels like Italy," she remarked, taking a sip of her water.

"Oh? Have you been in Italy?"

"No," she lied, with a girlish giggle. "I guess I should've said how Italy must feel."

Tillman toyed with his pasta, twisting the fork absentmindedly.

"You know I can't stop thinking about you, right?"

"Is that right?" Polyxena smirked. "Well, what does your wife think about that?"

Tillman shifted uncomfortably. "I, umm, didn't think my marriage was an issue with you."

"Let's talk truths," she said, "It was always going to depend on where you're trying to go with this."

He reached across the table and held her hand, gazing into her eyes.

"And to bed isn't the right answer?" He smile was a little sad. "I want you to be mine."

"Then it'll be on my terms."

"I wouldn't have it any other way," he vowed, speaking without hesitation.

Polyxena changed the flow of the moment, taking a bite of her salad.

"You know, I've got certain arrangements that I'm going to need someone high up to help me handle," she said, with an air of attractive confidence.

"Arrangements?" he echoed, eyebrow slightly raised.

"A girl's gotta eat."

"I see," he said, pausing as if he was thinking. "These arrangements, do they involve any illegalities?"

Polyxena smiled mischievously.

"You know what they say, some laws are made to be broken," she remarked, holding up her wine glass as if to toast her statement.

Tillman seemed to sit up straighter and cleared his throat.

"Well Polyxena, I need you to understand that's one of the main reasons they transferred me to this institution," he explained. "I run a clean shop. Now, if *you* need something, that's what I'm here for."

"Come on, Franklin, we all color outside the lines," Polyxena began, slipping her foot out of her shoe. "Because nobody can live in a straitjacket." She ran her foot along his inner thigh until she felt him, then she began to rub her foot slowly, using her toes to massage him. He hardened quicker than a glare from Medusa.

"Mmmmm, see?" she cooed, offering that knowing, pleasing smile she had perfected. "In your mind, you know what I'm doing is wrong, but it feels *so* right..."

Tillman subtly slouched and widened his stance, grabbing his wine glass for stability.

"This... is different."

"Is it? Adultery is a law this long black dick was made to break," she responded, massaging him the whole time. "Just imagine how it felt when I put you in my mouth, remember? How I ran my tongue all the way to the tip?"

He grunted, obviously thinking about it.

"I want to fuck you so bad right now," Polyxena whispered lustfully. "I want to feel you inside me so deep..."

The whole time, she kept her hauntingly exotic blue eyes locked on his. They were more hypnotic than the liqueur and more mesmerizing than the movements of a belly dancer. Tillman was stuck. The combination of her gaze, her seductive voice, and her foot action sent Tillman over the edge. He was helpless. The sudden fierce shudder gave him away.

"Damn," he gasped, trying to slow his spinning head.

"Now, was that so wrong?" she grinned, licking her lips like the cat that stole the milk.

Tillman sipped his wine, then dabbed his forehead with his napkin.

"These arrangements," he questioned, forcing himself to focus. "What is it exactly are we talking about?"

"Chiron Black."

"Chiron Black? As in the most dangerous man in the whole prison? Do I want to know what you need with him?"

"Someone slid a note under my door and said he has a cell phone," Polyxena replied, matter-of-factly. "I want him busted and put in isolation."

"I see. And who was this *someone*?"

"A nobody looking for a favor," she explained. "I need Chiron out of the way."

"I don't think you should get involved with a man like that, Polyxena."

A man like that is just what I need, she thought. Instead, she replied, "I've got you to protect me, right?"

He was reluctant to cross the line, but lust pulled him over. "Always."

Chiron will eat you alive.

After lunch, Polyxena watched Tillman pull off, as she touched up her lipstick in the rearview mirror. She knew he wouldn't hesitate to have the contraband unit raid Chiron's cell. He'd be shocked, but he'd think someone else snitched. It was prison. The place was filled with snitches and bitches. Polyxena knew Chiron would stop at nothing to get Achilleía back. She needed him isolated. Make him totally dependent on her. That was love, all her heart love. There was no way she was going to give him up without a fight.

You're dead wrong, a voice deep inside her said.

"She's supposed to be dead," she hissed at her reflection, fighting back tears for and against Achilleía.

Her mind traveled back to a time when she would've died for Achilleía, instead of wanting to kill her.

"My brother will *never* run this family," Achilleía seethed, as she paced the floor. "Over my dead fucking body. Daddy trained *me* to take over, not fuckin' Paris."

Polyxena had never seen Achilleía so full of rage.

They'd served in Afghanistan together, fighting and killing until they were both literally and figuratively soaked in blood, but still, Achilleía had never been as volcanic as she was in that moment. It didn't matter that they were in Polyxena's loft apartment, surrounded by luxury, Achilleía was back in the killing fields, in full on combat mode.

"But your father said—" Polyxena began before Achilleía cut her off with an icy, bloodshot glare.

"Whose side are you on??"

Polyxena went from zero to a hundred instantly.

"How dare you question my loyalty. Fuck you if you don't know me by now, Achie."

Both of them glared at each other for a moment, until Achileía, knowing she was wrong, broke eye contact with a frustrated sigh.

"I was buggin', aight? I'm sorry," she mumbled.

"Damn right you were! Despite your last name or my last name, bitch *we* family!" Polyxena stressed.

"I know," Achileía said. "Always. It's just... I can't believe the whole team is gone."

"We at war."

There was only time for blood and sweat. But in their hearts, they were mourning.

Jamaican Roxy.

Dead.

Maxi.

Dead.

Poo.

Dead.

Big Lez.

Dead.

The only one they didn't know about was Medea; she had just barely escaped the massacre.

"Have you heard from Chiron?" Polyxena asked.

Achileía shook her head, a worried crease running like a fissure through her brow.

"No. His phone is going straight to voicemail."

"So, what do we do now?"

She eyed Polyxena with a wicked expression.

"Show Paris he shouldn't have missed."

.   .   .

One of the family's main stash spots was in an apartment building with tighter security than the White House. There were shooters stationed on the roof, apartment security rode around in a white Taurus with the word 'security' emblazoned on the side, and there were more armed guards stationed inside. It was for the apartment on the fourth floor. They thought they were safe. Protected. But their armor was little more than a line-up of street goons, and they were weak where it mattered. Beneath.

Boc! Boc!

"I hate fuckin' rats," Polyxena spat, as she trained her infrared on two cat-sized rats and blew them into furry bits and pieces. Several other rats shrieked and ran off.

"Cut that shit out before they hear us," Achilleía spat.

In response, Polyxena stomped on a rat's head when the rodent was reckless enough to get too close. They sloshed through the sewer water. The women were outfitted for war. Kevlar vest, night vision goggles, and fully automatic weapons and live flash grenades.

The sewer reeked of shit.

Achilleía looked at the GPS read out on her phone.

"We're right underneath the building," she told Polyxena as she grabbed the first rung of the iron ladder dangling overhead. She hauled herself up. Polyxena came up right behind her. When she got to the manhole and tried to push it up, it didn't budge.

"It's stuck. I need your help."

Polyxena maneuvered up next to her and they both put their shoulders into the task. After several seconds of constant pressure, the sludge that held like glue finally broke and the manhole opened up, letting in the sounds of the boiler room—and a more unexpected noise; someone fucking.

Achilleía peered through the crack and saw a shapely cinnamon-toned chick bent over a washing machine, a light-skinned, bald-headed dude in a security uniform with his pants around his ankles servicing her like she was a rear loader.

"That nigguh don't fuck you like this, do he?"

Achilleía and Polyxena crept through into the room, coming straight from the sewer like Das EFX. The sounds of sex hid their footsteps as they tiptoed toward the unsuspecting couple.

"I'ma put this big dick in your pretty little ass," he grunted lustfully, then his heart leapt in his chest.

"And I'ma put this in your pretty little ass if you even take a deep breath," Achilleía hissed in his ear, pressing her gun to the back of his skull.

He sucked in his breath and held it.

"Yo-yo-you got it," he stammered, losing his erection in three seconds flat.

The girl's eyes swelled up when Polyxena put her gun to her cheek.

"Pl-pl-please don't make me," Polyxena mockingly replied in a sinister tone.

"How many inside?" Achilleía questioned.

"I don't know. At least twelve," he answered.

Achilleía snatched him by the collar, shoving him towards the door.

He shuffled up the stairs with his pants still around his ankles, too frightened to try and pull them up, with Achilleía behind him, while Polyxena kept the chick in check and followed them.

Two security guards stood around by the first floor door. As soon as one saw him coming up stairs with his pants down, they started to laugh. That mocking died the second they saw the barrel of Achilleía's fully loaded automatic MAC-10.

"Yo!" one reacted faster than the other, reaching for his gun.

He never made it.

Bbbbrrrrrrappp!

The barrage of bullets tore through his abdomen, chest, and face like a swarm of angry flesh-eating bees biting off fatal chunks.

"It burns," weren't very philosophical last words, but they were the best he could manage.

The second guard reacted a heartbeat later, trying to dive behind a pillar, but Polyxena picked him off mid-flight. He landed headless and twitching.

"Follow your friends," Achilleía told her hostage.

"Huh?"

Boc! Boc! Boc!

Achilleía hit him in the head twice and Polyxena dispatched the chick with one bullet under the chin that exploded out of the top of her skull. It wasn't the way she'd imagined her brains being fucked out only a few moments ago.

As the bodies dropped, three more guards raced into the foyer from the outside.

"They're in the lobby!" One barked into an earpiece, summoning more.

Achilleía spun and fired as she stepped back, using the stair-well as cover.

Another guard dropped, a bullet splitting his throat. Blood bubbled from his neck like a water fountain.

The lobby lit up like 42nd Street in the eighties until Achilleía and Polyxena made it to the elevator.

"They on the elevator! We got em!" More shouts down the earpiece.

On the fourth floor, a whole team of shooters got ready for their arrival. Automatics, shotguns, and pistols were trained on the elevator as they watched the numbers tick up from one to four and the doors slid open.

The guns sounded like an angry chorus of booming bari-tones, filling the elevator with smoke and bullets.

No one in that elevator could have survived.

But the elevator was empty.

The shooters moved in, cautiously staying on either side of the doors, trying to get a read on the situation as the smoke cleared. Two shooters lunged in, ready to blast, but found no one.

"Ain't—" one began to say until something metallic came bouncing out.

A flash grenade.

It sizzled and burst into blinding light.

It wasn't made to explode—it was designed to daze and blind —giving Polyxena and Achilleía enough time to drop back through the emergency hatch in the elevator ceiling and pick off the blinded shooters like fish in a barrel.

Their twin MAC-10s sang a duet of death as they sprayed up the hallway like the Orkin man, riddling shooter after shooter until the hallway was sticky with blood.

They ran up on the door at the end, and with one shot, blew the lock off, and kicked in the door until they were driven back by automatic gunfire.

Polyxena pulled the pin on another grenade and tossed it inside.

"*Clear!*" she barked, then she and Achilleía scattered away from the door in the opposite direction.

The detonation was brutal, shaking the concrete floor beneath them.

Black smoke filled the room.

They came in right behind the explosion, like the tail end of a tornado, blasting brainless anyone the grenade hadn't ripped to bits.

"In here!" Achilleía yelled.

They headed into the back bedroom, which was bare, except for a large waterbed.

"Help me move this," Achilleía told her.

It was a hell of a lot of work, but after a lot of grunts and some serious sweats, they got to the real treasure: the large floor safe hidden under the bed.

In the world outside, sirens were getting closer.

"Hurry up, Achie," Polyxena urged.

Achilleía flicked the dial back and forth quickly.

10-21-72.

Click! The safe opened.

"Damn yo, I'm robbin' my own safe," she remarked, not believing it had to come to that. The world was inside out and fucked upside down.

Inside, the safe was packed with stacks and stacks of shrink-wrapped money.

"We can't carry all of that," Polyxena surmised, looking at the bricks.

"Just get what you can."

They whipped out folded nylon bags, expanding them into the size of body bags and began to fill them up, fast.

Sirens grew louder.

Their hands worked like shovels, scooping and dumping, scooping and dumping. Once the bags were full, they tried to lift them. They were dead weights.

"Dump some out."

Polyxena dumped several stacks out, scattering them across the floor. It was hundreds of thousands of dollars, and the damned things were still too heavy to move.

"We gotta go!" Achilleía said, grabbing a double-fistful of bricks and tossing them.

They jetted.

Polyxena tracked over to look out the window. She saw all the police cars, strobe lights swirling like a disco down there.

"We'll never get back to the sewer," she told Achilleía.

"Then we use our wings!" Achilleía said, laughing.

Her adrenaline was pumping so hard, she felt invincible.

They hit the stairs, but instead of going down, rushed up for the roof door, slowing on the last spiral of the stairs expecting the stationed shooters to be in place.

Meanwhile, a long way down, the police were storming the building, S.W.A.T.-geared up.

Achilleía hit the bar across the door and threw it open in a blaze of fire alarms. Polyxena covered her. Nobody fired a shot. The alarm died the moment the door closed behind them, completing the circuit again. They made their way around carefully, surprised that the rooftop was empty and expecting an ambush at any second. Seeing the cigarette butts, still warm to the touch, Achilleía figured it out; the roof shooters must have gone down to protect the fourth floor and died in the attack.

The next building was only a long jump away.

Standing on the edge over the dizzying drop, they tossed their money over to the opposite roof. It was down twelve flights to sure death if they couldn't span the yawn.

"Ready?" Achilleía questioned, taking a deep breath.

"Ask me that on the other side," Polyxena said, grimly.

Achilleía was right behind her. Their feet intensely beat the asphalt, counterpoint to the slap of their hearts, and when they leaped, they felt the deadly fingers of gravity grab for their ankles.

And miss.

They landed on the other side, ducking and rolling, then came up running.

They grabbed the money and disappeared through the roof door, just as the police came bursting through the alarmed door on the opposite roof.

The cops spread out over the rooftop.

One officer walked over to the edge and looked down, then across.

She measured off the distance in her mind, then talked into her earbud.

"Check the next building over."

"Ten-four," crackled the reply.

But it was too late.

The police followed procedures, and procedures meant

delayed reaction; first they surrounded the parameter, blocking off escape routes, before they breached the building. By that time, Achileía and Polyxena were already in the basement, crawling through the manhole like ghouls returning to the crypt.

It would be morning before the police would discover the dislodged manhole cover and realized how they'd been screwed.

As the women rode away from the scene on twin jet Ducati's, Achileía got a call in her headset.

"Yo."

"Achileía?"

"Medea? What up, baby girl, where are you?"

"I'm at the lake house," Medea replied. There was something weird about her voice; it was strained and panicky.

"Okay, I—"

"Everybody's dead, Achie."

A sob down the long distance line.

"I know, but we're not, okay?" Achileía assured her. "Just relax, we got this. I'm on my way."

"This shit is crazy," Dominque lamented. "What the hell is going on between you and Paris?"

"I'll explain when I get there. We good. I'm on my way."

"I'll be here."

She killed the call and signaled for Polyxena to pull over.

They stopped, side by side, engines running.

Achileía unloosened the ties holding the bag in place on the back of her bike and handed it to Polyxena.

"What up?"

"Medea just called. She's at the lake house."

"The fuck she doin' at the lake house?"

"I don't know, but I'm going to get her. Take the money back to my crib and wait for me."

"Yo Achie, I'm not feelin' this. Somethin' don't smell right," Polyxena protested, feeling in her gut what she couldn't put into words.

"Don't worry, ma, we good. Baby girl one of us."

Polyxena looked her in the eyes and asked, "You sure about that?"

"You know our motto, no soldier left behind."

Polyxena couldn't argue against their core principle, but still...

"Just meet me at the crib. We good," Achilleía repeated, then began to pull her helmet back down.

"Achilleía."

"Yeah?"

"I love you."

Polyxena couldn't see it but she knew Achilleía was smiling behind her tinted visor.

"I love you, too."

They hugged then roared off in separate directions.

It was the last time Polyxena saw Achilleía alive, and Achilleía never knew they had come off with more than three million dollars, even after they'd been forced to dump all those bricks. That was a serious score.

12

"We need to get out of here," Quadir told Faith, gently shaking her awake.

Faith rolled over, groggy, unfocused. "And go where?"

"New York."

She opened her eyes.

"New York? I'm not going to New York. For what?"

"Achie—I mean—Faith, didn't you *hear* Chiron?" Quadir said. "This is not your life. Philly is not your home. You belong in New York. This war won't end until you come back and claim your throne. Believe me, ma, you're a queen in New York."

"I'm a queen wherever I am," Faith retorted, without conceit.

Quadir smirked.

"Achilleía, I hear you coming back."

She shot him a look.

"Stop calling me that. I'm... me," she replied, getting to her feet. "I've got to get home and—"

She momentarily lost her balance, wobbling on her feet.

Quadir caught her arm and steadied her, then sat her on the bed.

"You okay?"

Faith grabbed her head.

"Just a little dizzy and I still have a bitch of a headache," she responded. "I need my insulin."

"Insulin? You're a diabetic?" he asked, surprised. "Since when?"

She nodded.

"That's why I have to get home."

Quadir squatted down so he was eye level with her.

"Ma, you *can't* go home," he stressed. "Not an option. Your brother sent me to kill you, and when he finds out I didn't pull the trigger, he'll send more. A fuckin' army if that's what it'll take to stop you from getting back to the planet."

"The planet?" She echoed, not following.

"Of Brooklyn," he chuckled, using some old-school slang for Crooklyn.

She shook her head.

"I can't leave my daughter."

"So, lemme ask you this, would you rather lead them to her or away from her?" Quadir surmised. "With you back in Brooklyn, she's safe here in Philly."

Faith grabbed her head like she was trying to stop it from splitting.

"I need to talk to Hector," she said, then quickly added, "I can't do this. I can't think."

"Okay look, you don't have your phone so you can't call him. And you don't know who Paris has tailing him, so let me get you somewhere safe and then I'll bring your Hector to you. How's that?"

Faith thought about it. Whatever was going on, she the absolute last thing she wanted to do was endanger Hector or Jada. She nodded.

"Okay."

"Okay, let's see about getting you some insulin. Come on."

They pulled up to a pharmacy and parked. Quadir killed the engine and looked at her.

"So, how do I do this? Just walk up to the counter and ask for insulin or what? Or is there some special dose or something?"

"You can't just buy insulin, you have to have a prescription," Faith replied.

Quadir gave an exasperated little sigh. "Ma, trust me, they ain't gonna turn me away, if they got it, I'ma get it."

"Good luck with that."

"I'll be right back," Quadir jumped out and heading for the door.

The little bell rang overhead as he entered; old school. He looked around. It wasn't a large pharmacy, just a small neighborhood store. There were three other people in the place. Quadir waited until no one was at the counter before he approached the woman at the register. He grabbed two packs of gum and a magazine on the counter.

"Good morning, beautiful," he remarked, smiling.

Her coffee-brown complexion lit up just a little bit. "Good morning, beautiful yourself," she replied. She had a nice smile and pretty eyes. She was a big girl, but she carried it well. Not like some of the fat girls out there with tits that hung down around their bellies and bellies that hung down over their snatch.

"I'm sorry, I'm sure you get this all the time, but you really remind me of someone... Jill Scott, you know her?" Quadir said, turning on the charm. "I bet you can sing, too. Can you sing?"

She was blushing. "No, I can't sing to save my life," she replied. "But I like Jill Scott."

"I bet you sound good hittin' a high note," and there was something in the way he said it that told her he wasn't talking about music anymore.

Her cheeks flushed. "Ummm, that'll be—" she began to say, ringing up his order.

Quadir reached across the counter and put his hand on hers, gently.

"Listen, ma, what's your name?"

"Misha."

"I like that 'cause you have to smile to say it," he said. "Misha... Listen Misha, I need a favor."

"Okay," she replied, her tone saying *I'm listening*...

"I'm a diabetic, right, but I'm not from around here, and I don't have my prescription, but I need a shot to get me back home."

"I'm sorry, but you have—"

"No ma, don't do me like that," he soothed. "Besides, it's your fault. If you weren't so sweet, my sugar wouldn't be so high."

She shook her head, but couldn't help but smile.

"I'll tell you what—" Quadir said, pulling out a wad of money, all hundreds. "You go get your hair done, nails done, get a new outfit and some shoes and show Philly Jill ain't the only one living life like it's golden." He slid over ten hundred-dollar bills and put the magazine on top.

Misha looked down at the magazine.

She knew there was a grand under there.

She licked her lips, looked around then asked, "One dose?"

Quadir flashed her a smile.

"Whatever you can spare."

She looked him in the eyes.

"Long acting or rapid?"

"Whatever's the good stuff," Quadir said.

"I thought you were a diabetic?"

"And I thought you wanted to get paid," he shot back. "Bring me what you got."

She slid the magazine off the counter and walked in the back. She didn't come back for so long, Quadir thought she might've called the police. She came out carrying a small bag and handed it to him.

"I need needles and alcohol wipes."

"In the bag already," she winked.

"I like you lil mama, I'ma definitely check for you when I'm back in town."

"You do that," she replied.

When he got back in the driver's seat, he realized Faith had drifted off.

"You okay?" he asked, pulling out of the lot. He handed her the brown bag.

"Just feeling a little weak," Faith replied, taking the insulin out of the bag.

"You didn't tell me what to get, long or fast, I just got the best," he explained.

"Long or fast?" Faith echoed.

He looked at her.

"You don't know what you stick in your veins?"

"Hector always picks up my meds," she admitted sheepishly. "I guess I never thought to look at the bottle."

Quadir chuckled.

"Spoiled little house wife. Just wait 'til you wake up."

Faith smiled secretly, ignoring the implications of his comment. She wiped her forearm with the alcohol pad.

"You need me to pull over?"

"No, I've done this so many times I could give myself a shot on a roller coaster," she joked.

Quadir chuckled.

Faith glanced at him as he drove.

"Can I ask you something?" she began.

"No doubt."

"Who are you to her... Achilleía?"

Quadir smiled like he was reliving a pleasant past.

"In Achilleía's world, I didn't register a blip," he admitted. "I was a little nigguh in the game."

"And now?"

He looked at her, arrogantly.

"That was then. Now, I'm a boss."

She didn't respond to the last comment, because she was giving herself the insulin shot. When she finished, she recapped the needle and put it in the bag.

"The first thing—" Faith started to say, but then her whole body shuddered.

"Yo, Faith."

"I don't feel—" she tried to say, but her eyes rolled up in her head and she threw up violently.

"Faith!" he screamed, bringing the car to a screeching halt in the middle of the street.

He turned to her, but all he saw was the whites of her eyes while her body convulsed like she was being electrocuted and she foamed at the mouth.

"I'ma kill that bitch!" Quadir roared, thinking of Misha. But there was only time for one destination. The hospital. He floored the car and headed straight for Temple Hospital, driving like the Devil himself was on his ass.

He skidded up in front of the Emergency Room doors, flung the door open, then ran around to Faith's side. He opened her door. By this time, she was totally unresponsive, her eyes closed, her body clammy.

He feared the worst.

"Hold on ma, don't die on me, please!" He prayed, carrying her into the Emergency Room. He immediately started yelling, "Can I get some help! I need some help over here!"

Several nurses rushed over as Quadir laid Faith on a gurney.

A white nurse ran over immediately, asking, "What happened?"

"She's a diabetic," Quadir explained. "She gave herself a shot and then she started shaking and throwing up."

"Bring me the insulin!" the nurse demanded.

Quadir rushed out to the car and came back with the bottle

for the nurse. After handing it over, he tried to go past her and head toward the back.

"You can't go back there."

"I have to see her," Quadir said firmly.

The nurse put her hand on his arm, looking him in the eye sympathetically.

"Later," she said. "She's in good hands. She needs you out here, not getting in the way. Trust me."

Quadir sighed, shook his head, and headed over to the sitting area.

What the hell happened?

He thought to himself, pacing the floor. His first thought was Misha had given him something other than insulin, but he read the bottle before he handed it to the nurse and that was exactly what it was.

Is she dead?

He shook it off. He didn't even want to consider that possibility.

"Please don't let her die," he prayed under his breath.

It took four hours, but the doctor finally came out and spoke to him.

"She's in a coma," the doctor informed him gravely.

"A coma?" Quadir said, shocked. "But..."

"The nurse says that you told her the victim is a diabetic."

"Yeah she told me that."

"Are you sure?"

Quadir looked at him with a frustrated scowl.

"Of course, I'm sure, yo, I know what she said."

"No, I'm not blaming you," the doctor said. "It's just strange that a woman who isn't a diabetic would tell you that she was," the doctor explained. "When she took that shot, it dropped her blood sugar so low, her body went into shock and seized up."

"But she's gonna make it?"

"We're working hard to stabilize her."

Which wasn't an answer. And meant she wasn't stable.

Quadir shook his head, trying to wrap his mind around everything the doctor just said.

"Do you have any idea why she would be under the impression she was a diabetic?"

Quadir started to answer, but then heard Faith's voice in his mind. *Hector always picks up my meds.*

"Naw," Quadir lied. "No clue. When can I see her?"

The doctor looked like he wanted to say no, but then sighed and told him they'd send someone through to get him.

He'd figured on five minutes. It was more like five hours.

When Quadir entered the room, the antiseptic stillness and the *beep, beep, beep* of the equipment made his heart sank. Her saw her hooked up to the IV drip and the tubes snaking in and out of her.

"Hold on, Achilleía," Quadir whispered, with the force of prayer. "Now that I've found you, I know the mistake I made. I love you."

Quadir sat down in the chair, his eyes glued to Achilleía's sleeping face and thought about the day he had become her sworn enemy and her secret ally.

I'm the fuckin' man! Quadir's eighteen-year-old mind screamed as he watched the fake Beyoncé redbone strutting beside the worst Jennifer Lopez clone he'd ever scene, it didn't matter, they could have looked like Stadler and Waldorf as they played tag-team on his dick, he'd have still been the man. Redbone ran her tongue around the head, stopping to play with the tip while J-Clone licked the length of the shaft.

She looked up at him with the kind of lusty eyes only a porn star could pull off.

He had never been with two women before, but it was like crack, one hit and he was hooked. It was never going to be enough, especially not now that he'd moved up the pecking order, rising to the ranks of lieutenant in Sugar Ray's organization. He was as good as his right hand. This was had to be his new lifestyle. He deserved it. He was young and wild, sure, but he wasn't some dumb thug, he was a thinker. He knew when to turn up and he knew when to fall back.

Chiron had discovered him going hand-to-hand on the block when he was thirteen, recognizing a soldier when he saw one. He put him on the team. But it was Paris who *really* schooled him. Only three years older than Quadir, the pair hit it off immediately.

While he was laying there getting turned out, he had clue his life was rapidly approaching the fork in the road that would make or break everything.

Boooom!

The bedroom door came flying in and three seriously kitted goons rushed in before Quadir had time to react.

They'd caught him with his pants down, literally.

Had Redbone not been squatting over his face, he would've been able to reach his gun on the nightstand. But all he could think was that all that pleasure was going to be the death of him. Still, there were worse ways to go out...

But now, naked and shriveled, he sat frozen, staring down the barrel of three automatic pistols, the two hookers crying. All fear, no lust. How quickly life could turn.

Paris stepped into the room, carrying his own piece. He was icy calm.

"What up, Qua? Ladies," he smirked, checking the edge of the bed then sitting down.

Quadir started try and move.

"No. Stay where you are," Paris told him.

"Yo, Paris, what the fuck is goin' on, fam? I thought I was your man."

Paris nodded.

"You are. Only reason you're not dead," Paris said.

Quadir looked at him, a hand covering his junk.

"Sugar Ray is dead."

The air went out of Quadir. He'd known Sugar Ray was sick, but not that sick.

"Damn brah, I don't know what to say to that. Sorry to hear."

"Yeah, me too," Paris replied, his voice heavy with grief. "So, I'm doing what's gotta be done. Cleaning house. Starting with Chiron."

"Chiron?" Quadir echoed. "But that's your—"

"*Was*," Paris blurted out aggressively. "He's dead, along with everyone loyal to him and his crew. Nigguh was trying to take over the family, the family Ray left *me*."

Quadir knew exactly what Paris was getting at; was he loyal to Chiron?

"So, what's that got to do with me?" Quadir fronted.

Paris smirked and chuckled lightly.

"Good answer, but let's be real with each other, Qua. Who *wouldn't* say that in your situation, sitting there with your dick in your hand 'n all?" he quipped. "Thing is, we both know you got love for Chir. So what I'm asking is, can you forget him just like that?"

Quadir knew his life depended on his answer.

He looked Paris in the eye and replied, "And I still do. Chiron was a good nigguh, but even good nigguhs make bad decisions. He brought me into this family and he taught me to be loyal to the family above all else, feel me? So, if he turned, I won't. It's about family. That don't mean I'm wit you over him; I'm just loyal to the family."

Paris listened to every word carefully.

He didn't say a word.

When Quadir was finished speaking, the room was heavy with tension. The two looked at each other. The only sounds were the women's whimpers and the *tick, tick, tick* of the clock.

Finally, Paris nodded.

"Okay, I respect that. So, you recognize me as the head of this family?" Paris extended his hand.

Quadir shook it.

"It's your birthright."

Paris smiled.

"Indeed it is," he said. "But, I'm sure you'd understand if I tested your loyalty with an ask."

"What do you need?"

"Something handled. You take care of it for me, it will assure your position."

Pause.

"Who?"

Paris glanced around at all the faces. "Get dressed and we'll discuss it."

Quadir did as he was told, ignoring the goons and the girls as he pulled his jeans on, commando, and grabbed a dirty tee. As Quadir and Paris walked out, the goons nodded at the girls.

"What about the girls, boss?"

Paris stopped, smiled, and then shrugged.

"They're all paid for," Quadir said, "Enjoy."

"Chiron Black pled guilty in court today to charges of triple homicide. The infamous Brooklyn kingpin admitted killing his wife and twin boys," the reporter on the TV screen explained. "Black is believed to have been part of an underworld coup aimed at taking control of the Butler crime family. When questioned, Paris Butler had this to say."

The screen cut to a shot of Paris leaving the courthouse looking like he had stepped out of a magazine, sunglassed up and surrounded by a crush of reporters.

"I don't know where you people hear this stuff, it's make believe. There is no such thing as a Butler crime family," Paris said. "Let me ask you this: why is it that whenever a black man is successful, it's immediately labeled a crime family or some other slur deliberately intended to put us back in our place? Slave days are over, my friend. Chiron Black is simply a cold-blooded killer. It is as simple and horrible as that. I hope he burns in Hell for what he did to my sister and her boys."

Quadir cut off his plasma TV, tossing the remote aside.

"Yeah, cold-blooded is right," he spat in a disgusted tone, inhaling the smoke of an exotic blunt.

As he exhaled, he heard a knock at the door.

He got up, yelling out, "Who?"

"Guess!" came back the soft, feminine reply.

He smiled to himself as he opened the door.

Medea stepped inside.

He closed the door behind her.

"Paris just left the courthouse. It's done," Quadir told her.

Medea lowered her eyes.

"I know…" a beat. Uncertainty. "Do you think we did the right thing?"

Quadir tipped her chin up and looked her in the eyes. "I don't think, I know. We're survivors, baby, and this is a cold world. You wit me?"

Her smile returned, like the sun after clouds pass.

"Always."

He brought her close, kissed her forehead, then her nose, then her lips.

"You better go. He'll be looking or you," Quadir remarked.

Medea sighed.

"I'm so tired of this game, baby. How much longer?"

"Patience, sweetness. When the opportunity presents itself, okay? Believe me, you'll be the first to know."

"Promise?"

"Promise."

"I'ma hold you to that."

"As long as you hold me."

They kissed again, then reluctantly parted.

Quadir waited until he knew she was gone, then left the

apartment, going down to where his brand new Aston Martin Vanquish was parked up in the secure garage. Once he was in the driver's seat he picked up his cell and speed-dialed his man.

"Yo."

"We a-go?"

"Indeed."

"I'm on my way."

"Say no more."

But it was a meeting he'd never make.

Several police officers came from every direction and blocked him off before he'd even left the garage structure. Guns aimed at him from every angle.

"Hands where we can see them. Out of the car. Now!"

Slowly, he put his hands out of the window and opened the door from the outside, making sure he didn't give them an excuse to pull the trigger. He was a black man in a serious sports car. That meant he was a walking dead man as far as most the men facing him and to hell with Black Lives Mattering.

As soon as he stretched out on the ground, the police bum-rushed him.

He thought they were about to Rodney King his ass.

"Don't you fuckin' *move!*"

"I ain't!"

"Stop resisting!"

"I'm not resisting!" he barked, which earned him a cold-cock around the base of the skull as they snatched his arms behind his back, damn near pulling the bones out of their joints as they cuffed him up.

They hauled him up to his feet, sending lances of pain through the joints as bones bent ways they were never meant to bend.

When they threw him in the back of the police car, they made sure he hit his head on the door frame.

"Goddamn," he winced, "What the fuck am I under arrest for?"

"You want the good news first, eh? You'll like this. Murder."

"Murder? What the fuck? I ain't killed no one."

He knew the routine. Sure, he knew he'd committed the murder they were accusing him of, but they had zero evidence. It would come down to word against word, his against whoever was snitching on him.

"Fuck, this ain't right. I got rights here. In the constitution, I get to face my accuser? So, who the fuck lied on me?"

The blue blood shook his head, "Nigger, you don't have constitutional rights," and there was no doubting the race hate in those few words. The detective spat them in his face.

"Then fuck you, I want my lawyer," Quadir demanded.

"Nigger wants his lawyer? Bring on the dancing fucking monkeys," the cop rasped, but he knew the deal, lawyering up meant no interrogation.

They sent him down to holding, which was worse than a murder one rap because Chiron's regime ran the jail.

Once Chiron got arrested, he'd begun to rebuild a team of killers from the inside. He partnered with the Bloods to hold him down as he went to war with Paris. On the streets, Chiron's regime couldn't fuck with Paris. But behind the wall, Chiron was a God and his armies were like angels of death. A whole metric shit-ton of Paris's soldiers had met their maker lockup because Chiron's goons went hard.

Quadir knew he had to stay on point.

Murder one meant no bail.

As soon as he hit the pod, every eye in the place was watching him.

Every one of them knew who Quadir was, and who he ran with. It was only ever going to be a matter of time before the sparks to flew.

"Fresh meat!" someone yelled as Quadir bopped hard to his cell, mat in hand.

A few dudes snickered under their breath, lining up to watch him drop the mat. Quadir looked around.

"Yo, who the fuck said that shit?" he snapped, every muscle in his body tense and straining for action. The next few seconds were going to define his life in this hellhole.

No one responded.

"That's what the fuck I thought," Quadir stressed. "So lemme say this once, whoever said it can suck my muthafuckin' dick."

For two days, Quadir stayed on constant vigil, sleeping with one eye open, back against the wall. He'd tried to buy a prison knife, but every liar in the place claimed they didn't have one. That was when he knew it was going to get ugly.

It only took one more day.

Quadir was taking a shower, suds in his eyes, when four dudes, bodies as hard as steel, walked in and fanned out in a semi-circle around him.

He quickly spun around. Naked was vulnerable. It was like some law of the jungle. Strip a guy and he was weak. But it didn't have to be like that. He'd heard about some Russian guy who stripped naked before he murdered his hits, so if it got messy he could step in the shower, rinse the shit off, and get dressed again, leaving the scene looking fresh. There was something wildly primal about that, like an animal preparing for a life or death struggle.

The leader, Flex, spoke up.

"Chiron has a message for you, homie," Flex relayed. "He says welcome to his world."

With that, they rushed him from every angle.

Quadir caught the man on his right with a vicious hook, dropping him to one knee. He then dipped a wild haymaker, smashing the Adam's apple with a straight jab before he choked the dude cross-eyed.

While Quadir was busy defending himself, he took a bastard of a blow to the kidney that damn near made him piss on himself.

He stumbled but was able to hit Flex with an upper cut that had the other man bite his tongue bloody.

Quadir swung so much and so hard that he couldn't hold his arms up, but he kept on swinging, fighting through the punishment, adrenaline making him impervious to pain.

The goons were relentless.

They drove him back.

Quadir felt the wet tile against his back.

Boots and hands kicked and punched until he couldn't take anymore and his body betrayed him.

He blacked out.

Quadir woke up in the isolation ward.

It was a section of the jail where inmates were banged up for infractions—more often than not, fighting.

The guards had found him unconscious on the shower floor.

"Shit, the way he looks, I'd rather be raped," the racist cop joked, all smiles.

Quadir had two broken ribs, a fractured jaw, and a broken nose.

It felt a fuck of a lot worse than that.

He heard the jingle of keys. Time to eat. The key turned in the lock and an officer wearing a hairnet and plastic gloves walked in. The officer sat the tray down on the small lip of a table jutting out of the wall.

"You want my advice, I'd stay away from the oatmeal," the officer winked, smirked, and then walked out.

Quadir assumed that meant someone had jizzed in the oats, or pissed in it, even shit. So, despite his growling stomach, he didn't eat.

He picked the tray up and went to dump the food in the toilet, but felt something heavy.

Grunting, because every movement he made screamed, *pain,*

he used his spoon to fish around in the oatmeal and he quickly realized it was a cell phone tied up in a rubber glove so it wouldn't get wet. He ripped open the glove and turned on the phone.

As soon as it powered on a text popped up.

He opened it.

You had to be disciplined, the message read. *555-9812.*

There was no question who it was from.

He felt eerily self-conscious as he dialed the number, but didn't let the feeling stop him. After several rings, the phone was answered.

"I see you got my message."

"Chiron."

He heard a light chuckle.

"Sorry I had to go to such extremes, Qua, but you deserved it. You really ought to be dead, but I spared you because I know Paris's filled your head with all kinds of bullshit."

"Can't be no more bullshit than a nigguh that would kill his wife and kids," Quadir spat back.

The silence on the other end was so dense, Quadir could practically feel Chiron's anger radiating through the phone.

"I. Did. Not. Kill. My. Family," Chiron seethed. "You say that again, this conversation and your life are over. We clear?"

"So why'd you plead guilty?"

"Because that's the way this game is played, but I didn't call to talk about *me*,"

he said. "I called to talk about *you*. There's something you need to know."

"I know all I need to know," Quadir spat back.

"No, you just *think* you do, you dumb punk," Chiron sighed. "One thing about

you, Qua, your greatest strength is your greatest weakness, and if you don't control it, it's gonna control you. Now, like I said, I'm going to give you the history of this family—"

"You mean Paris's family," Quadir gritted.

Chiron laughed.

"Nigguh you don't know the half!"

At first, when Chiron began, Quadir wasn't interested. But, the more he heard, the more he *wanted* to hear. His lightning-fast mind began to whirl as he saw the angles and was dizzy with possibilities.

As soon as Chiron concluded, Quadir blurted out, "If that's how it went down, why ain't *you* runnin' the family?"

"Because Paris set me up," he said. "That's why I need you, nephew, to be my eyes and ears on that side of the fence, okay? You rolled with Paris because of your loyalty to the family, and family is everything, but now you see it was Paris who turned against the family, not me."

"Yeah, but goddamn Unck, you could've sent the message without half-killing me," Quadir remarked.

Chiron chuckled.

"Like I said nephew, discipline. Besides, Paris is sharp. He's one of the smartest dudes I know. I had to make it look good, feel me? Because if you would've came out untouched, you'd be a dead man to Paris. You know what you in for?"

"Murder one."

"You ever stop to think how they knew?"

"They said an informant."

"Yeah, but who informed?" Chiron said. Before he could answer, Chiron offered, "Paris's behind it, I guarantee. He wanted you to talk to me because he wants to see if your loyalty to him is genuine, feel me? Trust me, you'll sit about a month then this informant will turn up dead. Then the police will drop the charges. I know how Paris thinks. I taught him everything he knows. Just like I taught you."

Quadir knew exactly what Chiron was saying.

It was indeed a twisted game.

"Trust no one, Qua. Sometimes, not even yourself," Chiron warned, adding, "I'll be in touch."

A month later, it played out just like Chiron said it would.

A junkie woman was found OD'ed on a park bench.

An inconsequential death in all ways except one.

Paris was the one who told him about it his first day on the outside.

"I took care of that for you, yo," he chuckled. "The junkie bitch saw you do ol' boy. So I did her. Case dismissed."

Quadir gave him a gangsta hug but felt like he was in the embrace of a python. Straight snake. After what Chiron told him, Quadir would never look at Paris the same again...

13

As soon as Medea sped by in her silver convertible Alfa Romeo Roadster, Polyxena flipped down the tinted visor of her helmet and zipped out into traffic behind her. Polyxena kept a safe distance, using the agility of the bike to keep herself in Medea's blind spots.

In her mind's eye, she envisioned pulling up beside Medea and blowing her pretty little brain all over her hundred-thousand dollar car.

But it wouldn't be appropriate.

Yet.

"Soon, bitch, real soon," Polyxena seethed to herself.

She followed Medea to the mall.

It took her a minute to relocate her once she went inside, and by the time she did, Medea had a Gucci shopping bag in hand.

Polyxena waited patiently for her time to strike. Rushing meant risking a mistake, a mistake meant risking getting caught. She had all the time in the world. She followed from a safe distance. She watched, knowing it was only ever going to be a matter of time, and the time came when Medea disappeared into a dressing room at the back of an expensive boutique.

Polyxena crept down the back hall where there was a row of dressing rooms with their curtains pulled and doors closed.

She drew her .38 handgun, holding it firmly and kicked the safety with her thumb.

She walked down the line, checking the feet. She wasn't behind a curtain, which meant one of the doors. She approached the changing room Medea was in, snatching open the door and bum-rushed inside.

Medea had known she was there the whole time; the moment she'd pulled out onto the street, she'd heard the roar of her motorcycle. She *always* kept a constant check on her rearview, and there was only one person she knew who rode a silver Honda CBR900, Polyxena. Once she was in the mall, she used store windows and the angled anti-shoplifting mirrors to keep tabs on her tail.

The dressing room was too good a trap; she'd known Polyxena would make her move.

She was ready.

As soon as Polyxena burst through the door and put the gun in her face, Medea threw her own gun right back in Polyxena's face.

They faced off, both staring down a barrel ready to give and get.

A perfect balance.

"You always did underestimate me," Medea said. "Just because I didn't fight in a war doesn't mean I'm not combat ready. Remember, I was trained by the best."

"That doesn't mean you *are* the best, bitch," Polyxena shot back.

"Well, I am good enough to see you coming," Medea retorted, speaking with a flare of touché.

They stared each other down, both wishing they could put a bullet in the other. Finally, Medea put down her gun and turned to the mirror.

"My arm is getting tired. Shoot if you want," she put on the dress, knowing that turning her back made her vulnerable and not caring. It was a power play. An act. "How do I look?"

"I'm sure you know by now," Polyxena began, getting down to business.

"Of course," Medea replied, trying to keep her voice steady, but inside, she had chills.

Polyxena sensed it.

"For a yellow belly you sure do turn a ghost white."

Medea spun around and spat, "Fuck you, Polyxena! I have *nothing* to worry about!"

"You mean except the fact that you helped murder Achilleía?"

Medea got in Polyxena's face.

"I told you a million times, Paris set me up. I had no idea what he was planning!"

"Whateva," Polyxena replied dismissively.

Medea's anger melted into a nasty little smirk. "Maybe you ought to worry," she spat back. "After all, *I'm* not the one fucking her husband, am I?"

Now it was Polyxena's turn to boil.

"I can't wait until the day we can finally settle this shit."

"Wouldn't miss it for the world, but today isn't that day, is it?" Dominque said. "So, what *have* you got in mind, huh?"

Medea admired herself in the mirror.

Polyxena hated the fact that she needed Medea, but the situation was bigger than their beef.

"You already know I do," Polyxena said. "I love Achilleía but—"

"You love Chiron more," Dominque finished for her. "Of course you do. Go ahead and say it."

"You're a half-breed bitch," Polyxena spat, "But it's bigger than Chiron. Yes, I love him, course I do, but I love me, more."

"And you love that three million you stole from the safe house most of all," Medea snapped. "Does Chiron know about *that*?"

"I dunno, does Paris know you're fuckin' Quadir?" Polyxena sassed right back.

Medea sighed.

"Look, we *both* got shit on the other, that much is plain, but right now we need to be on the same page. Achileía *cannot* come back to Brooklyn. Period."

"I know. What the hell she's doing in Philly? And why she's been gone so long? It's not like Achie to hide out," Medea said.

"Better question is, who the fuck's been helping her? You don't go underground without support," Polyxena mused, thinking like the soldier of combat she truly was.

"Paris sent Quadir. He missed."

"I know, but we won't," Polyxena replied, looking Medea in the eyes.

Medea returned her gaze.

That shared look was like a handshake.

"We won't."

"I'll keep you posted, but as soon as we can both get away, we need to get to Philly,"

Polyxena turned to walk away, regretfully shaking her head. "In war, we make sacrifices to win. No matter how painful."

"Oh... and the dress in the Gucci bag? That's for you," Dominque said, casually. "Are you still an eight? You're looking more like a sixteen these days."

Polyxena knew what Medea was trying to say. That she had been onto her the whole time and she had the dress to prove it.

"Fuck you, you anorexic bitch," Polyxena smiled, taking the dress.

14

"Interview begins, 4:35pm with Mr. Hector Newkirk," Hoffman, the special agent in charge, said into the tape recorder, setting it on the table between himself and Hector.

Hector never liked Hoffman.

He reminded him of Archie Bunker.

"Listen, we're wasting time here," Hector said. "I need to be out there looking for my wife."

Hoffman shook him off.

"Protocol, Newkirk, you of all people should understand the necessity of doing things right. Now, for the benefit of the tape, how long has your wife been missing?"

"Too long," Hector huffed.

"Newkirk."

Hector sighed hard.

"Seven days."

"And when did you first lose contact with her?"

Hector eyed him hard.

"Seven days ago. Like I said, she's been gone for a week."

"And do you have any idea where she may have gone? Anything that you think might help us track her down?"

Hector licked his lips. The tape wouldn't pick the sound up. "Without her medication, there's no telling," he responded, sounding beaten. "How much longer are you going to sit here doing nothing?"

"As long as it takes," Hoffman replied smugly.

Hector snatched the pen from Hoffman's hand and slid the pad over to himself.

He wrote in big bold letters: **TURN OFF THE RECORDER OR I WALK!** He held it up for Hoffman to read.

Grudgingly, Hoffman picked up the recorder and said, "Interview suspended, 4:45pm."

Hoffman killed the tape and slid the recorder aside, then looked at Hector.

"Now, you want to talk, talk."

"We can't let the Philadelphia police charge Faith with murder," Hector started in. "We've both seen that footage, it was clearly self-defense."

"It's out of my hands," Hoffman shrugged.

"Bullshit. Make it go away. We can't let the state get mixed up in this and you know it."

Hector was seething.

He could tell the Feds were beginning to distance themselves from the situation, and Hector knew exactly what that meant: termination.

"Look, Newkirk, things have gotten out of hand. You lost control. Calling the state off, it's no small thing. It's gonna raise too many red flags. The situation has to play itself out."

Hector rose from his seat.

"Fuck you, Hoffman. I won't forget this. Trust me," Hector spat, slamming the door behind him.

Hoffman chuckled.

"I'm sure you won't... Lover boy."

Quadir felt good to be back in Brooklyn.

No other city in the world, not even another borough of New

York, could compare to Brooklyn. It was definitely its own planet. Under the smiling façade of its so-called gentrification, and the addition of the Barclay's Center, lay the heart of Crooklyn, chipped tooth and all.

But it was more than that.

He needed to distance himself from Achilleía/Faith.

While she lay in a coma teetering between life and death, he wanted to clear his head. He needed to prepare for either eventuality. With her living, and coming back home to claim her rightful place, it would make everything perfect. But if shit went the other way and she died, then things would continue to go as planned and there was no guarantee he'd be last man standing when the smoke cleared. It was a chance he'd been prepared to take, but finding Achilleía had been a godsend.

That night in the motel, it was like he had no control over himself. Her aroma seemed to fill the room, and even if it cost him his life, he had to have a taste. He didn't know what it was, but he remembered one night when he and Chiron were sitting on the balcony, looking out over Manhattan and drinking Cognac, Chiron had been planning a big party, over hundred grand for Achilleía's birthday.

"Yo Unck, I know that's your wife and all, and you love her, but goddamn, a hunnid racks? Ain't that much love in the world," Quadir remarked and Chiron had laughed like it was the funniest thing in the world and his nephew just didn't understand.

"Well neph, maybe you've never been in love like I've been in love, and maybe you've never felt the things that I've felt, but even a gangsta gets lonely. Young blood, let me educate you. I've fucked some of the baddest bitches in the world, some didn't even know English, except my name—"

"And that ain't even English!" Quadir joked.

Chiron gave him a dap.

"—No doubt, but there ain't another woman like Achilleía. Sugar Ray named her right, because she is bubbly, intoxicating, and trust me in this life only the best will do." Chiron said, shaking his head admiringly. "Motherfuckas bow down! That's my baby and I don't know what I'd do without her."

Now Quadir understand how Chiron felt.

He hadn't ever tasted her nectar and the thought alone had him crazy.

He was determined to possess her, even if it destroyed him.

"She gotta live," he murmured to himself, as he stepped out of his car and heading across the blacktop into Paris's cigar bar.

It was an ultra-exclusive joint. A gentlemen's club where the cigars were rare and expensive, the Cognac aged, and the females weren't any of the above. They only wore stilettos and walked around butt ass naked, waiting on the men. Stretch marks, excessive tattooing, and scars were shown the door. A woman had to be flawless, so flawless that Quadir never failed to get hard whenever he entered that place.

A svelte redbone with a perfect set of 36D's jiggled by all smiles, in a haze of cigar smoke.

"Hey Qua," she sang, her eyes saying so much more.

"How you, uh, Red," he greeted, forgetting her name.

She stopped, smirked, put her hand on her hip, and replied, "My name ain't Red. How could you forget me?"

Quadir's smile said, *you got me.*

"I'm sayin', ma, my bad, I just got a lot of shit on my mind."

She walked up to him, gripped his dick through his pants, then said, "Well come on in the back, I'll remind you."

He chuckled. "Let me handle my B.I. I need to see Paris," he said.

"That way," she nodded towards the stairs that led to Paris's back office.

Quadir headed up.

He knocked once, and then heard, "Come in."

He stepped into Paris's plush office. It was a king's throne room. The carpet was so thick, they had to cut the bottom of the door higher so it could open and close without dragging on the knap. Most of the right wall was taken up by an aquarium filled with all manner of exotics, miniature sharks, piranhas, and eels among others. There were other fish that were little more than chum for the predators.

Quadir looked over to watch them fight and die.

On the opposite side was a black leather couch.

Paris's bodyguard Wolf was sitting there.

Paris was behind his desk on the phone.

Quadir stood at the tank, watching the fish until the boss killed the call.

"Yo Paris, where the fuck you get this mini sharks?" Quadir questioned.

"They're not miniature," Paris responded. "They're sharks. Sharks grow to fit their environment. So those same sharks would be nine-ten feet if they were in the wild instead of three feet in the tank."

"Get in where you fit in, huh?" Quadir replied, sitting on the edge of Paris's desk.

"Exactly. What you got for me?"

Quadir shrugged.

"Like I said on the phone, she got away."

"Yeah, but what you didn't say is *how*? I'm interested in the details, Qua." Paris asked, his aggravation barely hidden.

"Come on big brah, this is Achilleía we're talking about, except she don't know it."

Paris scowled, saying, "Add on, God."

Quadir sat down in the chair in front of Paris's desk.

"I'm saying, I don't know if it's amnesia or what, but she ain't frontin' like Spook thought. She really doesn't know who she is."

"You talked to her?"

"For a second," he lied, not missing a beat. "We went in the store and I looked her in the eyes. She didn't recognize me. I could see it. The eyes don't lie."

Paris nodded.

"True indeed. She going by another name?"

"Faith Newkirk."

"Faith, huh? I wonder why she chose that."

"Or who chose it for her," Quadir noted.

Their eyes met with a look of mutual understanding.

"Okay. Faith Newkirk," Paris said. "I've got a few connects in Philly on the force. If she's still in Philly, they'll find her."

"Cool. As soon as I handle a few things, I'll go back, too."

"Naw, yo, you good. I need you here," Paris replied.

A red flag went up in Quadir's mind; he needed to be in Philly to protect her. Even though no one at the hospital knew her real name, if Paris had dirty cops, finding a Jane Doe in a hospital would be simple. He had to do *something*.

Chiron.

He need to facilitate a protection detail.

"Okay, cool," Quadir answered, keeping it calm even though on the inside he was feeling pressed.

Paris looked at his watch.

"I have to make a move, but tonight, me and you need to put our heads together."

"No doubt," Quadir affirmed.

As soon as he left the cigar bar, he was on the phone to talk to Chiron, forgetting all about the redbone waiting to be unforgettable.

"I'm sorry, the number you called is no longer in service. Please check the number and try again."

He knew he hadn't misdialed because he hadn't dialed. The number was programmed into his contacts. He tried it again anyway.

"I'm sorry, but—" the recording began again. He cut it off.

He flipped to Polyxena's number. She answered on the third ring.

"What's good, Qua?" she asked, walking naked to her shower.

Quadir clambered into the driver's seat, checking his rearview as he slammed the door.

"I tried to hit Chiron. What up with his phone?"

She sighed as she turned on the shower.

"There was a shakedown. He got busted with his phone."

"Damn! When can you get him another one? I got some hot shit to tell him."

"I can't, Qua, not right now. He's in the hole, and there are metal detectors going in and out," she explained, feeling herself for the plan was coming together, then added, "But what's up? I'll see him tomorrow and I'll pass the message."

Quadir thought about it for a minute. Chiron had told him, if he couldn't reach him, tell Polyxena.

He took a deep breath.

"Yo, ma," he began. "You ain't gonna believe this..."

Chiron paced his tiny isolation cell furiously.

He could barely pace four steps before he had to turn around, which made his movements short, bouncy, and erratic. He was heated. He couldn't believe some low-life janitor would have the nerve to snitch on him.

That was so much bullshit.

Captain Tillman planted the man's name in the report that Chiron got ahold of from Polyxena, this treachery costing an innocent man his life.

Chiron's men bum-rushed his cell, wrapped a sheet around his neck, and hung him from the vent of his room.

"Snitch ass nigguh," one of the attackers spat. "This is what you get!"

Despite multiple bruises from the beat down, the prison ruled the janitor's death a suicide.

"This shit is crazy," he mumbled to himself, pacing.

Without his cell phone, he really felt locked up.

He had no way of staying on top of the game, and his plans depended on staying on top.

At least I've got baby girl, he thought to himself.

Thoughts of Polyxena always made him smile.

She'd held him down through his whole bid.

He didn't know what he would do without her, but now that he knew Achilleía was alive, he didn't know what he would do with her, either.

He heard a rattle of keys approaching.

A white male officer's face appeared in the door's trap-window.

"You know the drill, put your hands behind your back, Black, and put them through the slot," the officer instructed in a lazy drone.

"Where I'm goin?"

"Nowhere," the officer said. "You got a visitor. Case manager's here to see you."

Chiron kept the poker face, but inside was smiling.

Baby girl always hold me down, he thought. *In more ways than one...*

Once Chiron was cuffed up, the officer opened the door.

Polyxena stepped in, her long, black, silky mane pulled back in a ponytail that reached the small of her back. She was dressed in that conservative skirt suit that always got him hard, and sensible four-inch heels that got him harder. She looked like a consummate pro, but he knew she wasn't wearing any panties under there. She never did.

"Mr. Black, please sit on the bed. You know the rules," Polyxena said evenly, before saying to the officer, "Thank you, Officer. I'll radio when I'm finished."

"Yes, ma'am," the officer stepped out, locking the door behind him.

As soon as his footsteps died away, a wicked grin spread across Polyxena's face then she straddled Chiron's lap.

"I see somebody missed me," she purred.

"I know you got your keys," he said, grinning.

She looked at him.

"Yep, but I'm not uncuffing you. Tell me you love me."

"I love you."

She knew the love he declared was more lust than love, and all he wanted to do was bury himself deep inside her but hearing those words made her feel whole.

"I love you, too, Chiron. I really do" She was crying. Not sobs, just a track of salty tears.

Chiron knew why.

"I love you, Polyxena, never forget that. How long before you can get me another phone?"

"Baby, it's too hot right now," she said, shaking her head and playing the role. "A lot of people are under investigation and I don't need to be one of them. That snitch really fucked the game up."

"Yeah, well, his game fucked up," Chiron gritted, wishing he could kill him again.

"Yeah, I heard he committed suicide. What a shame."

"Well look, I'ma need you to holla at Qua. Tell him to keep you posted on

Achilleía. And make sure you get at the connect. We need to re-up."

Polyxena kissed him softly.

"Doesn't mama always handle daddy's business?"

He chuckled.

"No doubt."

She hit the radio.

"I'm ready to come out."

"10-4," came the reply.

"Make sure you holla at Qua. Tell me what's good tomorrow."

"I won't be at work for a few days. It's my mama," she lied.

The footsteps were coming.

"As soon as you can."

"Soon as I can."

The door swung open. Her professional façade fell into place like as mask, covering her sexy façade, which in turn masked her conniving one.

"Okay Mr. Black, just keep your nose clean and you'll get out of here," she said on her way out the door.

"Yes ma'am," he replied, playing along.

Polyxena couldn't wait to get out of the building.

As soon as she was clear, she called Medea.

It went to voicemail, but she left a message.

"Pack your shit. We goin' to Philly."

15

I t seemed like an eternity...

From the moment she first experienced that head exploding pain until the cold turbulent shock of the frigid waters, Faith felt like she had been drowning all her life. The pain in her was so intense, it whistled in her ears, a high-pitched shriek. She wished for death, just to be free of it. But part of her refused to give up, gritted through the pain and fought against the current trying to rise back to the surface.

Fight! something inside of her screamed.

And she did.

Hard.

Harder than she had ever fought in her life.

The waters were dark and freezing.

She couldn't see anything, not even her own frantic movements as she thrashed about in the crimson, but she knew she wasn't alone. Not in any divine God looking over her sense, in a very real reach out and touch sense, like she was having an out-of-body experience.

Am I dead? she heard herself ask.

No was the comforting reply.

And then came the hand, plunging into the water.

Only she wasn't swimming.

Faith reached back and both of their hands clasped tightly. The hand pulled her up, clear of the water just as the last gasp of air was exploded from her lungs. The hand pulled her into the sweetest lungful of oxygen she'd ever drawn. It was like being reborn.

Faith lay on her stomach on some sort of wooden floor, coughing up water and trying to get her bearings. The pain in her head was still pounding, but it was like she had gotten used to it. She twisted, looking up at the night sky, not understanding how she could be on a wooden floor and under a moon so large and close, it was like she could reach out and touch it.

"It's called a Hunter's moon. This is the night for predators and nothing can hide... not even in the dark."

Faith twisted again to try and see who was talking. The voice sounded *so* familiar to her. It sent chills up her spine. She saw a figure standing in the shadows, watching her. It was the silhouette of a woman.

"Get up," she told Faith.

Faith struggle to her feet.

Everything hurt.

The world swam.

"Who are you? Where am I? Did you save me?" Faith questioned intently.

She laughed.

"You're just so full of questions, huh? In your place, I reckon my first question would be who am I?"

Faith bristled.

"I know who I am. Faith Newkirk. I wish everybody would stop trying to convince me I'm someone I'm not."

"Then you were right," she said, stepping into the moonlight. "Maybe the right question is who are you?"

When Faith saw who she was talking to, her knees buckled.

It was impossible. There was a dreamlike quality to it.

She was looking at herself.

Her other self was dressed in a pair of curve-hugging army fatigues with a large black pistol in her waistband. Her T-shit had the words 'Special Forces' emblazoned on it. Her hair was buzzed short.

"You're... me?" Faith tried to wrap her head around it, stepping back like she had been standing on the brink of madness and was afraid to topple over the edge.

"No," she snickered. "I mean, I don't know how this works, but since I was here first, I'd say that means you are actually me... and girl do I hate what you did to my hair."

Faith shook her head.

"This isn't possible. I'm dead, aren't I? This is Hell."

Her other self got serious.

"What's going on is I want my life back, Faith, dear. I'm Achilleía. I always have been, and that means you always have been- You're just me turned inside out. The problem is convincing you to basically kill yourself... I guess this would be the correct way to—"

"Kill myself? Are you fucking *crazy*?" Faith huffed, then turned to walk away.

But somehow Achilleía was standing in front of her again.

"No matter where you go, there you are," Achilleía quipped. "We don't have much time. We have to get it together."

"This has to be a dream," Faith tried to tell herself.

"If it helps you to think of it that way, knock yourself out. Look around," Achilleía inquired. "Do you recognize this place?"

Faith took a deep breath and did as she was told. She saw that they were standing on the dock of a lake house, hence the wooden floor and the open sky. They were in the woods. The memories came flooding back.

"Yes," Faith replied, surprising herself. "This is our boathouse, mine and my husband, Hector's."

For a moment, Achilleía was ecstatic, until she heard the name Hector. Then all the wind left her sail.

"Hector?" Achilleía questions. "You married Hector? Fuck that's worse than the hair."

"How do you know my husband?"

Achilleía shook her head, thinking, *like you wouldn't believe,* but she replied, "Just keep going."

"We have a boat," she recalled. "Nothing fancy, but it's nice. We come out here all the time."

"What else?"

Faith looked around, acclimatizing herself to the past.

"I remember a storm... We were on the boat. Just me and Hector, Jada wasn't with us."

"Who's Jada?"

"My daughter."

Achilleía felt like someone had punched her in the gut.

But now she knew who the little girl in the picture was.

"I have a daughter?"

Faith was too caught up reliving her memories to hear what Achilleía said.

"I remember being hit with something hard. It knocked me out of the boat. I can't swim—"

"Yes, you can."

"So, I was drowning," Faith continued. "Hector saved me. He reached down into the water. But the damage from the thing that hit me fractured my skull and put so much pressure on my brain. I went into a coma..."

"And you lost your memory," Achilleía added.

Faith shook her head.

"Only temporarily," she said. "Hector helped me regain most of what I lost."

"So, Hector told you what happened. That what you telling me?"

"No, he just helped me. I remembered on my own."

Achilleía sighed in frustration and began to pace.

"This is worse than I thought. Faith, listen to me. You don't remember, you only *think* you do. These things you're remembering, they ain't real, they're planted memories, cultivated to feel like the real deal, but they're as fake as Trump's Twitter."

"No!" Faith protested.

Achilleía took her by the shoulder.

"Goddamn, I'm hardheaded!" Achilleía said. "Chiron always said I was and now I see his point. Your memory isn't lost, it's being suppressed."

"What?" Faith asked, because for some reason Achilleía's voice seemed far away.

"I said your memory is being suppressed..."

"I can't hear you!" Faith screamed out.

Her vision began to grow hazy, like one of those old school Polaroid pictures, but instead of the picture slowly developing, the picture was slowly dissolving. Into blackness. She was aware only of her own breathing and the rhythmic beat of her heart. The blackness began to lighten, and continued, lightening all the way until it was blinding white.

Her eyes slowly fluttered open, the last remnants of the encounter seeping away with the blackness until it was totally gone.

Beep... Beep... Beep...

The machines around her hummed and whizzed; the mechanical whoosh reminding her that she was back in the world of the living.

Faith's mouth was dry and her body seemed to still be asleep.

She tried to lift her left arm to rub her face, but it only came up a few inches before it felt like her watch had caught on something. Except, she always wore her watch on her right arm, not her left.

She looked down.

She was handcuffed to the bed.

"What the—" she started to say, barely getting the words to sound in a craggy rasp from non-use.

A black female officer got up from her chair in the corner.

She walked over, her face set in a better-than-thou expression, like the badge made her that bitch.

"Sleeping Beauty's finally graced us with her presence, eh? It's called a handcuff, honey, and where you're going, you better get used to it."

"Am I under arrest?" Faith questioned.

"You think?" the officer replied sarcastically.

"For what?"

"Murder."

"Murder?"

The officer looked her up and down.

"Funny... you don't look so tough up close. Maybe it wasn't you on that tape."

"Tape?" Faith echoed. "What tape?"

The officer sighed and sat back down.

"That's it honey, you get the insanity in quick so your lawyer's got something to play with," she said, turning her back on Faith. "My show's back on."

Faith slammed her head back on the pillow.

She didn't know what tape the officer was talking about.

Nothing made a damned lick of sense.

But something, or someone, inside her screamed out a warning: she needed to get away. Fast.

16

"Desire, where is you hurryin' up to? You runnin' like immigration after your ass," the super-thick Latina stripper remarked to her partner, another thick stripper but not Spanish, just a redbone.

She was hurriedly shimmying into a purple sequined micro-dress and a pair of simple black open-tied stilettos that fulfilled a fetish.

"Girl, it's a cracker out there greener than an Eagle's jersey, just ready to trick off a grip!" Desire chuckled like she'd just hit stripper gold. "He offered me two grand just for a taste."

Her friend looked skeptical.

"Mo, you sure? Two G's? No offense but ain't nobody that green they're paying that for a taste of you, darlin'."

Desire sucked her teeth, then grinned and pulled her partner by the hand to the locker room door, pointing the dude out in the crowd.

As soon as her partner saw him, she knew he was that green, in his thick glasses and tight ass Dockers he looked like a refugee from a nerd convention.

"Ooh, you right girl!" she marveled. "Put me in the game."

"Sorry bitch, respect the hustle!" Desire grinned, throwing up the peace sign.

She sashayed over to the white dude, her thickness threatening to spill out everywhere.

"You ready, sug?" she said sweetly, in her little girl 'Daddy, fuck me' voice.

He pushed his glasses upon his nose.

"Am I ever!" he exclaimed, pure hick, pure gold.

She grabbed him by the hand and they left.

Like a lamb to the slaughter.

They stepped inside the small motel room. It was as cheap as she usually was. Desire wrapped her arms around his neck, all sugar and smiles. "Give me a sec to freshen up, sug, and I'll be right with you," she purred, running her nails ticklishly along his cheek.

"That won't be necessary," he replied, his voice different. It was suddenly a lot deeper, and gone was the soft weak Southern drawl she'd heard all the way from the club.

"Doll, I like that voice. Say something else."

"Sit down," Hector told her, taking off the fake glasses.

It was a Clark Kent Superman thing; without the glasses he was a completely different person. His strong features shone through. She understood now how Lois never figured him for a superhero.

"Are you the police?" she questioned.

He smiled.

"Not quite," he said.

"Then who?"

"I just want to ask you a few questions."

"Oh hell no, sug. If you ain't the police, and I ain't under arrest, then I'm out of here," Desire huffed.

Hector grabbed her forearm and hauled her back as she reached for the door.

"That wasn't a request."

Desire was a Philly girl, born and raised; she damn sure wasn't about to go out like no punk bitch.

She tried to knee Hector in the nuts, but he blocked it with his leg.

At the same time, she spat out a razor and barked, "Motherfucka!" as she slashed at his face.

He easily dodged the wild swing, shaking his head like he was such a disappointed Daddy. Hector backhanded her so hard, she pirouetted, all ballerina for half a second, before she came down off her toes and collapsed onto the floor.

He stood over her menacingly.

"It didn't have to be like this. I want you to remember that. Now get up and sit on the bed."

The force of the backhand had taken the fight out of her.

She scrambled her dizzy ass up on the bed, less a ballerina more like a punch drunk fighter using the ropes to pull himself onto his stool after a battering.

Hector grabbed the chair in the corner, planted it in front of Desire, and sat down. He reached into the side pocket of his jacket and pulled out a small medicine bottle and a syringe.

"Do you get high, Desire?"

"No. I don't do that shit," she squeaked, squirming away.

"I'm gonna say this again, and believe me I hate repeating myself, it doesn't have to be hard. I'm not going to hurt you," Hector said. "Unless you make me."

He turned the bottle upside down, stuck the syringe on the top, and filling it a third of the way up the measures.

Desire scrambled off the bed and ran into the bathroom—it was the only chance she had, a locked the door. The little bolt slid into place. He could hear her on the other side of the door, panting, crying, trying to think. "Please leave me alone," she called out, like such a simple entreaty could save her ass now.

Hector calmly walked to the door.

"Desire, I'm a forgiving guy, open the door and I'll forget you fucked up, but if you make me kick this door open, this only ends one way, and that's with you hurting," he said, his voice psychopath cool. "Do you want me to hurt you, Desire? Is that it? Do you have a thing for pain? That what gets you off?"

"No," she sobbed, wishing she had grabbed her phone.

"Then you know what to do. Open the door. It's as easy as that."

After a few seconds, the bolt slid back and she opened the door. She emerged from the bathroom, head bowed.

"Sit down."

She did as she was told.

"Good girl. Now, give me your arm."

She looked at him pleadingly.

He offered a reassuring smile.

"If I wanted to kill you, you'd be dead by now, that's all you need to worry about. I've got no intention of killing you, you have my word."

Reluctantly, she held out her arm.

Hector found a vein.

"You're going to feel a little pinch," he warned, as he slid the needle in like a pro.

"Why are you doing this?" she sobbed.

"It's okay, I know you're frightened but it's medicinal. It will help you remember all those little details your conscious mind has forgotten," he explained. "You'll get a little sleepy, but when you wake up, you won't remember anything. It won't even be a bad dream. I promise."

Even while he was talking, his voice began to change again until it sounded like the teacher in Charlie Brown.

Wonk, wonk, woooonk.

Her eyes fluttered and then she fell back on the bed.

Hector rested his arms on his knees and said, "Desire, can you hear me?"

"Yes," she mumbled, like she was talking in her sleep.

"Good. Now, I want you to picture the King of Prussia Mall. Do you see it?"

"I... see it."

"You're in a white Bentley. Remember it?"

"Yes," she confirmed.

"Who are you with?"

"I'm with Spook," she replied, her words as clear as when she was awake. "A guy I met in Brooklyn."

"Brooklyn? What was he doing in Philly?"

"Trickin'."

He chuckled.

"I see. He took you shopping?"

"Yes."

"Where did he take you shopping?"

"Fetish," she said wistfully, as if even in her comatose state, the name made her want to go shopping.

"What's that?"

"Shoes."

"You met a woman there? Faith?"

"No, Achilleía," she contradicted him. "Spook said her name was Achilleía. He made me ask her. She denied it, but I heard him on the phone, he was sure it was her."

"The phone? Who was he talking to?"

"Paris."

Hector's body tensed.

"And what did Paris say?"

"I don't know. I couldn't hear. But Spook sent me home in a cab and he stayed at the mall," Desire told him.

Paris.

Now he knew he had to find Faith.

He stood up.

"In the morning, you will forget what happened, okay?"

"Okay."

"You never saw me," he added.

She whispered, "Never."

Hector dipped out the door.

Detective Miles Porter thought he was God's gift.

He was 6'3" and 200 pounds, built like an athlete, because that was exactly what he had been once upon a time; a wide receiver at Florida State, before a career-ending injury destroyed those NFL dreams.

He became a cop for one reason: to get paid. There was no heightened sense of justice or sense that he needed to give back to the community. He was a hood nigguh from Compton, where half the force was either Blood or Crip, and even though he didn't bang, he was a go-hard type of dude.

He knew the first rule of law: *don't get caught.*

And the second: *he who makes the law can break it.*

He was a dirty cop. It wasn't a hard transition for a man like Porter. When he met Paris at a fight in Vegas last year, he'd quickly got down with his organization and been on the payroll ever since, making good bank for his services.

Porter had called Paris about Achilleía.

"You're not giving me much to go on, big brah," Porter said, as he stood beside his detective sedan with half a Philly cheesesteak dripping soft cheddar over the fingers of his other hand.

"Yeah, well, it's all I know," Paris said. "I already sent you the picture and I know her name is Faith."

"No last name?"

"Yeah, Findherass. Faith Findherass," Paris's voice was laced with sarcasm, despite the fact there wasn't a lick of humor in his tone. "That's what I'm payin' you for? I made it easy for you already. I told you where she works, now you do your thing."

Paris was frustrated that he didn't know more, but Quadir wasn't about to give up her whereabouts. What he didn't know was right at that moment her face was plastered across every screen on the news cycle.

"I got you, big brah. You know me, I always handle mine," Porter assured him, biting into his cheesesteak.

"Then handle it," Paris spat, before killing the call.

Porter finished his cheesesteak then got into the unmarked car.

He called the precinct, driving off. "Yeah, this is Detective Porter. Give me Detective Keys, please," he asked, waiting to be transferred. "Yeah, Keys? This is Porter from narcotics. How you doin'?"

Keys coughed into the phone. "Lousy," he offered up. "Seems like I've had this fuckin' cold for weeks. Probably some fucking pandemic shit trying to wipe us all out.... What can I do you for?"

"That mall incident a few days back," Porter said. "The one with the woman who killed those guys in the parking lot? I was wondering, have you made any headway?"

"Have we?" Ken guffawed. "Dude, where have you been? We've got her in custody. Well, technically she's in Temple Hospital in a coma, but when she comes around, if she comes around, we've got her dead to rights."

"What the hell happened to her?"

"Long and very fucking weird story," Keys responded. "Doesn't matter. The important thing is, we've got her. As soon as the doctor says she's good to move, it's off to county."

"Okay, thanks."

"Say, why'd you—" was all Keys got out before Porter left him spinning in the wind.

His mind analyzed the angles like some suped up super computer. He knew if Achilleía made it to county, it'd be just about impossible to kill her while she was in lock up. So, as loath as he was to put himself out there, he knew didn't have a choice. He was going to have to hit her in the hospital.

Porter did a U-turn in the middle of the street and took off for the precinct. First things first, he needed to find out who was on hospital detail.

Driving a rented black Dodge Charger, Polyxena and Medea arrived in Philly.

Both wore wraparound black shades. They looked sleek and dangerous.

"We need to source a getaway car," Medea remarked.

"Bitch, please. I was doing this when you were still tricking for loose change," Polyxena shot back, making a hard left.

Medea gave her a cold look.

"I'll be glad when this is over."

"Don't tempt me to hurry things along."

They headed into West Philly and shot straight to the hood, eyes peeled for a mark. They spotted one pretty soon; a pretty boy type dude that looked like a pale imitation of Drake pulled up beside them in a charcoal gray Benz 320.

He glanced over and winked at Medea, ridiculously pleased with himself.

"Got one," Medea flashed her nasty bitch smile, all clenched teeth, as Drake rolled down the window.

"What up, Jersey?" he flirted, proving that he could read the plates of the rental.

"How did you know?" Medea asked, playing her airhead.

He chuckled.

"I can just tell, you got a Jersey look about you," he lied. "Besides, if you were from Philly, no way I'd have missed your fine lookin' ass. I'm a connoisseur."

The light turned green.

"Pull over, ma. Let a nigguh holla at you."

"I thought you'd never ask," said the spider to the fly, and she led him to a McDonald's parking lot. It wasn't exactly a honey pot, but it would serve just as nicely.

"Work, lil mama," Polyxena winked.

Medea snickered and stepped out of the car.

Fake-Drake watched her strut around to the passenger seat of his car, edible in her skintight jeans, slung back heels, and off-the-shoulder halter top. She was so bad, she could've opened the driver's door saying, "Move over," and he would have done exactly that. He leaned over and opened the door. She slid in, cocking her curvy hip. The profile of her ass made him want to lick her jeans.

"Damn, ma, you don't waste time, do you?"

"Life is short."

"Yolo."

"Exactly."

They laughed, complicit, sharing the secrets of the universe in the front seat of a Benz.

"Me and my girl are looking for something to get into. Any ideas?" she purred, eyeing him seductively.

"Shiiiiit, you lookin' at it, ma," he smirked.

"Lead the way."

He pulled out and Polyxena followed him.

As they moved onto a smaller road, Medea ran her fingernails along the back of his neck.

"Just so we don't waste each other's time, if you got a little dick, let me know now," she told him. "I don't disappoint well."

"Naw, ma, we ain't got nothin' to worry about in that department."

"Let me see then."

"What? Now? While I'm drivin'?"

"Unless you got something to hide."

The challenge to his manhood had him unbuckling his jeans.

"Lemme just make it plain, I don't pull out my gun if I ain't gonna use it," he cracked, whipping out his dick, which was hardening off nothing more than the promise.

She looked. It was okay. Nothing to write a telegram home about. But nothing to be ashamed about.

"Mmmm, looks delicious. I got a hankering to taste it," she purred.

"Be my guest."

Fake-Drake sat back, feeling himself. He was about to get head from a bad bitch on G.P. He watched her bow her head and could almost feel her lips wrap around it.

But instead of something warm and familiar, he felt something cold.

The kiss of steel.

"What the—" he started to panic, realizing Medea was holding a straight razor at the base of his dick. It was enough to have the Benz veer across the blacktop. He caught it before the drift took it off the road.

"Relax and drive straight, sweetheart. One mistake and you'll be dickless. And we wouldn't want that, would we?"

He had a gun in his waistband.

Both of their eyes went to it.

"I double-dare you," Medea whispered. He didn't take the bait. "Smart man."

"Come on ma, don't do this. I ain't got no money on me."

"I don't want money, I want to borrow your car," she said. "Don't worry, you can come too. Now, be a good boy, take your left hand off the wheel and stick it out the window. Wave my girlfriend around then follow her. You got me?"

He nodded.

Polyxena had been waiting for the signal.

She saw Medea's head disappear from view.

"Nasty bitch, she probably sucking it for real," she mumbled to herself. She hated Medea. Real. Genuine. Deep-down hate. She couldn't wait for the moment this transitioned and she became the target. But she couldn't help but smile when Fake-Drake gave her the signal.

She accelerated around them, leading the Benz to an abandoned building not a million miles away.

They pulled into the parking lot.

Polyxena got out, her .45 caliber concealed behind her leg, and crossed the gravel lot to the Benz. She snatched open the door. Fake-Drake's pants were around his ankles and Medea had a straight razor to his dick. She had his gun in her other hand.

"Pop the trunk," Polyxena ordered.

He did it without hesitation.

"Now get out."

"Can I at least pull up my pants?"

Polyxena put the gun to his forehead.

"I *never* repeat myself."

Getting the message, he swung his legs out and stood up. He couldn't run if he wanted to. He shuffle-walked to the trunk, his junk flapping. Polyxena and Medea kept him covered every step of the way. Medea snatched the spare out the trunk and let it roll away.

"Get in," Polyxena demanded, shoving his head down.

"Y'all bitches on some bullshit," he mumbled, doing his best to get comfortable in the cramped confines.

Polyxena pulled three sets of plastic zip ties out of the pocket of her cargo pants, then strapped his ankles together, his hands behind his back, and ran another zip tie through the other two, so he was hug tied. "Wouldn't want you jerking off and ruining the fabric," she chuckled.

"These shits too tight." Fake-Drake complained.

"Imagine what a coffin feels like," Polyxena quipped, putting an end to his protests.

Polyxena pulled a small metal ball—no bigger than golf ball, but with a lever-like handle—out of her pocket. She pulled, what looked like a grenade pin from the side, keeping the lever depressed with her thumb.

"Now, open your mouth."

"For what?" Fake-Drake knew. He couldn't take his eyes off the metal ball in her hand.

Boc!

Without hesitation, Polyxena shot him in the thigh.

It was a glancing blow, no danger to the femoral or anything else, through and through the meat, meant to scare him more than hurt, but even so the bullet's grace ripped a chuck out of his thigh.

He opened his mouth to scream, which was all Polyxena had wanted him to do in the first place.

She stuffed the metal back in his mouth.

"See?" she smiled. "Fits perfectly. And yes, it's a grenade, and yes, it'll blow your head all over the interior if you fuck this up. But as long as you keep your mouth shut the lever stays depressed and you don't end up like brain salad splashed all over the trunk. But, and I cannot stress this enough, if you so much as try and whistle, *Boom!* Feel me?"

Tears rolled down Fake-Drake's face, mixing with the balls of sweat rolling. He was breathing hard through his nose. He'd come here thinking about being blown. Now, lying here, he couldn't imagine a fate worse.

"Remember, closed mouth and you live. It's as simple as that, no need to complicate shit," Polyxena shrugged then slammed the trunk closed.

Medea laughed.

"A grenade? I knew you were crazy."

"Not as crazy as you?

"Huh?" Not getting it.

"You're driving," Polyxena smirked, then turned and sashayed back to the Charger. Medea boiled a moment, growling, "I hate that bitch."

"Daddy, when's Mommy coming home?" Jada asked from the back seat.

Hector smiled at her reassuringly through the rearview as he drove.

"Soon, doll face. I promise."

"You said the last time, and the time before that. and the time before that," she replied exasperatedly, then added, "Is Mommy in trouble?"

Hector frowned slightly.

"Why would you say that?"

"Because the man on TV said Mommy did a bad thing," Jada answered.

Hector hated the fact that his daughter thought anything bad about her mother.

"No baby, he doesn't know what he's talking about."

"Oh."

His phone rang. He looked at the caller I.D.

Hoffman.

"Yeah?" he answered.

"Have you seen the news?"

"They found your wife."

Hector damn near slammed on the breaks.

"Where?"

"Temple Hospital. She's in a coma and under arrest."

"Shit," Hector barked, then hung up to Jada's giggles. She covered her mouth and pointed at him. For a second Hector didn't realize that he'd said a bad word.

"Sorry baby, Daddy was...," he let his voice trail off because his mind was on fire.

He had to get Faith out of the hospital for both their sakes. If she went into the county jail, termination wouldn't be a rescindable order, it would be a fact of life. But what was he supposed to do with Jada? It wasn't like he had time to take her home. Not that he could leave her alone. No, he had to take her with him.

It would be dangerous, but the alternative was worse because if he didn't save his wife, he'd have to kill her.

Faith laid back with her eyes closed, her face totally relaxed, willing herself to breathe deeply.

Think, she told herself. *Think.*

She could feel her whole being calming, relaxing, centering...

And then she knew.

"Officer," she said in a deliberately weak voice, letting the pain seep through into that one bitter word.

The officer looked up from the magazine she was reading.

"What?" she asked, all attitude.

This was important. Dangle the carrot. "I know about several other murders."

The officer's ears perked up.

"What do you know?"

"I did them," Faith whispered.

"What? I can't hear you."

"I committed them."

"Speak up."

"I can't. It... *hurts*," Faith lied.

The officer did just as she anticipated; she rose from the chair and came over to the foot of the bed.

"Tell me about these murders," the officer said. "I want to hear."

"Okay, I... need some water."

"Water?"

Faith nodded.

The officer turned to grab a pitcher of water on the side table and Faith made her move. She arched her right leg over her left and wrapped it around the officer's neck, using her left leg like a wedge to bend the woman's spine at an angle it wasn't made to bend. The officer tried to grab, claw, and pry Faith's leg away, but it tightened like a boa constrictor.

"Do I look tough now, bitch?" Faith growled, taunting the officer's preconceptions.

Faith pulled tightly, lifting her left leg and straining her right until she heard an audible snap—a branch breaking.

If that branch was the woman's neck.

Her body went limp as the life force drained from her.

It wasn't easy, and involved gymnastics that would have made a porn star proud, but Faith managed to pry the keys off the dead cop's belt before she fell to the floor. She uncuff herself and rolled out of bed, breathing hard, adrenaline on 1000.

Faith stripped the cop. They were of a size. A couple of minutes after taking her life she took her uniform and left the corpse in her place in bed, dressed a bra and panties. She cuffed the cop to the bed rail, then partially covered the face as best she could to obscure her identity.

Faith wanted to know what had gone wrong. Insulin had never done that to her before. She flipped through her chart. As she read, there were more questions than answers.

Not a diabetic? A bullet in my head?

Faith was dizzy, but she pulled herself together. She didn't have time for a freak out. She snatched her report off the clipboard and stuck it in her pocket. She pulled out the service revolver, cocked it, and then clicked off the safety with her thumb, heading out the door.

As she stepped of the room an elevator opened at the other end of the hallway.

17

Polyxena and Medea put their grey wigs and frumpy dresses on in the bathroom on the ground floor of Temple Hospital. The only thing that would've give them away were the Nike Air Maxes on both of their feet, and even then, nurses were all about the comfort so plenty wouldn't think twice seeing the new sneaks. Underneath the dresses, they wore Spandex bottoms and halters, making the fast-change costume change for their escape as joggers easy.

They had it all planned out.

"You ready?" Polyxena called out from one stall, as she slipped on her old lady glasses.

"No doubt," Medea replied, putting hers on.

Meanwhile, Fake-Drake was in the trunk of his own car, bleeding, crying, and whimpering; his jaw was all pain from having to keep the grenade lever down.

Two car spaces down, Hector parked his car.

He turned around in his seat and looked at Jada.

"Listen baby, Daddy has to go inside. I want you to wait here, okay? All the doors are locked, but if anybody tries to get in, you scream, you do not let them in, okay?"

"Like this?" she asked.

Before he could protest, his little girl let out an ear-piercing scream that was a decibel or two from cracking the windshield.

"Yeah baby, *just* like that," he chuckled, then got out and made sure all the doors were locked.

He walked right by Fake-Drake's Benz, oblivious to the fact he'd abandoned his daughter within blast zone.

Polyxena and Medea rode up on the elevator, both locked in their own thoughts.

They'd been friends who became enemies, and now they were about to become partners in killing a friend. It was a fucked up world they lived in.

Both loved Achilleía, but circumstances had pitted them against each other, and it was better she died again rather them dying for the first time.

"She should've stayed dead," Polyxena remarked quietly.

Medea nodded in agreement.

As soon as the elevator opened they saw the female officer emerging from the room. They were half-a-second from missing it, but the angle was just right. The cheekbones, the profile. It hit them. That wasn't a cop. It was a ghost.

"Achilleía!" Medea gasped, shocked to actually see her, even though she'd known Achie was there.

Faith looked up at the two old women and saw them reaching to pull guns from beneath their dresses.

For the whisper between heartbeats there was silence, then Faith bellowed, "No!" and pulled her stolen piece.

Boc! Boc! Boc! Boc! Boc!

Shots rang out like wicked church bells from three different directions, intent to damn the women to Hell.

Polyxena and Medea took aim at Faith, buzzing her so close, forcing Faith to dive behind the nurses' station for cover.

Pandemonium broke loose.

People ran screaming and yelling in every direction.

Bullets whizzed and zipped all around.

The two assassins went after their prey.

"Shots fired! Shots fired! Third floor!" another officer, this one sat watching the main door, heard crackling from his walkie-talkie as Porter entered the hospital.

"What's going on?" Porter questioned, flashing his Detective's shield.

"A shoot out on the third floor."

The third floor was Achilleía.

"Shit!" he raced for the bank of elevators.

Porter ran by Hector, not recognizing him, as Hector headed for the stairs.

As soon as Hector hit the stairwell, he pulled out a nickel plated nine and screwed a silencer over the barrel. He took the steps two by two, expecting Faith to burst through one of the doors above him at any moment.

Boc! Boc! Boc!

More shots echoed from above.

He abandoned all trace of caution and ran up the stairs.

Faith, Polyxena, and Medea realized they were out of bullets at the same time.

Faith went for the extra clip hanging from her police belt, but Medea and Polyxena rushed her before she could ram it into place.

Medea had a straight razor and Polyxena had a Rambo knife.

This was all about finishing Achilleía by any means necessary.

"So sorry I've got to spill the Achilleía," Medea quipped, slashing at Faith's face.

"Who are you?" Faith huffed, arching back to avoid the slash. She delivered a backhand to Medea's throat that sent her reeling back, holding her neck.

Polyxena lunged at Faith, knife poised to strike, but Faith grabbed her wrist while simultaneously tripping over an overturned chair; she fell on her back hard, Polyxena still on top of her.

The two former friends were eye-to-eye, close enough to kiss, and that's when Polyxena realized Faith truly didn't recognize her.

"Achilleía?" Polyxena said.

"My name is Faith!" she grunted, wrapping her legs around Polyxena's waist. She tipped her over, reversing their position.

Now she was on top, she used the leverage to twist Polyxena's wrist, damn near breaking it.

Polyxena cried out as Faith pried the knife from her hand. She started to plunge the blade at her, but Medea slammed into her, knocking the knife out of her grip.

"Don't play with me, bitch! You know who I am!" Medea spat.

"Fuck I do!" Faith barked, "But you're about to know me!"

Medea slashed at her face.

She nicked her on the cheek, just as Porter burst out of the elevator.

There was another trip-hammer heartbeat as he struggled to take it all in and react. He yelled, "Freeze!" aiming his gun.

All three scrambled for cover.

Shots rang out.

Boc! Boc! Boc!

Porter let off three shots, barely missing the mark.

Faith rolled over, snatched the clip from her belt, popped it in, cocked it back and came up firing all in one smooth motion.

Boc! Boc! Boc!

Her shots sent Porter diving back into the elevator for cover, the bullet's pitting the drywall where his head had been a fraction of a second before.

Life could be measured in millimeters.

Hector came running through the exit.

He saw Faith and yelled out her name.

"Hector!" she cried with relief.

Polyxena popped up.

"David? What *the* fuck?"

"Polyxena!" he gasped, two worlds colliding.

Seeing Faith and Polyxena, he made a mental leap, assuming they were together because of their history. Which could only mean one thing: Achilleía had awakened. That meant she knew the truth.

He had to terminate her.

His heart ached, but it was what it was. He knew what had to be done. He'd always known there was a chance it might come to this.

He raised the gun and aimed at Faith.

In that moment Faith was so shocked; she was in the open, exposed. If it hadn't been for Polyxena pulling out another golf ball grenade and tossing it in Hector's, he would've broken Faith's heart. With a bullet.

The explosion wasn't big; the miniature grenade wasn't large enough to do serious damage, but it packed a punch.

Hector barely stepped back, but the force of the blast blew him another six feet, slamming him hard into a wall.

Medea kept Porter pinned down inside of the elevator, firing off shots to make sure he didn't risk sticking his head out.

Boc! Boc! Boc!

"Pink!" Medea barked, calling Polyxena by an old code name. "We gotta hustle! Go!"

Faith used the seconds the chaos bought to sprint down the hall, head down, focused on the corner and getting around it before—

Boc! Boc!

Polyxena cracked off two rounds, but she was too late.

Faith was gone.

The pair took off after her, while behind them Hector staggered, groggily to his feet. Dazed. Confused. Porter risked emerging from the elevator as the doors tried to close on him again, and jogged up behind the two assassins, not knowing that Hector was behind him.

Faith aimed for the stairwell and started to go down, but heard several footsteps and the squawk of police radios waiting for her, so ran up to the fourth floor, three and four risers at a time. She pushed past three people on the stairs, who looked at her with sheer panic in their eyes, trying to decide if she was a threat; the entire hospital had heard the gunfight. But she was in that stolen uniform, meaning it wasn't fear, it was salvation they were looking for from her.

"Officer, what's happening down there?"

A nurse asked, seeing her come out through the door.

"Everything's fine. No need to be alarmed. Nice and calm, I need everyone to exit through that stairwell, now, nice and orderly, and assemble in the lot out front," she instructed.

She sent them to the stairwell, knowing the two blood-hungry old ladies were coming up in hot pursuit. It would be enough to slow their roll. Sure enough, when Medea and Polyxena reached the door, people were pouring out like the flood that floated Noah.

"Move! Move!" Medea barked.

"Get the fuck out of the way!" Polyxena spat.

They elbowed and shoved their way through the crowd, but the cramped confines meant the people really had nowhere to go where they could get out of their way.

Finally through the press of people they each headed in different directions down the hallway, fanning out to look for Faith.

She wasn't hard to find.

She was standing in front of the elevator.

She'd pried the doors open and was staring into the elevator shaft. The elevator was coming from the top floor. As it sped by, Polyxena happened to turn the corner. She saw Faith as she leapt into the shaft, trying to understand the suicide attempt she was seeing, and fired two shots to help her on her way. They hit the back of the shaft.

Faith landed on top of the elevator car as it clattered by.

Medea heard the shots and came running, rounding the corner in time to see Polyxena cock back her arm.

She threw a golf ball grenade through the open doors into the shaft.

The explosion echoed like a bass drop at an EDM concert, rising up out of the shaft. If the elevator car had been on a higher floor it would've crashed into a ball of flame. But, luckily for Faith, the car had already begun its deceleration and was near the basement level when the explosion severed the cable and blew the anchor arm of the top of the car, peeling the lid like it was a can of sardines.

The drop was less than fifteen feet.

The impact was no worse than a fender bender.

It was the flash bang that had totally dazed Faith. The two doctors in the car stared up at her, shaken, not understanding what was going on as they saw the female cop come crawling in through the ruined ceiling. Faith was bleeding from the ears and she was dizzy, as she staggered to her feet, shaking off their instinctive help to fight with the doors. She needed to get out of there. Fast. She could barely pry the door twelve inches apart, so she wriggled through, stepping out in the morgue.

She looked back at the two doctors.

"You never saw me."

"What the Hell was that?"

"An explosion?"

"Sounded like they're demo'ing the basement!" someone else said, lost.

Porter ran by heading for the first floor.

The place was swarming with police.

Even though he couldn't hear them, he knew helicopters would be hovering overhead. Standard threat response. His heart sank. There was no way Achilleía could have escaped, the place was swarming with cops and security. As good as she was, the odds were just stacked against her. Which meant the chances of him killing her were slim to none. No pat on the back for a job well done. No cash reward for taking care of business. He thought about trying to get to her county and all the challenges that would entail for a guy like him. It was easier for a guy like Paris with he connects, not for someone like him. Lockup wasn't his world. If he tried and succeeded, there would be an investigation and someone, somewhere, would crack. If he tried and fucked it up, it would be worse.

Miles Porter wasn't an idiot. There was no way he was going to risk it; Paris was just going to have to be disappointed this one time...

Medea and Polyxena stripped out of their granny wigs and dresses, letting their beauty be its own disguise as they hurried out of the hospital.

"I'm not leaving Philly until I know that bitch is dead," Polyxena vowed, as they walked fast toward the getaway car.

"That's on you," Medea replied. "I've got to get back to Brooklyn before Paris misses me."

It got quiet for a moment as they walked, then Polyxena said what they were both thinking.

"She really didn't recognize us?"

She shook her head. She knew it wasn't the flimsy disguises. She saw it in her eyes.

"Faith? An alias?" Medea questioned.

"What the fuck was David doing here?"

"Who the fuck is David?" Medea wanted to know.

"I'm out," Polyxena replied, knowing she had said too much already.

Fake-Drake was so drained, he couldn't feel anything.

He'd shit and pissed on himself, struggling to keep his entire body clenched along with his jaw.

The pressure was getting to be too much for him. It felt like his mouth was pushing back. The lever had become a weight, like the jaws of life trying to pry his teeth apart, only that wasn't right, it was more like the jaws of death. His mind spiraled. He was beyond scared.

There comes a time when nothing else matters, when things go beyond fear into acceptance, and we just know... it's all too much and all we want to do is let go.

Fake-Drake was done.

He had crossed the tipping point.

Fear had become acceptance. Acceptance had become relief.

He let the grenade fall from his mouth.

Hector walked out of the hospital, crossing the underground lot as he headed for his car.

"Polyxena," he murmured to himself, shaking his head, trying to fathom what she'd been doing there, and what she did or didn't know about Faith.

Even if she wasn't faith anymore, he couldn't afford for Achilleía to emerge.

He would always love her, but this wasn't about love.

The last thing he thought about was Jada.

He would have to raise—

The explosion came from around the corner...

Where Jada was waiting for him.

He was screaming as he raced around the corner, into a nightmare he would never forget.

Medea and Polyxena were coming from the opposite direction when they saw the getaway car's trunk rip off in a ball of flame.

They saw flaming pieces of Fake-Drake's dismembered body sprayed in every direction.

The sheer decibel force of the explosion was amplified a thousand-fold a heartbeat later as it ignited the gas tank, blowing the windows out of the two cars parked behind it, the sheer force of the explosion flipping them like they were paper cups.

"Plan fucking B then," Polyxena spat, as they turned away and jogged off.

Faith knew she was trapped.

Through every window, she saw police.

She heard the helicopters above.

She looked around.

There wasn't much to see. The place was freezing. The walls were lined cold storage cabinets where they kept cadavers.

Her eyes landed on a body bag on a gurney.

The corpse was headed for the funeral home.

A smile spread her lips as a macabre idea formed in her mind.

She unzipped the bag.

Inside, there was a purple white man, ugly and naked and very dead.

Knowing he was past giving a shit about how people treated him, she knocked the body over on the floor and then peeled it out of the bag. She didn't have much time, she hauled the dead weight to a closet freezer drawer and manhandled it onto the shelf and slid it inside. She ditched the cop uniform, stripping naked. If she was going to play dead, she knew she had to play it all the way.

She padded back over to the bag, her pistol in hand, locked and loaded and put the body bag back on the gurney.

It wasn't easy, but she climbed inside and zipped it up as far as she could from the inside.

Sealed in there, she was overcome with the stench of death.

Prison cell smell a whole different level of worse, a voice inside her warned.

That settled her stomach.

Moments later, she heard a door swing open, footsteps and voices, then she felt the gurney moving.

"Where is the wife?"

"Ask the mailman."

The two men began laughing.

The gurney bounced and rocked until she felt it being lifted and tossed on something hard.

She heard a car door slam and then the engine started.

Her heart danced as she felt the car moving. She relaxed, allowing her mind to blow off the tension that wound her up tight.

When the police swarmed the morgue, they'd find the missing corpse along with the discarded police uniform, and the logistics of her escape would drop into place, but by then it would be too late.

The driver, a medical examiner, had his mind on a cold beer and was too wrapped listening to more Rush Limbaugh spleen venting to hear the tiny buzz of a zipper slowly moving down in the back.

The fresh air rushed in and Faith took in a lungful before sitting up.

The timing was flawless. The medical examiner glanced in his rearview and saw a beautiful, naked, black woman, sit up out of the body bag. He mashed the brakes and yelled out of pure blind superstitious panic.

Faith leveled her gun at his face.

"It's your lucky day. Take off your clothes."

He gave her his pants and shirt.

"You're a doll," she winked, putting the shirt on. He was a big man, raised on a diet of heart attack burgers and animal fries, so the shirt was like a dress. She decided wear it as that, and unlooped his belt from his pants, to finish the makeshift look.

"Cell phone and car keys," she said, holding out her hand.

He obliged.

She pocketed the keys and smashed the phone on the ground.

"Now, be smart, don't move," she told, beginning to walk away.

Kill him the voice inside urged.

She whispered to herself.

The voice raged.

She protested.

He'll tell them I'm in the area, what I'm wearing, and which way I went, she thought to herself, not recognizing the cold logic of the killer whispering into her mind. But there was no denying the wisdom of it; she took a deep breath and mumbled, "You're right."

Her next thought was, *who the hell am I talking to?*

She turned back to the driver.

"I'm sorry about this, but you understand—" she didn't finish the thought, there was no need, he wasn't alive to hear her excuses.

Boc! Boc! Boc!

She put three bullets in his face, blowing his eyes back up into his head and his brains out of his eye socket.

She dipped off and disappeared from the scene.

Polyxena dropped Medea off at the airport. Medea was determined to charter a jet and get back to New York as soon as possible. Shit had hit the fan, so she wanted to be as far away as possible from the blowback.

Polyxena, on the other hand, couldn't push herself to leave.

She was a military vet, Special Forces, when she went on a mission, she expected to succeed, but at the very least she saw it through to the bitter end. Her pride wouldn't allow her to admit she had failed. She drove the streets of Philly aimlessly, unable to shake the upside down world that made her best friend her enemy.

"Damn you, Achilleía. Why didn't you just stay dead?" she rumbled, hitting the steering wheel in frustration.

Polyxena had mourned Achilleía's death more than anyone— more, even, than Chiron. They'd been the only two partners in the pain of loss, while everybody else was fighting for gain. Now, five years later, seeing that face, barely changed, barely aged, brought back all of that grief she thought had died with Achilleía.

Who was Faith?

And what the fuck was David doing there?

So many questions swirled in her head, sending her mind reeling back to the early days of her loss and how she fell in love with Chiron.

"Nigguh, you got some nerve calling me," Polyxena rasped into the phone, holding it tighter than a grudge.

She was in the back of a limo, alone, coming back from Achilleía's funeral.

The black dress she wore had nothing on the blackness that clothed her heart.

All around her, the streets were swarmed with bloodshed, crews loyal to Paris going to war with those loyal to Chiron. Polyxena had made it abundantly clear to Paris that she was done. She wasn't going to roll with him and she damn sure wasn't going to roll with Chiron after what he had done to Achilleía. She was out.

"On the strength of your love for Achie, I'm going to respect your decision, Polyxena. Don't make me regret my kindness," Paris had warned her at the funeral.

Polyxena nodded, then eyed Medea, who was standing beside Paris, trying to project the kind of regality her status didn't deserve. The two women eyed each other colder than penguins frozen in ice floes. The truce didn't extend to their relationship. Polyxena had walked away, walking away from the lifeuntil her phone rang ,Chiron was on the other end.

"Polyxena, listen to me, you're the only one I can talk to. Please, don't hang up. I need you to hear me out," Chiron spoke firmly and evenly, no desperation, but urgent. He wasn't the kind of man to beg, but that urgency kept her from hanging up.

"Talk."

"I didn't kill Achileía."

"Nigguh, fuck you. You're a fuckin' liar. All I need to know is what Medea had to do with it, because when I find out, she as dead as you."

The other end got so quiet, Polyxena thought the connection had broken.

"Hello!" she shouted down the line.

"I know you're upset. I am, too. But I didn't kill Achie. Now, don't ever threaten me again." The coldness in his voice sent an unnerving chill up her spine. It wasn't the time to vent the venom of emotions churning inside her.

"Just say what you have to say."

Chiron sighed heavily.

"Ma, you don't know what I'm going through... I lost my heart. Achie was my heart, so to kill her would be like killing myself. You know me, I strike you as suicidal?"

Hearing him put it that way made her look at it with a whole new light.

"No," she admitted, reluctantly.

"Just because things seem a certain way doesn't make them true," he continued. "See things as they are, not as they appear to be. You of all people should know that, Polyxena."

"Meaning?"

"I know all about what happened in Afghanistan. Achileía told me everything."

Polyxena got tensely silent.

"Don't worry, ma, I'm not trying to use that against you in any way," he assured her. "I'm just making a point. Facts can be manipulated, no?"

"True," she answered, relaxing her nerves.

"I'm going to need your help. Shit is going to get real crazy. I may even have to plead guilty to her murder, but I need you to believe and trust me. We will revenge Achileía's death. You have my word."

The strength in his voice warmed and chilled her at the same time.

Intuition said he wasn't lying.

Despite how it all appeared, she believed he was telling the truth, meaning their new relationship began with solid trust, a strong foundation for any relationship.

She would visit him in the county jail under an alias. The things he told her made it undeniable that he was supposed to be the head of the family, not Paris. And while she knew he wasn't telling her everything, what he did tell was enough to give her unshakable faith in their cause.

At first, that cause was avenging Achilleía.

They were bonded by a mutual love and a devastating loss, so laughter and tears watered and nurtured the early days.

"No, no, remember the time Achie smacked that waitress," Polyxena cackled, doubling over on her bed with raucous laughter.

"Shhhh!" Chiron shushed her, trying to contain his own laughter. "The sound in here carries."

He was in his cell in the county jail. He'd had a female office that he'd hooked bring him a phone. Chiron went to the door to check the tier, but it was two in the morning, everything was dead quiet.

He laid back down.

"Yeah, that shit was crazy. She did it so fast, nobody in the restaurant even seen it," he added, speaking fondly and nostalgically. "But boy did they hear it."

"She had it coming. Acting all snooty and shit like we didn't belong in Paris."

"Nigguhs in Paris!" Chiron cracked.

They both laughed.

"But Achie was so calm, right? 'Excuse me, miss' type shit. Man, the look on that white bitch face? *Wap!* One punch. Eyes big as a dope fiend on blast, bottom lip quivering like she was gonna bawl—"

"—And Achie on some 'That was for being a bitch, the next one will be about me acting like a crazier one, we clear?'"

Chiron laughed.

"Yeah, she got that 'are we clear' shit from you," Polyxena reminded him. "I swear, sometime I thought y'all were brother and sister, y'all acted so much alike."

After the laughter subsided, they both got quiet.

Polyxena rolled over on her side in a fetal position, the phone between her head and the pillow.

"I miss her so much," Polyxena fought back the tears.

"Me too," Chiron replied, fighting back his own. "But we've got to stay strong and focused. We can't afford to slip now. Believe me, Polyxena, if I had to choose a partner in all this, I couldn't have chosen a better one than you. You're a special woman. A broken mold if I ever I saw one."

As he spoke, the tears lined her cheeks.

She didn't know if it was the pain or Chiron's kind words or both.

At some point, she'd closed her eyes and the soft pillow had become Chiron's chest. The words coming out of the phone became a heartbeat, each word throbbing in her ear. Just as she was relaxing into the image shimmering in her head, she stopped cold, shocked, scared, and embarrassed.

Chiron sensed something was wrong.

"Polyxena, you okay?"

"I have to go. My battery is dying," she lied, because she needed the cover of a lie to distance her from the truth of what had just happened, day dream or no day dream.

She hung up, without waiting for his reply.

Oh my God! What is wrong with me?

Fantasizing that Chiron had been in the bed with her had made her body respond in ways she's hadn't expected; it wasn't like she was attracted to him. Of course, he was fine, gangsta as fuck, rich, and by the way Achilleía glowed, she knew he had to have some good lovin', but he was Achilleía's husband and that was that. Polyxena wasn't cut like that. Friends were more important than dick.

Yeah but Achilleía's dead, her more indulgent side reminded her.

She shook it off, put the pillow between her legs, and went to sleep.

At first, she tried to deal with her budding emotions by not talking to him late at night and never when she was lying in bed. But, night after night it became harder to deny how much she found herself looking forward to his calls and hearing his deep, raspy baritone.

"Go pick up that money from Brownsville and give it to Flatbush," he instructed her, never mentioning names, only sections of Brooklyn.

She had become his eyes and ears on the streets.

He even started sending her on missions that ended in bloodshed.

"My angel of death," he'd jokingly referred to her, but all she heard was 'my angel.'

She even gave him money to flip so he could get better prices.

"What can you do with two hundred grand?" She had asked one day.

"Triple my profit," he chuckled.

She never told him the money came from the safe house robbery, so, technically, the money was his. But the investment made them partners in crime, as well as partners in pain. Their bond was growing wings.

And it got even stronger when Polyxena landed a job at the prison where Chiron was being kept.

It was all a part of the plan they had devised.

She was going to work her way up in the system so she could

be in the position to break Chiron out when the time came. It was a long game, and they had it all planned out so smoothly, they'd never know he was gone.

"The quickest way out is if I have pending charges with the Feds," he'd explained. "Let's say, I'm facing life with federal charges while I'm going to trail. I wouldn't be in the jail system at all. The computer would say I'm in federal custody, but what if I didn't have a federal charge, Polyxena? If someone can plant that info in the system, then the State will think I'm with the Feds and the Feds wouldn't know I existed. It would be months, even years, before they'd figure out what happened."

He laughed like he had figured out the cure for cancer.

As he talked, the vision got clearer for Polyxena.

She could see it.

"Damn that's gangsta, Chir!" she said, nodding appreciatively at the simplicity of it. A few strokes on a keyboard. That was it. No guns blazing. No blood. "I see that shit. How long do you think it would take?"

"Maybe three years, four tops," he answered. "Long game, but let's make it happen. We can do this."

With her I.Q. and background in the military she got hired as a prison C.O. in no time. Every officer in the place was on her. Perfect. She played each one like an instrument, creating her own orchestra.

The bitch was so bad she needed a theme song.

With Polyxena inside making moves, Chiron locked down the prison and began to spread his power to others. He was making close to fifty grand a day in three different prisons and Polyxena was his queen bee.

"You're a genius, you know that?" She told him one day when she came to make her rounds on his tier.

He winked and kept it moving.

They kept their interactions to a minimum. He didn't want anyone to know who his connect was. For her part, Polyxena stayed off the radar, but she couldn't help but watch him. Talking to him was one thing, but seeing him on a daily basis was another. His swagger, the way he wore his prison blues like they were designer brands, the way he moved as if he wasn't in prison, but just in a different world. He was a man among men, but when he had to be, he was a beast among animals.

She saw him bare-chested and working out; he looked like an action figure. He was so cut up, his eight-pack was putting every six-pack on the yard to shame.

She had to have him.

It had been over a year and a half since he first called her, and, little by little, Polyxena had been falling in love with him.

She hadn't wanted to. She'd never intended to, but once she admitted it to herself, she was torn.

I'm in love with Chiron. I'm in love with Achilleía's husband. But Achie is dead. It's not right. It's not wrong either...

She went to him in her confusion. She switched shifts with the other house officer where Chiron worked and signed for him to stay behind when everyone left. He grabbed a broom and swept his way back into the storage room where she was waiting. He looked around then closed the door behind him.

"Everything okay?" he asked with genuine concern, reading the expressions of her face.

"Yes."

"The drops going good?"

"They're fine," she replied.

She tried to will herself to stop trembling, but she couldn't. Being this close to him was like being within touching distance of raw electricity.

Chiron stepped closer.

"Are you sure you okay? You're shaking."

"I've been thinking," she began, but found herself in able to continue.

"About?"

All she could get out was, "You."

It wasn't a special night. It wasn't magical. There were no fireworks or chorus of angels. She knew he hadn't returned her love, how could he, but that was okay, Achilleía would always have that special part of him and that only made her more determined to make him love her too.

"I think Paris sent Quadir at me."

"What you mean?"

"He got him knocked on a murder charge to see if I would get at him," he explained. "I did blast first and I taught him a lesson."

"I'm surprised he's still breathing," she remarked sourly. "I brought him in after. I think he understands now."

"You saw him?"

"He's on our side."

"You can never be sure of that, Polyxena. Never say never, right?"

Looking at how their situation had developed she was forced to agree.

"I guess not."

"And he reckons he's got Medea under his wing."

She narrowed her eyes at him.

"So, what you sayin', Chir?"

"Give her a pass."

Polyxena sucked her teeth.

"You better be right, boy."

"Ain't I always?"

Polyxena shook her head. Her heart and body were singing out, but her mind was telling her this would end badly.

She just didn't know *how* badly.

Polyxena picked up her cell phone to check the news. The first thing she read was about the car explosion, the poor bastard blown apart in the trunk and what happened to the little girl sitting in a car parked two bays away.

18

Paris stepped out of his chauffeur-driven Rolls Royce, buttoning his tailored suit and walking the sidewalk like he owned Manhattan.

His bodyguard shadowed him inside the fancy restaurant, only a couple of blocks away from Wall Street. It had stars, both in terms of chefs and guests, and was more often than not frequented by Hedge Fund managers, investment bankers, and government officers working to cut themselves into the action.

He stopped at the Maître D's station.

"The Randolph party," he said, before interrupting himself. "Never mind, I see them."

They weren't particularly hard to spot given they were the only black faces in the place that weren't waiting on tables and busing dishes.

When Patricia spotted him, she gave him a polite smile, but her eyes were much more vocal, and brutally eloquent.

Her husband beamed brightly. He had that look about him, like a man used to getting his way. Arnold Randolph was the biggest black real estate developer in the city. He was on the board of three publicly traded companies, as well as being an

NAACP board member. He was power. Arguably, he was the most powerful black man in New York.

And that wasn't counting his bond with Sugar Ray.

It had been Sugar Ray's money and connection that had made Arnold the man.

He'd gone from being Sugar Ray's lawyer to a multimillionaire, maybe even billionaire on paper at least, but he hadn't forgotten where he came from. And now he was in the position to repay his obligations to the Butler family.

"Paris, how are you?" Arnold stood up to receive him.

Paris gave him a hug.

"Uncle Arnold, you're looking *good*. Hello, pastor," Paris replied, bending down to give Patricia a hug.

"*I'm not wearing any panties*," she whispered, then added louder, for the benefit of everyone at the table. "You're not looking too bad yourself."

"Paris. Boy, your daddy sure knew how to name his kids for confidence. I'm surprised he didn't name one of you God," Arnold laughed. "Or at least Jesus."

Paris chuckled.

"Knowing Pops, he probably thought about it. No doubt Ma set him straight."

Paris settled into his seat.

"Confidence is imperative for a black man in his work. Everything in the country is designed to say you can't," Arnold said, grunting. "You have to have that thing inside gut that says, 'Yes I can.'"

Paris nodded in agreement.

He liked Arnold.

He was a strong black man who was loyal to his father.

But that didn't stop him from fucking his wife because Paris was loyal to no one but himself.

The waiter brought a bottle of wine to the table. He poured

Arnold a taste in his wine glass and waited for him to pass judgement.

Arnold swirled it, smelled it, and then tasted it.

"Ah, excellent."

"Very good, sir," the waiter replied, filling all three of the glasses before walking away.

"I know you're a busy man, Paris, so I'll get right to the point. We're talking about a *lot* of money so I want to be damn sure we're on the same page," Arnold began.

His demeanor was friendly but all business.

Paris nodded.

"I agree."

"And the only reason I'm even considering getting involved is the love I have for your father and the respect I have for you. Other than that, I wouldn't be caught dead being involved with a son of a bitch like the General, piece of—" Paris held up his hand.

"Please, Uncle Arnold, you and the General are two of my father's oldest friends. I would never let him badmouth you, so please."

Arnold nodded and sighed hard, "You're right. I'm sorry I was out of line. Bottom line is, it's a fuck of a lot of millions, but I'm in."

"No, the bottom line is we're going to be a fuck ton richer than we are now," Paris said. "This deal will give us a fast hold in the military defense market. That's priceless. It puts us in a position to build up our position and Nigeria at the same time."

Arnold chuckled.

"No disrespect, son, but making more money doesn't excite me at this stage in my life. A man starts to think of his legacy. I look overseas and I see what those terrorists are doing to our people... They're cowards and I want to be a part of the force that knocks them on their ass. Simple as."

The waiter brought their food then left again.

"Well, I for one, am proud to be able to do my part for the

motherland," Patricia chimed in, digging into her salad. "My ministry will extend the love of others through the many churches we've established, tending to the souls of the flock."

"Amen," Arnold nodded. "I have to admit the General and I may not see eye-to-eye, but he's definitely put together a hell of a plan, no denying that."

Paris raised his glass, "To the motherland and to empowering the black man!"

He toasted, adding in his mind, *and to robbing your ass blind!*

Paris had no intention in cutting Arnold in on the deal, just like the General had planned. It was ironic that the General had a hell of a plan, just like Arnold said, even if he didn't know he was little more than a pawn in it. It all rested on Patricia. Paris looked at her out of the corner of his eye and caught her glancing his way. Her holy roller horniness was hooked.

"And to freeing the black woman and giving her a voice," Patricia added to the toast.

The clink of glasses signaled the conclusion of business.

Arnold looked at his watch.

"I'm sorry to have to go, Paris, but you know how it is, the city never sleeps, so I can never rest," he said, standing up. "Make sure you get the rest of the paperwork to my lawyer and everything should be a-go. Sweetheart, I'll see you tonight." He gave Patricia a quick peck on her cheek.

"Have a good day, love," she lied, seeing no reason to protest her husband's lack of attention. She had been doing it for years. Now, she had someone who gave her all the attention she craved.

Arnold shook Paris's hand.

"I'll have it sent right over," Paris promised.

"Enjoy your meal. It's on me."

As soon as he was out of earshot, Paris quipped, "I assume you're the main course?"

"I definitely can be," Patricia said.

"Hold that thought. I've got to make a run, but the next time I see you, I want you naked with your ass in the air and your face in the pillow."

"Just tell me when and I'm there, baby. I love you," Patricia confessed.

She'd never had anyone who made her feel like Paris did. She was hooked on his thug lovin'. Little did she know, it was all a game to make her rich ass cum money.

"Half hour, rent the room, and text me the room number."

Quadir sat in his Lexus, watching the screen on his iPhone like he was watching some Michael Bay movie. Temple Hospital looked like a warzone, live on CNN.

"Yes Bob, it has truly been a tragic day here at Temple Hospital," the reporter said, explaining the situation. "There are reports coming out that several lives have been lost, including a police officer, Amanda Jenkins. She was assigned to the guard of murder suspect, Faith Newkirk. Ms. Newkirk is believed to be the shooter involved the mass homicide at the King of Prussia mall which left four men dead."

The screen cut to the surveillance video from the mall parking lot. The video was grainy, but Quadir saw the van pull up and attempt to abduct a woman. Her face wasn't clear, but he knew it was Achilleía. The van rocked violently and the dude outside the van tumbled backwards, apparently from gunshots. He saw Spook's Bentley pull up while Achilleía slipped under the van. Then Spook got into the van and just as he was about to get out, Achilleía came out from beneath the chassis and shot him dead. No jury would be able to say it was her for sure, but Quadir knew. Of course he knew.

"Goddamn, baby girl 'bout that life."

The screen went back to the reporter, with Temple University in the background.

"Ms. Newkirk is also believed to have killed a medical examiner seven blocks away from the hospital while making her escape," the reporter continued. "But in what can only be described as a dose of Shakespearian irony, in the process of making her escape, her own four year old daughter was caught up in one of the explosions, and is currently in Temple fighting for her life."

"What?" Quadir barked at the screen. "What the hell was she doing there?"

Then Hector was on the screen.

"We were here to see my wife," Hector began. "I can't believe she is capable of the things she has been accused of... I know here better than she knows herself and she isn't the person they say she is... Jada had been asking to see her Mommy... so I brought her here... I only left her alone for a minute..."

Hector tried to explain, but broke down in tears. It was a painful end to the soundbite. The kind of thing the pain porn hunger viewers lapped up. Anything that made them feel like someone had it worse than them was golden.

Quadir shook his head in disbelief as the camera cut back to the anchor in the studio. He hated that he had left her. Had he staged it, it wouldn't have come this. Achilleía charged with murder? He was glad she'd gotten away. But it was all so far out of hand it wasn't funny. He had to get back to Philly. He had to find her. It wasn't just about ensuring the plan worked, he needed to do it for himself. He was just like anyone else; he'd do anything for the woman he loved.

He clicked to his contacts then selected one.

She picked up on the second ring.

"Hello?" Medea's voice sounded weak and groggy.

"What's wrong with you?"

"My period," she lied, and not well.

"Oh, you talk to Paris?"

"Not today, why?"

"Did he meet with Randolph?"

"I'll find out."

"You do that," Quadir replied.

He hung up, adding, "Conniving ass bitch," for his own benefit.

Quadir let her lie go because sometimes it was better to let people think you've fallen for them. You could use it to your advantage later.

He got out of the car and walked inside the mosque.

Forty men lined up, shoulder to shoulder, offering prayer.

Quadir had been raised Muslim. He understood every word the Imam chanted, his prayer sounding like a beautiful song. He'd long since abandoned his faith. There was no God outside the game, and the game owned his soul. Even so, he couldn't deny the sweet feeling of nostalgia he got from hearing those familiar words of the Quran recited.

He caught himself swaying slightly as the prayer rolled out to the heavens. He looked along the line of penitents and worshippers, and, as the chant concluded, caught the eye of two heavily bearded Afghan men further along the line. It's a fairly common mistake in American society, people tend to think of Afghanis as Arabs, but most Afghanis consider themselves Caucasians.

These two looked it, despite their craggily and wrinkled sun burnt skin; their blue eyes nestled above their beards, giving away their true identity. They crossed the room to Quadir.

"As-salaam Alaykum, Quadir," Muhammad, the taller of the two, greeted him.

"Wa-Alaikum-Salaam, Muhammad, Akil," Quadir returned, with a familiar smile.

The dumpier of the pair answered with a nod and a grunt.

Even in prayer, he kept a gun on him.

But that was no surprise; he was a man who was only comfortable in war.

"Come, we can talk in the basement," Muhammad suggested, ushering him to follow.

They made their way through worshippers who were shaking hands and hugging one another.

Today was a holy day, Jumu'ah.

Muhammad led them down a long, dark staircase. Akil followed behind Quadir. In the dark, Quadir couldn't help but feel a little uncomfortable. He had his gun on him, but as dangerous as he was, he knew they were the real killers.

They entered a small concrete room.

His initial impression was that they'd wandered into an open sewer, the stench was that strong. They turned the corner, stepping into a smaller room. A young, naked and badly beaten black dude was tied to a chair in the middle of the room. The stench was down to the fact they'd literally beaten the shit out of him and left him sitting in it.

His face was swollen like the Elephant Man.

"Not interruptin' anything, am I?" Quadir joked. "I mean, I'd hate to get in the way of work."

Muhammad chuckled mirthlessly while Akil continued to watch Quadir like a hawk.

"No, no, my brother, you're *just* in time," he said, his voice echoing. "This is D.P. He used to be a friend of ours. But he doesn't want to be our friend anymore. We find that quite... disappointing. We don't love disappointment. Isn't that right D.P. you want to break up our little friendship?"

D.P.'s lips were so swollen and purple, he could hardly speak.

"Man, I'm gonna get your money," he slurred, his words barely more than a whisper.

Muhammad waved him off. "Forget the money, my friend, it's not about that now. It's all about friendship. I take friendship seriously, don't you, Quadir?"

Quadir nodded, looking Muhammad in the eyes.

"Very much so. Friendship is sacred."

"I agree," Muhammad said, nodding. "But sadly not everyone does. D.P. didn't. So now, I must introduce him to another one of my friends."

Muhammad went over to the corner and came back with a transparent trash bag.

He moved to a small table and grabbed what looked like a modified electric saw, but instead of a blade with teeth, it had a blade that was smooth, like a straight-edged razor. The way the light from the bare bulb overhead reflected on the blade made him think of a deli counter meat cutter.

Muhammad walked up behind D.P. He was in no hurry. Everything was utterly methodical. He checked the bag, making sure there were no rips or tears, then put it over D.P.'s head, pulling it tight at the neck.

The plastic sucked in around D.P.'s face, making a smooth featureless mask out of his screaming mouth as fresh tears cut down the tracks of old ones.

Muhammad started the saw.

It came to life with a metallic scream.

"To friendship," Muhammad said to Quadir, going to work on D.P.'s neck.

The bag was to catch his blood.

As soon as the blade bit into D.P.'s neck, the clear cellophane turned bloody red.

That modified blade cut the nigguh's head off smoother than the slices of a turkey on rye.

D.P.'s head tumbled into his lap, eyes still wide and mouth open in a scream that would never be silenced inside Quadir's own head. Muhammad looked at him. Quadir looked at the stump on D.P.'s shoulders, still gouting the last pulses of blood.

Quadir knew what Muhammad was trying to do here; instill fear in Quadir with the bloody demonstration and assure compliance. What the Muslim butcher didn't know was that Quadir had been taught the art of violence by Chiron and they didn't call Chiron The Butcher for nothing.

"I see the young brother got *ahead* of himself," Quadir cracked, offering a grin.

Even Akil cracked a smile at that, no doubt his version of offering props considering Quadir hadn't flinched at the gruesome decapitation.

Muhammad nodded at Akil.

Akil moved in to clean up while Muhammad and Quadir took a seat together by the door.

"So, tell me, what do you have for me?"

"The truth. Can you handle it?"

"Try me."

"Paris is about to cut you out cold," Quadir laid it old cold, no prettifying the betrayal coming down the pipe.

Muhammad and Akil looked at each other.

"How do you know?"

Quadir smiled.

"Have I led you wrong yet, my *friend*? The bottom line, the General is switching allegiances. Afghanistan is old news. The war is over, and whatever the fools say on TV to placate the nation and make America feel great again, the Taliban won. He's scheduled to get that third star pinned to his chest and he's off to serve as the NATO Chief Commander for Africa. You, my friend, are about to become yesterday's news."

Muhammad thought about it for a moment then spat, "That Bastard! He cannot abandon us like that!"

"That's the American way, Mu," Quadir mused. "No disrespect, least not from my side, but Afghanistan was always beside the point. A usual ally for a while in an enemy of my enemy shit, but now, as you say, you're going to have to make new friends."

"Like who?" Muhammad asked.

Quadir smiled.

"Chiron Black."

"I am not sure how useful a friend in jail can be," Muhammad replied.

"Chiron's reach is long. He might be temporarily indisposed, but I'm not. I'll be his agent on this deal," Quadir said. He nodded to himself, like he was thinking through all the angles and only seeing up sides. "Besides something, or should I say, *someone*, just fell in my lap and I foresee a lot of problems in Paris's future."

A smile spread across Muhammad's face. He was no fool. "This isn't about Chiron at all, is it, my friend? This is *your* deal?"

Quadir shrugged. "Let's just say I have every intention of being the last man standing and leave it as that."

"A question for you. Do you know why we always manage to drive invaders out of my country?"

"No, tell me."

"Because we long since learned how to play them off one another. It is the only way you survive, and looking at you, I see you have a little Afghan in you!" Muhammad told him.

He stretched out a hand to seal the deal.

Quadir to it.

He was a pawn but he had plans on becoming king.

All he needed was the queen.

19

Hector sat by Jada's bed, holding her hand. The infernal beeping of the machine was like the devil's hammer chipping away at his sanity; all the tubes going in and out of her made him feel so utterly helpless. There was nothing worse in his world than feeling impotent, all that rage and pain built up inside him with no valve to let it out. He'd never forgive himself for getting Jada hurt. He didn't even want to think about what would happen if she died; him eating a bullet rather than live the rest of his life in regret.

The doctor had given her a 50-50 chance, without putting it in so many words. They didn't like to commit one way or another for fear of law suits. That was how fucked up the world had become; it was all about protection the hospital from malpractice and more frivolous writs that could run up millions because of a carless promise that went to shit in a body bag.

"We're at the point where we've done all we can," he had told Hector. "Now it's up to that little lady of yours in there. If you're a religious man I'd be looking to cash in a few favors, never hurts to put in a word with the Big Guy."

Hector did the only thing he could, he went down to the little chapel and he prayed, and he prayed and he prayed. It wasn't something he'd done before, but for his little girl, he was willing to try anything, including trading his soul for hers if God was up for that kind of deal.

"I don't know how to do this," he said to the empty room, "but if you're up there, all I want is for you to save my little girl," tears tracked down his face. "I don't care about me, so if you have to take someone, a soul for a soul, if that's how it works, take me instead. Look, I'm not gonna lie to you, what's the point, you see all and know all, right? So you know I've I know I've led a life of lies, but in my defense, look into my heart, you gotta see I did it for love. I've never wanted anything so bad. Truly. So, if you're listening, don't punish Jada or Faith for my lies. That's on me. Take me instead."

He heard a soft knock on the door.

"Yeah," he called out.

Special Agent Hoffman walked in, grim-faced and forbidding. He extended his hand. Hector stood up from the cramped wooden pew and shook it.

"I'm very sorry about your daughter, Newkirk," Hoffman said. The words sounded sincere.

Hector nodded.

"Thank you."

"I didn't want to disturb you, I understand how rooms like this can give solace, but this city is going crazy and Washington wants answers, you understand, especially since explosives were involved."

"Let's just get it over with. Ask what you've got to ask."

Hoffman nodded. "The internal surveillance video shows you involved with the shoot-out, so I've got to ask, what were you doing engaging the assailants?"

"What do you think? Protecting my wife," Hector replied, staring Hoffman down.

The agent took a deep breath, then shook his head. "That's not what the tape shows, Newkirk, and you know it. Playback shows you firing *at* your wife."

Hector turned away and looked to Jada's bedside.

"I don't know what you're talking about."

"Avoiding me wont—"

Hector turned back and locked eyes.

"I said I don't know what you're talking about, do you understand?"

"What the fuck is going on, Newkirk? First your wife now—"

"I want that tape gone. Suppressed," Hector stated.

"Are you out of your mind?" Hoffman questioned.

Fire in his eyes, Hector said, "Check my record, Hoffman. You have any idea who you are dealing with here? I'm ex-CIA, which, I'm sure you know, and I still know where the bodies are buried. Now I'm tired of this little protocol dance you think we've got going on. I told you to stop the murder charge. You're a piss ant S.A.C. in a backwater city. Let me spell it out for you. You get on the phone, you call Washington, and you tell them you've got a situation that's bigger than you. You know what Washington's going to do? They're going to bury the tape. Now do it, or so help me, I'll have you stationed so far away you can verify the climate change glacier by melting fucking glacier."

Hoffman was rigid with anger, but he knew Hector wasn't playing.

"Just tell me on thing."

Hector looked at him, then replied, "National Security."

Hector turned back to the cross and Hoffman turned to the door. With their backs to one another, Hoffman said, "Even if we bury this tape, your wife will still be wanted for murder."

"My wife," Hector began. He couldn't help but smile, adding, "Let's just say she hasn't been herself lately."

Hoffman sensed a deeper meaning, but had no idea, how deep. He let it go and walked out. Hector waited a few minutes to be sure he was gone, then headed back up to his daughter's room. All he wanted to do was take her hand.

His mind drifted back to the last time he sat by a hospital bed.

20

She emerged from her coma coughing.

Hector knew the reason behind the coughing was almost certainly psychological, no doubt because she'd been locked in that drowning nightmare. Looking at her waking face, his heart lifted, knowing she would finally be all his. She was by far the most beautiful woman he had ever laid eyes on, black or white. She had a cat-eye gaze that was half panther half goddess. She had the kind of beauty that made men lose themselves, like the most exquisite work of art. And yes, he'd stolen her...

"Where am I?" she whispered, her long eyelashes fluttering up as she tried to turn, to see the room around her. She was met by his smiling face, stained with the track of tears.

"Who are you?" she asked.

Hector smiled and smoothly replied, "Hector. I'm your husband, Faith. You know me."

It was like being born into the world all over again.

"My name is Faith?" It was the question of the lost looking desperately to be found. "I don't remember..."

He bent down and kissed her lips.

She allowed herself to be kissed.

Hector sighed and sat down, holding her hand.

"You're in hospital," he told her, patiently, tenderly. "There was an accident on the boat... You knew you couldn't swim, but weren't wearing a life jacket. I had to dive in. You were down there a long time. I couldn't find you at first... but I got you... You don't remember any of this?"

Faith shook her head.

"No, I... no," she admitted, overwhelmed with confusion.

Hector kissed her on the forehead.

"Don't worry, it's natural. The doctors said you'd probably have a little memory loss, you took a serious whack to the head, but it'll come back in time."

Faith nodded, trusting him. She wasn't sure about anything he was saying, but there was no doubting the love in his eyes. She knew deep down she could trust *that* at least, so she allowed herself to be led.

A few days later, they came home.

Faith looked out at the strange house in the strange neighborhood as they pulled into the driveway. None of it was familiar.

"It's good to be home, eh?"

She didn't say anything.

"Don't you recognize the house?" He asked, struggling to keep the disappointment out of his voice.

"No," she admitted.

"Okay, well, let's give it a few more days before we start to worry. It'll come back," he promised. And that became his mantra. It'll come back.

Once they were inside, he took her from room to room, reminding her of the life that didn't feel like hers. She eyed all the clothes and shoes in her closet. They were her size, but she couldn't remember the look or feel of a single item in her wardrobe. They might as well have belonged to a store manikin.

He showed her their wedding album.

She saw herself in a beautify wedding dress in Hector's arms, smiling.

"Who is that?" she'd ask from time to time, pointing out a stranger's face in the background, and he'd explain, leading her through their shared lives.

He told her how her parents had died and how his folks didn't approve of him marrying a black woman, so he'd disowned their racist asses.

"So, it's just me and you, kid," he winked, doing an abysmal Bogart impression as he softly punched her chin.

She looked down at her wedding ring and couldn't hold back the tears.

"Why can't I remember?"

Hector pulled her to his chest and held her tight.

"It'll come, just give it time, okay? Don't worry, I'll be right here."

He kissed her gently, and then again softly.

She pulled back.

"I don't," she began, but stopped mid-sentence.

"Hey, we've got the rest of our lives. You get comfortable, I'll go get your insulin."

"Insulin?"

"Yeah, you're a diabetic," he told her.

"I am?"

He smiled reassuringly. "I can't imagine what it's like trying to learn yourself all over again. Scary, huh?"

Faith nodded.

It took a few days, but little by little, things began to come back to her.

"We were married in Jamaica!" she told him one morning at breakfast.

Hector laughed. It was a good sound. It made her feel happy. "Well, at least you know I am not an imposter," he joked.

This time she kissed him back.

Up until then, Hector had been sleeping in the guest bedroom, but that night while he was sitting on the couch watching the Black Hawk's hockey game, Faith came and stood in the living room door, naked and vulnerable as she asked, "Aren't you coming to bed?"

Hector scooped her up and carried her to their bedroom. He laid her down on the bed and began to cover her body with soft gentle kisses that grew more and more urgent the lower his lips traveled until he was ready to consume her.

Something deep inside her knew she had felt him before, which only served to confirm what she already knew: he was her husband.

Two weeks later, he heard the sweetest words in the world.

"I'm pregnant," Faith threw herself into his arms.

His wildest dreams had come true: they were a family. Step by step, their life took a monotonous normalcy. That was right up until the night she didn't come home and he found her splattered with blood.

What was Polyxena doing there? he asked himself, as he held Jada's hand.

If Faith was gone, all he had was Jada.

He prayed again that he wouldn't lose them both.

He couldn't.

21

I t was only in her moment of deepest need that Faith realized how classified her life had been.

It was true that she ran a very successful business, equally she very hands on in their daughter's life, her marriage was fulfilling, and her husband was attentive, but now, with her back against the wall, she was on the run for multiple murders.

Desperation forced her to question her own identity and everything she thought she knew about herself. She had no place to go. No one to turn to. She and Hector attended church and she knew plenty of people socially, but none remotely close enough to appear on their doorstep after she'd been branded Philly's most wanted.

The only person she felt owed her enough to keep her mouth shut was Kareema, and even then it was a big ask.

She headed to her place, taking all the precautions she could think of to stay off the radar.

Every police cruiser had her turning her head, ducking behind cars or cutting through alleys, trying not to cut her bare feet on broken glass or do something much worse. Finally, she made it to Kareema's street and was thrown for a loop when she saw the yellow crime tape across her short Philly front porch.

She felt it deep in her gut; this was another part of the thickening plot her life was becoming.

Faith looked around then dipped between Kareema's building and her neighbor's.

It wasn't exactly a row house, but the space between the two was so tight, she had to turn sideways to inch her way to the back.

She came to a window low enough to see in through if she stood on her tiptoes. It was Kareema's kitchen. She used the other house as leverage, wedging her back up against it, then put her feet on Kareema's wall and crab-walked up to the second floor. Suspended between the two houses, a full twenty feet in the air, she tried Kareema's bedroom window. It didn't budge.

She was already wanted for murder, so breaking and entering was hardly going to add to the sentence if she got caught.

Faith pulled the sleeve of the shirt over her fist and punched through the glass. It shattered on contact. Someone was going to have heard it, but there was nothing she could do about that. She quickly reached in, unlatched the window, and pushed it open, climbing inside headfirst.

Once she was in, the first thing she wanted to do was take a shower.

She needed to get her head together and a shower always did the trick.

Faith took off her stolen shirt and headed to the bathroom, naked.

She stepped into the tub—not knowing it was the same one Kareema had been drowned in—and turned on the water.

For the first time, she was happy that the city's administration was so disorganized: the water was still on. The water was so hot, it scalded her skin, but she stayed under the spray.

Hector had taken a shot at her...

At the time, her adrenaline had been pumping so she'd

barely processed what had happened, but now that it begun to sink in, she struggled to wrap her mind around it. It was heartbreaking to think that that the man who had nursed her back to health, stood by her side, helped her in every way imaginable, the father to her brilliant beautiful daughter, had tried to put a bullet in her.

And what about the one in my head? her mind screamed.

She'd never been shot, or so she thought, until a few hours ago. Now she wasn't just questioning her identity, she was questioning her sanity.

She needed to talk to Hector. He was the only one who knew the answers to the questions plaguing her.

And, she realized, despite everything, she needed to hear his voice.

The problem was, she didn't know his number.

She hated to admit it, but technology made memory obsolete.

All of her numbers were in her phone and her phone was at home. And home was the one place she couldn't go—because not only were the police looking for her, her husband was apparently trying to kill her.

Then it hit her.

Her own words...

Technology had made memory obsolete. What she didn't know, she could Google. It was all out there being remembered by some computer somewhere. Faith stepped out of the shower, not bothering to shut the water off. She grabbed a towel and headed straight for Kareema's bedroom. Her friend's laptop was on the dressing table. She opened the lid one-handed and turned it on, drying off in the few seconds while it booted up.

As soon as the web browser came up, she typed in the name Achilleía Black.

The first hit was an article with the headline: *Mob Heiress Slain, Body Unrecovered.*

She opened the page. *Achilleía Black, daughter of the infamous*

'Sugar Ray' Butler is believed to have been killed, along with her twin sons, by her husband Chiron Black. The bodies of the two children were recovered from the Black's lake house in New Jersey, though as yet the body of Achilleía has yet to be found. Police divers are dredging the lake nearby. Chiron has been taken into custody.

Chiron, that was the name of the man on the phone who had claimed to be her real husband. She blew out a heavy sigh. Whoever Achilleía was, he had killed her. *But he knew so much about me,* her heart protested.

She read on.

The next article's headline told her: *Black Pleads Guilty.*

Chiron Black, after having vehemently denied having killed his family, pled guilty to his wife's murder. In a deal with the District Attorney, Melvin Shultz, not to seek the death penalty, Black entered a guilty plea this morning in court. Those close to the case say it was in Black's best interest to plead guilty because, despite his strenuous denials, he had been caught with the murder weapon, and it was likely any jury would've found him guilty. Black's lawyers issued a simple statement of regret.

"Bastard," Faith grumbled, until she scrolled down and saw a picture of him.

Her breath caught in her throat. It wasn't about looks, it was something deeper.

She kept clicking on relevant articles everywhere the name Achilleía Black appeared, several included pictures of her. It was obvious why everyone kept mistaking her for the dead woman. They could have been twins split from the same egg. Even confronted with the evidence of her own eyes, she refused to believe they were the same person.

The first picture was of Achilleía in a little black dress with a pair of heels so fierce they made Faith's calves ache just looking at them. Achilleía seemed to exude confidence. She was provocative. She challenged the camera when she stared it down, like she was daring the world not to look.

Even her haircut screamed fire. It was cut in a pageboy with icepick side burns, which looked sharp enough to have cut the dimples into her cheeks.

Twins.

The next few were of her and Chiron.

The way they smiled at each, always in contact, holding hands or each other, it was the look of love she saw.

The pictures of the twin boys melted her heart. Who could hurt children like that? Knowing what had happened to them, she couldn't bear to linger on those pages.

Next she saw Paris.

It was obvious he was Achilleía's brother. They were male female versions of the same person, though he was a shade darker.

There was a link to a news clip of Paris as he left the courthouse.

"I don't know where you people hear this stuff, it's make believe. There is no such thing as a Butler crime family. Let me ask you this: why is it that whenever a black man is successful, it's immediately labeled a crime family or some other slur deliberately intended to put us back in our place? Slave days are over, my friend. Chiron Black is simply a cold-blooded killer. It is as simple and horrible as that. I hope he burns in Hell for what he did to my sister and her boys."

She could see the man was overcome with emotions.

Yet he's the one who supposedly tried to kill me? she remembered Quadir's words.

Her life was upside down and inside out.

Nothing made a damned lick of sense to her.

Quadir. Had he poisoned her, was it really insulin in that bottle or was it like the chart said, she wasn't a diabetic?

Every answer was more confusing than the question. She was beginning to believe that Chiron had sent the hit squad to kill her, but once she flipped the script, Quadir had simply played along. That was easier to follow than all this other craziness, wasn't it? After all, he said he was talking to Paris, but with his own gun in his face quickly called Chiron. So, if he was with Paris, why the hotline to Chiron? And why didn't he kill her instead of taking her to the hospital?

She read on about Paris.

She saw a picture of him standing with Pastor Randolph, and a woman she recognized as the pastor of a mega church in Brooklyn and several satellite churches in other cities. Her heart warmed to see how Paris had helped open several centers for children around the city. In her mind, it was becoming clearer and clearer who the killer was, and how she'd been lied to and manipulated by everyone she thought she could trust.

When she checked in on her own life what she saw almost blew her heart out of her chest: Jada was in the hospital, branded a child of an escaped killer and victim of her own destruction.

The digital front page of the *Philadelphia Inquirer* had a picture of Faith, taken from a surveillance camera, in the police uniform blasting her gun. Right next to the still photograph was one of Jada hooked up to the machine in a hospital bed.

She wanted to race back to the hospital and hold her baby, consequences be damned. But if she went, it would be the last time she held her before she went away for life.

It was time to get out of Philly.

She went in Kareema's closet and looked around. Her friend was smaller than she was so instead of trying to squeeze into her jeans, she grabbed a Nike running suit and a pair of Air Maxes. She turned to the top once more but she heard the sounds of strained voices outside. They were distorted. Crackling. Radios.

She risked a glance out the window.

Two cruisers parked outside. There was another one coming down the street.

"Just kick it in! We've got activity inside!"

The front door was torn off its hinges. She had to get out. She quickly scrambled through the window, but instead of going down she scaled her way to the roof. She heard them storm into the bedroom beneath her.

"The computer's still on!"

She stayed low on the back slant and peered over the guttering at the street below. The three police cruisers had turned into six.

She stayed low as she scampered along the slant, then launched herself the few feet to the neighboring roof. She came down lightly, fingertips grazing the tile, as an officer stuck his head out of Kareema's bedroom window. Instead of looking up, he did the natural thing and looked down. There was an officer making his way between the houses.

"Anything?" the officer on the ground shouted up.

"She can't have gotten far," he called back.

Faith slid on her belly away from the edge then leapt to the next.

She made it to the end of the block one rooftop at a time, disappearing into the city minutes before they closed off the entire block.

New York, here I come, she thought, as she ran off up the street.

22

"Martinezzzzzz, I'ma gonna kill you! I swear!" Achilleía screamed in agony, her legs propped up and cocked wide.

"Don't worry, ma, we almost there!"

"We—"

"We? Nigguh, ain't no we in this!" Achilleía swore.

"Push, Mrs. Black, I can see the head! One big push, that's all we need," the doctor urged.

Achilleía dug her nails in Chiron's arm hard enough to draw blood, and gave it all she had, bellowing her agony out in a cry that became he's son's welcome to the world.

He came out kicking and screaming.

Chiron kissed her on the forehead. "Just one more."

"Another one?" she said, so drained of energy.

"Ma, quit playin', you know we havin' twins, now you got this, push!"

She growled, catching a second wind and imagining the grueling regime of boot camp. Fuck it, boot camp had been a cake walk compared to giving birth to twins, but the memories put steel in her spine. She concentrated her energy.

The second boy came out, screaming and punching.

"That's my baby, Achie, that's my baby!" Chiron exclaimed, the proud father.

They named the boys Amir and Amar. It wasn't long before they became the center of Chiron's world, his reason for being, his meaning and purpose.

"This, or should I say *these*, are what it's all about," Sugar Ray chuckled, sitting in his wheelchair. He held his sleeping grandsons, one resting in the cradle of each arm. "People say tomorrow isn't promised, but they're wrong, children are the promise of tomorrow."

Chiron nodded in agreement, "Yeah, Pop, feel you one hundred percent on that."

Sugar Ray was a rock of a man, even in his last days. It didn't matter that he had shrunk to half his size. Seeing tears trace the leathery creases of his hard face, Chiron knew Sugar Ray was having an important moment.

"I'm going to die, son, and not so far from now, but I can still look forward to tomorrow," Sugar Ray said.

Chiron dropped his head.

"We're all gonna die, Pop. If I can accomplish half the things you did in this world, then I'll hold my head high."

Sugar Ray looked at the ceiling-to-floor windows of his bedroom at the new Brooklyn, a Brooklyn he'd helped create. In the distance, he could see the Barclay's Center. That was somewhere he'd made happen. A lot of folks thought it was all Jay-Z and that cult of celebrity, but in reality it was really Sugar Ray who moved the Nets to Brooklyn.

Despite the beauty of the skyline, it was the beauty asleep in his arms that made him reply, "You already have, Chiron. As black men we have so much ground to cover to take back what rightfully ours. What I did, what you do, is only so these two don't, you know? In fifty years, I want you to be to black power what Joe Kennedy was to Irish power, you feel me, son?"

Chiron looked him in the eye.

"I won't let you down, Pop."

"I know you won't. In a few days, I'll be seeing P. Dupree," Sugar Ray told him. "After that, you and I are going to talk. Don't tell anybody, not even my daughter, okay?"

"Word."

Sugar Ray nodded then chuckled.

"I think this one just shitted on me."

Chiron picked up Amir. Sugar Ray was not wrong. He chuckled.

"My fault, Pop."

"Fault? The smell of my grandbaby's shit is sweeter than roses," Sugar Ray said with a smile, but Chiron knew he was dead serious.

When he looked back, right before he left, he saw Sugar Ray staring out the window again. The sun hung over his right shoulder, but from the angle Chiron was looking, it looked like it was setting in the old man's breast pocket.

That was the image that would always stay with him.

Chiron stared through window of his isolation cell.

He was still seeing Brooklyn in his mind, right up until the second he heard a dull knock at his metal door.

"Cuff up, Black, your case manager is here to see you," the officer told him.

Chiron walked over to the door, put his hands behind his back, and put them through the slot in the door. He'd done it a hundred times. The officer cuffed him. Chiron stepped back, like it was choreographed.

The door opened and Polyxena walked in, a ray of sunshine in a yellow skirt suit.

Her yellow and white ostrich Gucci mules echoed off the concrete.

"Thank you, Officer."

"You know the routine, ring when you're done."

Chiron leaned against the steel lip of a table that was affixed to the wall. It was where he kept all his worldly goods; deodorant, soap, lotion, pens, and paperclips. It wasn't much to sum up a life. He picked a paperclip up and unbent it, straight, without Polyxena suspecting a thing. Hands behind his back, he worked it into the keyhole of the cuffs as she walked towards him.

Polyxena wrapped her arms around his neck.

"Hey baby," she breathed, all big, sexy smiles right up until he turned his face away as she tried to kiss him.

"I need to get out of here," he said coldly.

She stepped back and looked at him.

"I know and I'm working on it. I mean you did get caught with—"

That's all she got out before Chiron had jammed the cuffs open. The metal sprang and he reached around to grab her by the throat.

He pinned her to the wall.

"Do. Not. Play. With. Me." He growled in her face. "I don't give a *fuck* what I did or didn't get caught with, that's why you suckin' the Captain's dick, the sole reason, ain't it? To make the moves I need you to make?"

His words hurt more than the hand around her throat.

"No! I'm suckin' his dick so I can get you out and we can have a life!" she said. "Jesus how many times... I fucking *love* you, Chiron. Real grown-up love. That means I'm willing to do *whatever* it takes to get you free. You see anybody else making the same kind of sacrifices? Do you?"

Even heated he knew not to push it *too* far.

Polyxena had her limits, and she was his lifeline.

He couldn't afford to kill her just because he was impatient.

It was vital to remember freedom was a long game.

But he couldn't help feeling frustrated. Achilleía was alive. Not only was she back in his life, she could testify who had killed their children and tried to kill her... if only he could get her to remember who he was.

He pulled Polyxena into his embrace.

She sobbed into his chest.

"I'm sorry, truly, it's just being in this hole is startin' to get to me, feel me?"

She looked up at him.

"No, Chiron, let's be real, no shit between us, we both know you're too much of a soldier to let the hole get to you. It's her. Now that you know she's alive, you can't on your hands and wait. It's like you're willing to blow it all up suddenly. And you are a smarter nigguh than that."

Chiron sighed.

"Am I?"

"Maybe not," she said, "But I really do understand, however much you think I don't, I do, but on some real shit, I didn't see her beating down the door trying to get you out."

"She don't remember me," he admitted.

"So she says. Don't remember, or maybe she don't *want* to remember," she signified. "Maybe she's got another life that means more? It ain't like she didn't do it before."

And that last was the killer blow. Chiron shot her a menacing scowl, but Polyxena saw the pain in his eyes. She hated to hurt him, but her point was made.

Achilleía was no angel.

"Thanks for reminding me," he said, sourly.

"I'm sorry I didn't mean to go there. Look, I'm just sayin', baby, I'm *here*. I've been here for five years; where has she been?" She shook her head. "Can't remember? Really? That's some twisted shit right there. This is Achilleía we're talking about. Be sensible, baby, and believe what's staring you in the face," she kissed him, trying to take the sting out of her truth.

"I hear you, ma, I do. But with her back, she can prove I wasn't the one who tried to kill her. That's gotta be something for *us*."

She nodded.

"True. Or, and hear me out, she could put the final nail in the coffin. Do you wanna take that chance?"

He'd already thought of that.

"I have to."

Polyxena understood. She looked at her watch.

"Well, I need to go and we didn't even get a chance to talk about what I came to tell you."

"What did you come to tell me?"

She looked him in the eyes, fronting him, "I'm pregnant."

Chiron had no words for that.

23

No sooner than Polyxena was back in her office, than Tillman barged in, slamming the door behind him.

He was seething.

"Good morning to you too, Frank," she said, turning away from her computer to look up at him.

"He's dead," Tillman hissed, trying to keep his voice down, but his anger wouldn't allow it.

"I assume by 'him,' you're referring to your informant?" she smirked. "Don't worry, in prison, there'll always be another snitch to take his place."

"Don't play with me. A man lost his life playing your little game. I did not sign up for this."

Polyxena punched at a few keys.

"I'm taking to you," he said.

"And I'm *listening* to you. Now, let's see... Leroy Thomas, 48. Habitual criminal. Third and final felony, molesting a ten-year-old girl. I ask you this in all sincerity, do you think the world will miss that piece of shit?"

"That's beside the point. We aren't fucking executioners, we abide by the law. We see justice is met. When I agree to get Black locked up and blame it on an informant, I did not agree to have the man *killed*." Tillman sounded like a man who regretted fucking the devil.

"This is prison, Frank," she replied, drily. "Shit happens."

"Not anymore, it won't. Not if I have any say," he spat then turned for the door.

"Before you go, Frank, one more thing you ought to know."

"What?" He snapped.

"I'm pregnant."

For the second time in one day, she'd made a man speechless. He turned back around.

"You *what*?"

Polyxena slowly stood up and rounded the desk, walking up to him, lips twitching as a smile played with them.

"That's right, Frank, you're going to be a daddy again," she said.

"You can't be...My wife—"

"—Will never know. Believe me, I know how to play this game. I need you now more than ever. But you've got to be a big boy about this. I've got big plans and I need a big man. Are you that man, Frank? Tell me yes, Frank. Say yes to me."

"Yes," he said, getting ready to fuck the devil again.

Polyxena smiled and lowered herself to her knees.

She needed a slave for the final phase of the plan. From here on in it was about making sure he was that slave.

"Damn you look good, baby," Paris came up behind Medea and wrapped his arms around her waist, then kissed her softly on the neck. She could feel all of him against her.

"Oh, it's like that, Poppy?" she purred.

"Naw, it' like this," he replied, turning her to face him.

Five hundred million... The number rolled around in his mind, giving him chills.

It was the type of money that would make him untouchable.

Above the law kind of money.

Just the thought made his dick hard, but Medea thought it was all about her.

"I missed you," she whispered, unbuttoning his pants.

He chuckled. "You talking to me or him?"

"Both."

"So tell him that."

With a wicked grin, she lowered herself to her knees. By the time she reached his pelvis, the fragrance of another woman was obvious.

She comforted herself with the fact that even after he fucked these other women, she was the one he came home to.

She was the one on his arm at all the events.

The taste didn't bother her; in fact, it made him taste even sweeter.

Paris looked down at Medea, watching her.

"I've been thinking a lot about you lately," Paris expressed.

"What about?" She asked, looking up at him.

"How much you've stood by my side, how loyal you've been to me and the family. Things that can't be over looked," he replied, looking her in the eyes.

"It's because I love you, but the loyalty part is just who I am you know?"

"And who *are* you?"

"I'm me, you know, just trying to be all I can," she answered, not really knowing how to answer.

Paris smiled.

"Naw, you, you my wife," he said. "That is, if you say yes."

"Are you asking me to marry you? Now? When I'm on my fucking knees? Meant to be you down here, not me, fool."

"Yeah, I am, so?"

"Yes, yes, yes. I'll marry you, yes!" She started to get up, grinning. "Where's my ring?"

"I can do you a pearl necklace if that works for you?"

That earned him a slap. He laughed. "I tell you what... How about we see if the jeweler makes house calls?"

"Married?" Quadir said, shaking his head after Medea told him her big news the next day.

"Yes, married. Why you lookin' like that? You act like it's the end of the world," she tossed off flippantly, sitting down on this couch. Quadir shook his head again.

"Ma, we talked about this. I told—"

"Yeah, yeah, Quadir, I *remember*, you told me he would *never* marry me. Does this look like never?" she said, holding up her 3.5-karat engagement ring.

Quadir sighed hard and sat down next to her.

He could see his plan going down the shitter faster than a deuce, just as it was about to take off.

"Medea., I know the nigguh probably painted a pretty picture, but *trust* me, please, I'm begging you, Paris ain't got no intention on marrying you."

"Ninety thousand is a hell of a price to pay for a lie."

"It's an investment," he said, not impressed. "Paris is smart. Fuck, he's as close to a genius as I ever seen, so I *know* he's got something up his sleeve. I don't know *what*. But he'll never marry you because you're a half-breed."

Medea waved him off even though his words hurt.

"Please, all that Egyptian science shit died with Sugar Ray. Paris fucks white girls and all that."

"You know for yourself how Paris felt about Sugar Ray."

"Paris's his own man."

"Is he?" Quadir challenged, looking her in the eyes.

She blew out her cheeks. "So why the game? Tell me that?" The problem was she knew deep down that Quadir had a point.

He took her hand in his and replied, "Paris's making a move and whatever it is, that ring on your finger ain't an engagement ring, it ain't even a token. It's a joke. He's a muthafucka like that.

Just give me a little time. I'll work out what shit it is he's trying to pull."

Quadir traced her cheek with his fingertip as she pulled away.

"Don't," she said, standing up. The move put distance between them. "I'm tired of all these games, Qua. Everybody trying to fool everybody else. For what? I just want to be happy. So, you know what, even if that means believing an some bullshit fake-ass illusion, let it be. I'm done hurting."

Quadir understood her pain.

Medea wasn't like Polyxena or Achilleía. She wasn't a soldier. She was a good woman. He came up behind her and wrapped her in his embrace.

"Remember that night I promised I'd take care of you? Have I let you down yet?"

"No," she admitted.

"So, stick with me. Yeah, it's a crazy game we're playin', but we're in too deep to just walk away, both of us. And a slip could cost us our lives. Stick with me and we walk away on top, and then it'll be you and me. I promise." He kissed her neck.

She shook her head, trying to get away from the confusion clouding her mind.

"I don't know what to do, Qua."

He turned her to face him, tipping up her chin to look into his eyes.

"Yes you do. Trust me."

He took her silent gaze as consent, and kissed her again to seal the deal.

But her silence was more calculating than that.

She had an ace in the hole, too. The only difference was if she played her card, it would bring the house of cards down on all their heads.

Quadir's phone rang, ruining the moment.

He looked and saw it was Paris.

He put his finger to her lips as he answered.

"What up big brah?" Quadir answered, as he slipped that same finger in Medea's mouth. He liked the idea of talking to Paris while his bottom bitch sucked on his finger. He slowly traced down to her breast.

"Where you at?"

"Manhattan. What's good?"

"I need you to meet me at the spot."

"Everything okay?"

"I don't know," Paris answered, "It's Achilleía. She just walked in."

24

Hoffman lifted his glass to his mouth and sipped at the scotch.

He changed his mind, and downed the double in a second swallow, then filled it back up.

He was in his own living room, but in his mind, he was still in Kareema's bedroom.

He'd arrived at the scene not long after Faith's escape. It was so close, the steam from the shower she had taken still had the bathroom mirror clouded up.

"We've blocked off the area for a six-block radius, sir," one officer informed him.

"Any sign?"

"No, but we're going door to door."

"Don't bother," he said, the cold hard reality was if she could escape half the police force at the hospital she'd disappear without a trace in an open-ended dragnet. "So, tell me, what else do we know?"

"She went online," the officer reported back.

"Laptop or smart phone?"

"Laptop, sir."

"She take it with her?"

"No sir, that's it right there."

The laptop was sitting on the bed. He sat down and opened the lid. He saw what she was looking at last. Paris. Hoffman worked his way backwards, screen by screen, through her search history until he saw her: a picture of Achilleía Black.

He couldn't believe his eyes. His first instinct was to follow the same line of reasoning Faith had at first, that he was looking at a twin. But the more he read, the more sure he became that Faith Newkirk and Achilleía Black weren't twins, they were one in the same.

Hoffman glanced up at the activity around him.

The Philly police were dusting for prints and other forensic evidence, but the only evidence worth a damn was on the laptop.

Hoffman deleted her searches.

He knew it would be nothing for an IT technician to pull the pages back up, but he also knew that no one would bother.

He sat the laptop back on the bed and walked out.

And now he sipped at another glass of scotch, contemplating everything he knew—and he knew everything.

Once he got back to his office, he did an extensive search, pulling up everything on Achilleía Black. And it was a lot of stuff to pull up. She was the daughter of a black mafia kingpin, married to another black mafia don, the sister of the prince of the city. He knew she was presumed dead and that her husband was doing life for the crime he didn't commit.

But the kicker was her military service.

She'd been Special Forces, her assignment taking her to Afghanistan.

But after that, the trail ran cold.

Everything else was classified above his need to know.

"Newkirk, you son of a bitch. What the fuck is going on?"

He knew this was so much deeper than a mall shooting.

If he was going to get any answers, he'd have to get them himself and there was only one way he'd be able to do that.

He picked up his phone and dialed a number from memory.

"Hello Special Agent in Charge Johnson? This is Special Agent in Charge James Hoffman of the Philadelphia office. I'm sorry to bother you but I was wondering if I came up to the city to talk to you, would you have time for a few particulars? I'm hoping you can help straighten a few things out for me... Great, Tuesday is perfect. I'll see you then."

He hung up with New York on his mind.

25

S tan never had any good luck in his life.
He was fifty pounds overweight, a truck driver by trade,
and could never get over the hump. Good shit always happened
to the other guy. So, when he saw the beautiful black woman that
reminded him of some singer whose name he couldn't remember
standing by his truck, he didn't know what to think.

He'd just pulled into the truck stop to take a piss, grab a bite
to eat, and catch a few winks, but when he came out and saw her,
he couldn't take his eyes off the woman. She was too pretty to be a
prostitute, surely? "Hey, Daddy, lookin' for me?"

He damn near choked on his chicken sandwich.

"Naw, but I am now."

She smiled, "Well, I'm definitely going your way."

"Hop in?"

And they were off.

"What's your name?"

"Candy," she purred. "My daddy named me that because he
said I taste so sweet."

"Damn, you must've had a freaky ass daddy."

"And he taught me everything I know. Get me to Camden and

I'll show you," she promised.

"Say no more. Camden here we come."

He couldn't get there fast enough.

By the time they reached the truck stop in Camden, it was almost four in the morning. Stan parked his eighteen-wheeler then glanced over at Candy, ready to claim his reward.

"Welcome to Camden."

"You got a cab in the back?"

"And a bed."

"Then what are we waiting for?"

He didn't need telling twice. They clambered into the back of the cab, where, true to his word, he had a mattress. Candy climbed on top of him and looked down with a butter-wouldn't-melt smile.

"You ready for me?"

"Fuck yes. I want you to fuck me like you used to fuck your ol' daddy."

"Exactly the same," she promised, and then from the small of her back, pulled out a pistol.

He didn't have time to regret the choices he'd made in this life. There was no life flashing before his eyes come to God moment. There was only

Boc! Boc!

two headshots pointblank.

They made what was left of his face look like a chewed-up tomato.

Blood splashed back into her face and all over the shitty little mattress.

Faith got up and wiped her face, checking for blood in the small, dingy mirror.

"Sorry, Stan, but we all gotta go sometime," she told the dead man, digging in his pockets. He had over four hundred dollars and a loaded .38 snub. It wasn't much but now that she was out of Philly, it would get her to New York.

She chose to come to Camden because she knew it was an outlaw city. A city even the city police didn't like to patrol. Gangs and thugs ran the streets, making it a perfect place to hide out in until she could get to New York.

She hopped down out of the truck and looked around.

Besides one other truck, the truck stop was deserted.

Nobody, not even truckers, wanted to be in Camden after dark.

She quickly learned why.

"Hey mami, how you doin, eh?" a Spanish creep driving an Escalade called out.

Faith just kept walking.

The Escalade pulled up beside her.

That's when she realized he wasn't alone.

There were two other people in the car. Three against one was uncomfortable if things went south in a hurry.

"Ma, you ain't gotta be like that," the passenger called out. "It's too late for a pretty bitch like you to be out there by yourself. I know you need a ride. Why don'tcha just get on in?"

"I'm good," Faith replied, no eye contact.

"Now, you know *anything* could happen. This ain't a safe place. Come on, you, get in."

"Please, just leave me alone."

"Stupid bitch, I'm tryin' to look out for you. Ayo José, stop the truck!"

The passenger jumped out of the car, bulked up like he'd just come home from a weightlifter's prison. He was about as over-stacked as a plastic He-Man doll.

He stood in front of her.

"I said get in the fuckin' car," he growled.

Instinct. Familiarity. Calculations. Faith's mind assessed her predicament. He wasn't armed, but she statistics said someone else in the car was. This was Camden. People got murdered in broad daylight here on Main Street. A back block in the middle of the night? If she blasted the dude out of his shoes, it'd escalate into a shoot-out and three fresh corpses would draw unnecessary attention.

But assuming she got in the car, odds were they'd drive her to a quiet place looking to fuck her sore. Quiet was better.

"Damn, you ain't gotta be so mean," she retorted, with a ghetto twist to the neck.

His scowl broke into a smile.

"I won't if you don't make me. Come on, ma. Me and my nigguhs just hanging out."

She saw the way he watched her, and knew he was thinking about getting a shot of that ass.

He was definitely going to get a shot.

She clambered into the back between two dudes with dreads. They looked like twins in the dark.

The driver pulled off.

"See ma, we ain't about no bullshit. We just trying to party," one dread said, holding up a wad of money.

Jackpot, she thought, maintaining her composure.

"I'm definitely down with that," Faith giggled. It was a shallow act, but she could play it just fine.

The other dreaded man threw his arm around her neck, leaned in and said, "I don't give a fuck what these other nigguhs talkin' bout, I'm first."

"Oh, really? What makes you so sure of that?" Faith smirked, giving him a playful glance.

He pulled out his dick. He was hung like a mule.

"Cause one shot of this is like heroin," he chuckled. "Believe me-"

She looked at him, "With a dick like that, you can be last or first. Or both if you're up for it, sugar."

They were too cheap to get a room, choosing to go to the driver's apartment instead. The guy looked like Fat Joe, but it didn't take long to figure him for the muscle man's yes man.

They never made it upstairs.

The only reason they even made it out of the car was because she didn't want to get blood all over the upholstery. It wasn't as if she could drop by some car wash and get it detailed if it looked like a crime scene photograph.

A parking lot in the back of an apartment building in the middle of the night; the same thing they thought was their advantage became their downfall.

"You gonna dance for us, ma?" Fat Joe joked as they headed for the door.

"I don't dance, sugar, but wanna see your moves," she replied. "Dance for me, fat man."

"Huh?"

Boc! Boc! Boc! Boc!

They never knew what hit them.

Faith slipped the two guns from the small of her back and brought her arms up like eagle wings, delivering headshots to both dreaded men simultaneously.

Two more shots hit Fat Joe in the face and his muscles in his chest.

The dreads were dead before they hit the ground.

Fat Joe was barely conscious.

Only Muscles witnessed the savage transformation.

He laid on his back, coughing up blood.

"You skank bitch," he gruffed. "You know you wanted the dick."

"You know, I want it so much I think I'll take it with me."

She pulled out his dick, put the .38-barrel to it, and with a single curl of the finger made a girl out of him.

Muscles opened his mouth, but nothing came out. It went beyond pain.

"Second thoughts," Faith said, looking at the bloody sausage of flesh in her hand. "A man and his meat should not be parted."

She grabbed him by the hair and forced he head back. He

gritted his teeth, earning a bitch slap with the pistol's butt, and as his head came back Faith stuffed what was left of the dick down his throat so far he gagged on the head.

She stepped back to admire her handiwork.

Boc! Boc!

Two shots pointblank opened the back of his head and blew his brains out, forming a red halo around his now-empty skull.

Faith stood up and looked at his face, frozen in horror; his eyes open, watching the angel of death with a mouthful of dick.

"Guess you were right about it being a dangerous town," Faith snickered.

She took everything of value, loading up on money, watches and jewels.

She thought about going upstairs to ransack Fat Joe's apartment, but she'd collected the best part of five grand in cash and probably another six or seven platinum chains and designer watches. That was more than enough for what she needed.

"Sure am glad I ran into you boys," she told the corpses as she jumped behind the wheel of the escalade. She adjusted the seat, then found a smooth listening R&B station on the radio, and pulled off, rolling over one of the dead dread's head's and crushing the bones beneath the tire. She felt the resistance, followed by the bump, then it was smooth again.

Like stepping on roaches, she thought.

Instead of going straight to New York, she took a detour to Trenton first.

She intended to stay in urban areas. The big risk was keeping the Escalade too long. The Camden cops would find the bodies soon enough, and the first thing they'd do was run vehicle and license checks. She had made four or five hours before her wheels became too hot to be worth the risk.

On the city limits, she dumped it and got a room in a run-down crack motel. It was the kind of shithole where no one would ask questions.

She stopped at the store, got eggs, grits and all the good stuff for breakfast in a 24hr diner, then crossed over the street to pick up an electric clipper, and a box of blonde L'Oréal hair dye from a drug store.

The first thing she did when she got back to the room was take a shower.

It had been relentless, hustle, move, kill, move, hustle, kill. No time to think. But now that she had, the only thing she *could* think was, *what is happening to me?*

She had never thought of herself as a killer but then again, she'd never been in a 'kill or be killed' situation.

Or had she?

Just thinking about the fact she didn't know her own life did her head in, but there was no denying that every time she pulled the trigger, she felt something, a creeping cold sensation not dissimilar to déjà vu come over her. There were no jitters, she felt no remorse for her actions, and most tellingly, no fear.

She didn't even think about the lives she took.

Which begged the question: *was I really always cold-blooded under my housewife façade?* And the follow-up: *does anyone truly know themselves?*

The problem was that Faith couldn't lie to herself. She felt good about getting as far as she had. Every time she found herself in a no-win situation, she found a way to defy that outcome and walk away a winner. Her confidence was on one thousand, even if she couldn't explain it.

She stepped out of the shower and stood in front of the hotel vanity mirror. She could see her whole body, head to toe, if she stepped back far enough, but up close she was cut off at the knees. She wasn't in ripped shape, but looking at herself she loved her body in a whole other light. It wasn't about being sexy or looking like she'd stepped out of a glamor mag. It was about the fact it was lived in. It had given birth. It bore the stretch marks of life well lived and the scars of experiences hard learned. And it was strong. The way she handled those two women at the hospital, especially the one with the hypnotizing gaze. She'd never seen a woman so dark with eyes like that. They were an aberration. She knew they were real. She'd seen them up close. And she'd seen something else, too. Guilt.

The woman wanted to be cold, but she couldn't hide it.

When they were locked in battle, her hypnotic eyes betrayed her guilt, but about what? What could be worth killing for?

You said it yourself, betrayal, that voice inside growled. *That's the only thing. Always the only thing.*

Faith brushed it off and picked up the clippers.

She needed to change her look.

If it wasn't already, her face would be plastered across every screen in the country soon enough. She had to disguise herself, or at least make herself unrecognizable. Normally, with disguises you added stuff, that was always easier than taking stuff away. You added layers of fat, jowls or wrinkles, you added a wig and make-up. But she was starting out from the opposite position, taking stuff away. She grabbed the clippers and shaved her head down to a buzz cut, and then she used the blonde dye to finish the transformation, coming out of it with a brand new Amber Rose look that had her starting at a stranger in the mirror.

Faith put her hand on her cocked hip, tilted her head to the side as she admired her reflection, and said, "I like it."

She sat down on the bed and put on the TV.

The morning news wasn't saying anything about Camden or Philly. She breathed a sigh of relief. Satisfied, she killed it, checked the window, then laid down, keeping her guns close but out of sight, and closed her eyes, figuring she'd just doze for a couple of hours, refresh and start over. Before she knew it, she was...

"Can you hear me, Faith?"

She heard the voice, but it took a minute to process her thoughts; her mind felt groggy. Heavy, but at the same time, clear.

"Faith, can you hear me?"

Hector.

It was Hector.

She wanted to open her eyes, but she couldn't.

She could still talk, albeit barely above a whisper.

"Yes. I can hear you."

"Good girl. You are my good girl, right?"

She felt a smile creep across her face.

"I'm your good girl."

"Okay, I need you to talk to me, okay? Can you do that?"

"I can."

"Afghanistan."

As soon as he said the word, it was like her inner eye and she found herself dumped into the middle of one of those first-person shooters. But this wasn't computer generated; it was real and she was there. She could feel the sweat on her face. She could smell the cordite, the iron of spilled blood, the stench of death.

"Incoming!" someone yelled.

Boom!

The explosion was close enough to feel the ground shiver beneath her feet, but not close enough to threaten. She stayed calm, her M-16 to her cheek, looking through the scope. Any enemy combatants and... *BBBRRRRP!*

She cut him in half, sending him to hell hollering like a bitch.

"Faith."

Hector's voice was like the narrator of a movie, in her mind, but not quite there at the same time.

"This is me, baby, Hector. Your husband."

Hesitation.

Facial contortions.

Torn.

"The General. I need you to tell me about the General."

26

He had the kind of presence that meant when he made an entrance people felt the urge to stand and salute. He commanded attention. Even when he was dressed impeccably as a civilian, albeit in five thousand dollar suits, the military air still followed him, like the scent of cologne, and General Priam knew it.

He was one of few black generals with three stars.

His gray hair and reddish hue added to the gravitas.

The man oozed power.

He stepped out of the back of his black Lincoln, security detail in place. They looked like Secret Service, but were hand-picked, men who had served under him for years. That kind of loyalty couldn't be bought. One opened the door of the cigar bar for him. He walked in.

Inside, Paris and two of his goons waited.

They stood when he entered.

"Uncle Joe," Paris smiled, giving the General a warm hug.

"You're looking more like your father every day," the General replied, returning the hug, and adding with a chuckle.

"I ain't Sugar."

"That's true, you're more like black ass molasses," the General said, earning a genuine laugh from Paris. There was real love here. And real respect.

They dismissed the security and took a seat at one of the booths facing the door.

A topless waitress brought them over a bottle of Hennessey, two glasses, two cigars, a lighter, and a cigar cutter, all on a silver tray.

"Can I get you anything else, boss?"

"All good."

The General clipped the top and Paris lit him up.

"These babies won't be the same now that we're opening the doors to Cuba again," the General remarked, puffing until the tip lit up.

"Yeah, Unck, ain't no fun if it's legal," Paris replied.

The two of them puffed on their cigars. Paris poured his uncle a drink.

"So, you talked to Arnold?"

"Yeah, he's on board."

"Just like I knew he would be. Fuckin' pussy," the General cussed. He would never respect Arnold. The two had too much history.

"Yeah, but pussies are made to be fucked. Ain't that what you and Pop always taught me?"

The General nodded and brought his glass up for a toast.

"Your father was always a better man than me," the General remembered, though that might have been those rose tinted Ray-Ban's coloring the past. "If it would've been up to me, I would've been killed Arnold. But your pops knew on a house nigguh level Arnold would make us rich." He sipped his drink, then added, "And bless him, he did. He played them crackers at their own game. I gotta give it to him. He's a smart bitch."

Paris nodded, a sly grin spreading across his face.

"And... I'm getting married."

"When's the funeral?" the General retorted, only half-joking.

"Naw, it ain't like that. Just crossing T's on this one," Paris explained. "Five hundred mil is a lot of money. All eyes are gonna be on, Hell, I know Interpol's gonna be all over this once we're done, so somebody's gotta be in a position to take the fall if it comes down to it, and it damn sure ain't gonna be me."

The General downed his drink.

"Setting up the woman you love, you're a cold motherfucker, nephew."

"Who said anything about love?"

Another toast.

"Now this is our next..."

He began to scheme, laying out the foundation of his thoughts, but then he saw something that damn near took his breath away. He couldn't believe his eyes. In all his years, he had seen things that made miracles seem impossible, but for the first time, his cynical heart skipped a beat.

"It can't be...," he breathed, his eyes affixed on the vision.

Paris turned to see what he was looking at, and he was speechless for a whole different reason.

She came here?

It was like a mouse walking into the cat's crib bold as fucking brass. Like a sheep coming to the slaughter with the straight-edged razor in her teeth waiting to be sheered.

Faith recognized Paris from the Internet, but the older man staring at her wasn't someone she knew.

But the tender look in his eyes made her feel almost normal for the first time in forever. She allowed herself a moment of weakness—but only a heartbeat—because she needed to be comforted. She'd made it from Trenton, taking the train to New York. Once she arrived at Penn, she'd caught a cab and told the driver, "Brooklyn. The Ultimo bar on Atlantic Avenue."

She had read about it online.

She knew it belonged to Paris. It was the only business they'd listed in any of the articles she'd read, making it her best bet for getting to him. She had nowhere else to go. Everyone else wanted her dead.

The General slowly approached, with Paris a few steps behind him.

"Baby girl?" the General gasped, not believing his own eyes.

She walked into his embrace. She could feel the concern in his strong-but-gentle touch. She may not have known who *he* was, but his touch exuded love, and in that same strange haunting way, felt so, so familiar.

"My God, where have you been?" the General asked, shaking his head, eyes red with unshed tears.

"I don't know," Faith found her voice. "I don't know anything. I don't even know who I am..."

She collapsed into his chest, allowing all the pressure, pain, stress, and confusion to be free.

The General couldn't stop shaking.

He looked back at Paris.

"Your sister is alive?"

Paris allowed himself to be pulled into the three-way hug, pretending to be in the moment. His mind raced. The only thing on his mind in that second, clutching onto Achilleía like a lifebuoy was: how he could kill her?

They went back to Paris's apartment, which was located in the upper reaches of Trump Tower. As they stepped off the gold elevator onto his floor, Faith started to tell her story, beginning with the boating accident she thought she had all the way up to the escape from the hospital in the face of two murderers.

She left out the murders she committed on her way to New York, but laid everything else on the line.

The General shook his head, still unable to grasp the enormity of her return. It was like a gift from the gods. "All this time... I thought you were dead," he said for the umpteenth time. Shaking his head some more, he told her, "I'm just so happy, I don't know what to do." His grin was infectious, even as he admitted, "I thought Chiron had killed you."

She nodded along. "I don't know what to believe. I read about Chiron Black, not much, but everything I could find online and then there were those girls—" the General cut her off.

"What girls?"

"I told you about them. The murderers who hit the hospital."

"No, you said murderers. You weren't gender specific," the General clarified.

"There were two of them. One, she was dark with these incredible blue eyes."

Paris nodded, even though he knew without being told who had paid his sister a visit. "Polyxena."

Faith looked at him, "You know her?"

"You do, too. I would have said she was your best friend, but trying to kill you makes me think those days are in the rearview," Paris told her. "Word on the street is that she's been fuckin' Chiron."

"But he's in prison."

Paris laughed, not cruelly, but with no genuine warmth, either. "Sis, this Chiron we're talking about, he run the prisons."

The General was boiling. "That fucking Chiron. I should have taken him years ago."

Faith wasn't listening, now she knew what the guilt was for in those blue eyes. That bitch was fucking her husband.

"You said there were two of them. What did the other one look like?" Paris questioned, keeping up the pretense of ignorance.

"Spanish," Faith replied.

Paris nodded, poker faced.

"Don't you worry. We're going to get you the best doctors. You'll get your memory back," the General promised.

"Easier said," She reminded him, "I'm a fugitive. It's not like I can go back to the hospital."

"Then we'll bring the hospital to you," he said, winking. "You may not remember, but this is your city. The Butler family owns this place lock stock and two smokin' barrels, the cops, the courts, and the streets. All of it. This is ours. And you, my dear, a *fucking* soldier. I trained you myself."

"Was I in Afghanistan?"

The General squeezed her shoulder affectionately. "We'll talk," he answered, without really answering, then looked at Paris. "Take care of her, nephew. I don't know what's going on, but I'm counting on *you* to take care of her."

"No doubt, Unck. Achilleía is my heart. They'll have to kill me to get to her," he vowed, the lie easy on his forked tongue.

The General nodded, satisfied that his family was whole again, and turned to the door, leaving them to catch up.

"Damn ma, I can't believe you're alive. Damn that Pop ain't here to see you back from the dead," he looked at her seriously, pushing just a little. "Is there *anything* you remember?"

Part of her wanted to tell him what Quadir said about her own brother wanting her dead, like it was the most preposterous thing in an already fucked up world, but something deep down warned, *No. Wait. Watch.*

"Nah, it's a blank in here, whole different life that I never lived exists where you all used to be," she answered.

Paris smiled, "Welcome home sis. Lil brah missed you."

27

Hoffman wasn't the only one hot on Faith's trail, and ironically, it was the not so Special Agent who'd tipped Hector off when he used the computer in his office to try and look up Achilleía Black's military history.

The inquiry into her classified files triggered an alert higher up the food chain. That alert resulted in a phone call to Hector.

"The project has been breached. Terminate the subject," came the order from above.

"Please, sir. Let me—"

"This is not for discussion. The decision has been made."

There was no getting around what terminate meant. Faith's death warrant had just been issued. It was hard, even though Hector had been fully prepared to do just that in the hospital, now, on the other side of impulse where things became pre-meditated he didn't know if he could simply blow her brains out.

In a combat situation, the adrenaline, the rush of action was nothing short of a high. Whatever else he had become, Hector was a soldier first and foremost. He could do anything in the heat of battle, including kill the woman he loved. But, cold blood? Could he do that? He loved her. It might be a fucked up kind of love, but that didn't make it any less potent. The whole project had been initiated because of that love. He'd sacrificed his career for that love. He'd imprisoned her in her own mind for that love.

Truth be told, it was more than love. It was darker than that. It was obsession.

Once he used Hoffman's search to guide his own search, he knew *exactly* where Faith was headed: Brooklyn. It was sadly predictable, given the fact Achilleía was waking. He ran inquiries about recent robberies, car jackings, and unsolved murders between Philadelphia and Brooklyn over the last 48. He knew that if Achilleía was awake, her path would be lined with bodies. That was just who she was.

There were two that could be laid at her door looking at the M.O.. A trucker and four gangbangers in Camden. The trucker was out of Philly, but his body in up a Camden truck stop. The four gangbangers were found in a parking lot, one with his dick shoved down his throat, like he was being given a message.

If she wasn't fully awake, she was definitely stretching, Hector thought, because that macabre maneuver was classic Achilleía.

One of the gangbanger's vehicles turned up in Trenton, but there was no sign of Achilleía.

He used his contacts in Washington to access footage from the city's traffic cams and drones to zero in on the vehicles. Until, finally, at a red light, he got a clear view of the driver. There was no mistaking his Faith behind the wheel.

But the next shot made his heart sigh with the grief of nostalgia.

Using traffic cams and surveillance footage, he was able to trace the motel she'd stayed at. The motel itself had no cameras, but a taxi had picked up a woman from that address and dropped her at the station the next morning.

"Yeah, I remember her. A blonde chick," the cabby told him over the phone.

"Blonde?"

He was about to dismiss it until saw for himself.

She was at the train station, keeping her head down like she was trying to avoid the cameras. For all the changes, her profile as she got on the train was unmistakable. Her hair was in a buzz cut and dyed blonde.

Just like it was when they first met.

"You're a cutie, but I don't do the white boy, David," Achilleía had told him bluntly, as they both exited the mess hall, adding, "Besides, I'm married."

David smiled. He knew the last part was more for her than for him.

"Well, would it help if I told you my father's mother was a Navajo? So not really all that white. More off-white."

"No, but you get an 'E' for effort."

"Ah well, can't we be friends?"

"We already are," she winked, walking to catch up with Polyxena.

David couldn't help himself; she looked beyond good in those army fatigues. But it was the way she wore her buzz cut that stopped his heart.

Back when she'd first enlisted, her whole mane had been dyed blonde, and it was pretty fucking obvious to anyone with eyes to see she was the most beautiful woman at the base, but she really didn't enjoy the attention, hence the buzz cut.

"Now all you gotta do is imagine I got a dick," she would tell all the gawkers and admirers to steer them clear.

David loved the way she handled the situation.

She knew she was beautiful with or without hair. It was always such a fucking cliché when people said shit like the hottest thing about her was she didn't know she was hot. That was utter shit masquerading as a compliment. She knew. Of course she fucking knew. But she wanted them all to know how little being beautiful meant to her. And that was special.

David couldn't stop thinking about her.

He watched her constantly.

During their drills when she had to crawl, covered with mud, or run ten clicks with a twenty-five-pound pack on her back, the intensity and focus showed on her face.

Boldness would win him a smile, but pretty much nothing else. And that killed him.

"You shouldn't stare at people. They may get the wrong impression," Achilleía told him one day.

"And what impression is that?" David cracked a dimple."

"That you're trying hard to imagine them naked. That's not what you're doing, is it David?" she replied, a teasing tone behind her flirtatious words.

He knew she was toying with him, same way a cat plays with a mouse before devouring it. He liked the game, even if he was the mouse.

And then one night, it happened.

It was a rainy summer night.

David had been on guard duty in the barracks. He'd put a raincoat on to go out for the perimeter checks. Lightening hissed and sizzled with brutal elemental fury, illuminating the night sky, then disappeared, taking all the power with it.

For several minutes, the whole camp was plunged into darkness, the only light coming from his flashlight.

"Fuck," he cursed under his breath as he cut the corner, heading for the rear of the barracks.

The rear exit was recessed from the exterior wall with a brick partition. When he cut the corner, there was someone behind the partition: Achilleía.

"Bang, bang, you're dead," she smirked, making a gun of her finger and thumb.

The back-up generator kicked in and the base lights came back on, yet she and David were hidden in the shadows.

"What are you doing out here?" he questioned.

"I'm going AWOL."

"Why?"

She shrugged, "Because I'm horny."

Those few words sent a tingle down David's spine.

She began to walk off into the rain.

"You can't go AWOL, Achilleía."

The rain had soaked her already, her T-shirt sticking to her and her sweatpants moving so freely, he knew she was wearing nothing underneath. She turned to face him but continued walking backwards.

"Who's going to stop me?" she challenged then turned and ran off.

David didn't know if she was serious or not, but he was a soldier, he couldn't just let someone go AWOL. He gave chase. Woods surrounded the base. It only took a few minutes before Achilleía was swallowed up in the forest of darkness.

"Achie?" He called out, trying to keep his voice low.

The MPs patrolled the bases perimeter constantly.

"This is crazy," he mumbled, until he saw something hanging off a tree limb: her wet T- shirt.

His breath hitched. She was somewhere nearby, topless and horny.

He stood still, listening.

He could hear her moving through the leaves up ahead, giggles floating in the wind like a fucking wood nymph.

David found her sweatpants next.

He picked them up.

He had to find her.

Then all of a sudden, the trail went cold.

No giggles.

No leaves rustling.

The rain muffled out sound and drenched everything around him.

But he *knew* she was close.

He could smell her perfume.

He closed his eyes and concentrated on the fragrance.

He turned to the right and pushed through a tangle of vines.

The scent grew stronger, and stronger, until he saw why.

He had been wrong.

She'd been wearing a black thong.

He found it dangling from a branch just like the soaking tee.

David took it down and put it to his nose, inhaling her fragrance.

A hand snatched his gun out of his holster and held it to the back of his head. "And all this time, you thought you were chasing me," Achilleía whispered in his ear. "Turn around," she told him.

He did. A bolt of lightning lit up the sky, silhouetting her.

She was naked, but not remotely vulnerable.

"Damn, you are beautiful," he said, only wanting to worship her.

Achilleía stepped up to him lightly and peeled the raincoat from his shoulders as she kissed him.

"And let's not forget horny," she reminded him.

"How could we?"

He didn't need telling a third time.

He quickly stripped down, wrapping his nakedness around hers. He started to try and lay her down, but she was having none of it, she pushed him down into the dirt, and straddled him. The warm rain cascaded down her body.

It wasn't beautiful. No love songs would be written about it. And when it was over, she leaned forward and kissed him, "Thanks, I needed that."

And just like that, she gathered up her clothes and she was gone.

David...

He hadn't thought about his real name since the project began.

And just like that night, once again, he was chasing her in the dark.

But this time he was determined not to fall for the panties-on-the-branch trick.

That's where Desire came in.

He looked down at her.

He'd injected her with Neuritrinol, the same drug he'd been shooting her up with for the past few days. He'd developed a level of expertise thanks to five years with Achilleía. Hector sat down beside Desire. Her skin was covered with freckles. Her complexion reminded him of cherry vanilla ice cream. She had the kind of body that could drive a lesser man out of his mind.

"Desire, can you hear me?"

"Yes," she responded, her eyes closed but fluttering.

Her mind was in a dreamlike state, highly sensitive to suggestion.

"You like Brooklyn."

Her face frowned slightly.

"No. I don't like New York."

"Yes, you do," he told her. "New York is a wonderful place to like. You used to hate New York but now you don't."

"Brooklyn."

"Yes, Brooklyn. Lots of money. Do you like money, Desire?"

"I love money."

He smiled.

"Then you need to be in Brooklyn. Neil will help you. You can trust Neil."

"Yes, I trust Neil."

"And Neil trusts you," he replied, referring to himself by the name he gave her.

"Brooklyn. Neil."

"You'll love it in Brooklyn. You're moving to Brooklyn."

"I'm moving to Brooklyn."

"Moving to Brooklyn."

"Moving..."

"Now," he said, standing up and unbuttoning the front of his jeans. "Why how about you open wide? You want to, don't you?"

"Always," Desire said, and spread her pretty lips wide.

"Brooklyn? Since when you wanna go to New York?" Desire's friend, Lola, questioned, as they sat in her apartment smoking a blunt.

"Girl, please, I used to hate New York, but now? Brooklyn is blowin' up and I've got to be there," Desire cackled. "Center of the universe, where else a woman like me gonna be?"

In her mind, she'd gone through this long, drawn-out decision-making process. She had no idea her thoughts had been manufactured.

She inhaled the blunt.

"Man, I got all the blowin' up I need right here in Philly," Lola replied.

"Local bitch," Desire joked. "You gotta expand, like my pretty little white boy, Neil. He's starting some tech company or whatever, and girl, you know these white boys. He's liable to be the next Facefuck or whatever you call it."

Desire and Lola high-fived.

"I hear you girl. But shit, I know he green and shit, but Brooklyn? What if he gets tired of you? You sure you can trust him?"

"Neil? Absolutely."

She passed Lola the blunt.

"Well, you sound like you got your mind made up. Not this bitch's place to try and convince you otherwise."

"Absolutely," Desire agreed.

Lola was only half right. Desire had her mind made up, though it was Hector who'd done the making, not her and not her make-believe Neil.

28

Quadir rode the elevator up to Paris's apartment, knowing the next few minutes were going to come down to kill or be killed.

He had his .45, safety off and one in the chamber.

He'd always known there was no way he could avoid the situation.

Paris was expecting him.

The variable he couldn't control was Faith. What would she say when he walked through the door? And what the fuck was she doing there in the first place?

He'd told her that Paris had sent to him to kill her, so why the fuck would she run to him?

Nothing about it made sense.

His only option was to stay on point.

If anybody made a false move then everything went out the window and it'd come down to the last man, or woman, standing.

He rang the bell several minutes later.

Paris opened the door.

As soon as he saw Quadir, he smiled.

"What up, lil brah?"

He embraced Quadir tightly.

"I'm good, yo."

Quadir returned the embrace, but he wasn't going to be rocked to sleep that easily. He stayed on point as he stepped inside. His and Faith's eyes met.

Her gaze said, *I remember you.*

His said, *what are you doing here?*

A subtle smirk was as close as she came to a reply.

He couldn't lie though. She looked more like herself with the short hair. So much so he had to ask, "Is it Faith or Achileía?"

She regarded him coolly.

"That's what I'm here to find out," she replied.

Paris put his arm around Faith.

"You remember lil brah, sis?"

Quadir's whole body tensed, waiting for her to sign his death warrant, ready to start blasting. She looked at him for what he seemed like forever, as if she were weighing her response, then shook her head and answered, "No. I've never seen him before."

Slowly, Quadir relaxed, although he still hadn't grasped what was going on.

"Well, then, let me re-introduce you to Quadir, one of the family's most loyal soldiers, ain't that right, Qua?"

"You already know, big brah."

"I have a headache," Faith said, touching her fingers to her temple.

"My bad Achie, come on, I'll show you where to lay your head."

"Please, don't call me that, okay? My name is still Faith," there was no conviction in her tone.

Quadir poured himself a drink while Paris took Achileía in the back.

A few minutes later, he walked in.

"Achie just walked in, cool as you fuckin' like," Paris said, shaking his head. "I couldn't believe that shit, fam. And the

General, he havin' a Ricki Lake moment. If it wasn't for him, I would've put her ass down on the spot."

"The General was there? Damn."

"Exactly. So now we stuck with this bitch for the time being. But I know this much, that shit that went down in Philly at the hospital? Polyxena was there," he told him, neglecting to mention Medea.

"Polyxena?" Quadir echoed .

Paris nodded.

"And the bitch tried to kill her," he added.

Now shit was starting to make sense across the board.

H knew why Medea lied.

She'd been in Philly with Polyxena.

"So, what do we do now?" Quadir questioned.

Paris struggled. "We wait. She don't remember who she is."

"But what if her memory comes back?"

"Then we're in trouble, Qua. But for now, she's under the General's protection."

Quadir nodded, perfect poker face, but inside, he was smiling so fucking hard.

Once again, Achilleía had found a way to step into the lion's den and tame the savage beasts.

"Yeah, yo. It is what it is."

29

Chiron felt good being back on the yard, because truth be told, the walls of the hole were had been closing in on him. It was brutal for the mind. Not because he couldn't handle it, but knowing that his wife was alive, and out there fighting for her life, made him crazy to find her.

He *hated* feeling helpless.

"Eight, nine, come old man, push! There you go. Ten! One more, one more, gimme one more. Go on, money!" Chiron's man Bang urged, as he lifted all 280 pounds of pure steel dumbbells back into the rack.

Chiron popped up off the work out bench and playfully, but powerfully, shot Bang a two-piece to the ribs.

"I still got them hands like Evander with the power of Iron Mike!" Chiron bragged.

Bang laughed.

He absorbed the two body blows and then squared up to throw a few punches of his own.

Chiron was taller, but Bang was wider and built like a Texas bull.

He kept his long dreads in a ponytail. Bang was a straight

gangsta. He was fifteen years deep into the first of three life sentence bids. He'd murdered two cops and the dude who had ratted on his cousin in broad daylight, coldest of blood, while they were coming out of the courthouse.

When Chiron met him, he was a gangbanger, running around the prison extorting nigguhs and raping white boys just for the fun of it. Chiron had taken him under his wing and over the last few years, and Bang had become his second-in-command. Trusted. True. He hadn't stopped banging, but the only color that mattered to him was green. With Chiron's help, he had stacked over a hundred thousand dollars and was on his way to getting a re-trial.

"Aight, Unck, I do work with these like Hercules," Bang spat back, cockily.

The two playfully shadowboxed until a female C.O., Hargrove walked by, shaking her head. "Okay, you two, y'all know no horse playin'."

She wore her uniform like she was a stripper who just so happened to be dressed like a cop for a bit. Despite the fact she wore her clothes big, there was no hiding her buffed body underneath.

"Come on ma, you know you ain't no playin with this horse," Bang cracked, grabbing his crotch.

"Hey Black, glad to see you back," Hargrove smiled.

"I'm glad to see you back and front," Chiron shot back, smoothly.

She nodded and kept it moving, giving them something to talk about as she walked away.

"I'm telling you fam, that head game is a fool," Bang grunted, remembering the night before in the broom closet.

"I might just have to see for myself," Chiron replied, then added, "That thing go down smooth? Who you put on it?"

"I put myself on it, Unck. I did that personally," Bang

answered referring to the murdering of the snitch that they thought told on Chiron.

Chiron shook his head, "Fam, how many times I gotta tell you? You can't get your hands dirty anymore. We gettin' too much paper to get sloppy now."

Bang nodded. "Yo, I hear you Unck, but with all due respect, that's who I am. You like my big homie, you gave me the way to get outta here. So far when a nigguh tries to violate you personally, I violate him personally."

Chiron didn't agree with his logic, but he definitely respected it.

"Say no more. I'm going hit the showers."

"I'ma go shoot some back and loosen up."

The two men parted ways.

Chiron headed back inside the dorm.

He didn't know he had company.

Two white boys with shaved heads and shaved eyebrows followed him. They were so pale they looked like skulls, which just so happened to be the name of their clique. The Skulls were a branch of the Aryan brotherhood and the darkest things on them were their homemade prison tatts. They were covered with them. One even had tattooed the whites of his eyes with red ink, making him look like a pure devil.

"He's going in his cell," Red Eye said, gripping the knife in his sleeve tightly.

"Nah. Not there. Too dangerous. I know he's got weapon in there," the taller, lanky one said. "He's gonna have to hit the showers in a minute. We do it there."

Several minutes later, Chiron come out of his cell in his shower shoes and shorts, a towel draped over his shoulder, wash cloth, soap dish, and boxers in his hand.

The two skulls checked for the guards.

None were in sight, making it a perfect time for a killing.

The Skulls moved in.

Chiron's mind was in a world of its own.

All he could think about was Achilleía.

"It's time to make it happen," Chiron mumbled, speaking to himself, but they got the message loud and clear.

He knew Polyxena wasn't in the ideal position to put his plan into motion, but waiting any longer wasn't an option. Achilleía needed him. He could feel it in his gut, and bottom line, nothing was going to keep him from her.

He turned on the water after having set his towel and boxers on the opposite wall so they wouldn't get wet.

The hot water felt good.

The bathroom quickly steamed up.

Chiron heard footsteps approaching.

"Ayo, get the fuck outta here," Chiron growled.

The two Skulls came stepping through the steam, like ghosts out of the fog.

"Don't worry, this won't take long," Red Eyes growled, holding a blade, seven inches long and icepick sharp.

Chiron, naked except for his shower shoes, squared off, back against the wall. The two Skulls spread out. The lanky one was on Chiron's right, his blade was curved, razor-sharp and perfect for slicing a throat.

"You crackers musta lost your minds," Chiron spat.

"Fuck you, Black, this is business! The General sends his regards."

Chiron's mind didn't have time to process the words.

Both men moved at the same time.

Chiron had a gift; he could look in a man's eyes and read his soul. So, despite the redness that clouded his irises, Chiron knew that Red was the weaker of the two.

He moved hesitatingly, unsure, even with the benefit of the numbers, Chiron didn't. Chiron lunged at Red, causing Red to lash out with the blade too soon, a downward thrust. Chiron weaved the attempt and cold-cocked Red with a rock-solid jab to the temple. The impact staggered him.

But the lanky one was on him.

Chiron dropped low and spun a backwards leg sweep that caught the lanky one just beneath the ankle. Because his assailants were wearing boots, the slippery wet tile became Chiron's advantage.

Lanky grunted as he felt the floor slip out from under him. He hit the wet tile hard.

Chiron went to stump him, but rolled away just as Red came at him with a straight knife jab chest high. Chiron dodged the tip like a bull fighter side-stepping the bull's horns, but he allowed Red's knife to graze his side, knowing it would go to his advantage even if he bled; he caught Red's arm between his own and his side, with the knife dangling helplessly behind him. Chiron yanked Red in and head-butted the racist bastard across the bridge of the nose, rupturing it.

He hollered in pain.

But Chiron was only getting started.

He went straight psycho in that shower, hitting the lanky one over and over, in his face, neck, and chest. He beat him bloody until his upper torso resembled a zombie's rotten flesh. Then, and only then, Chiron, covered in blood, let the body slump to the ground.

Chest heaving, he rolled Red over on his back and put the knife to his throat.

"Please man, don't kill me! They paid us, it was only business!" Red begged, the weakness coming out of him like the strong, nasty stench of piss that filled the shower block.

"Who paid you? Who?"

"Steinbech! He paid us to say that shit about a General! I'm begging you, Black, it was only business."

"Yeah, well, believe me, this is pleasure," Chiron stabbed him dead in the eye so hard and deep, the tip of the blade stuck in the bone at the back of his skull. It he'd have rammed it in any further it would have chipped the tile.

Chiron let the water cleanse him of the blood then returned to his cell.

By the time they found the two Skulls, almost two hours later, most of the blood had been washed down the drain, along with their lives.

Steinbech...

Jonathan Steinbach, age 27, had been a corrections officer for four years.

Four.

That number stuck out to Polyxena.

He had been there the whole time, dormant, waiting?

Or was it coincidence?

Nah, she knew there was never coincidence where the General was involved.

The whole situation made her realize just how deep the game they were all playing went.

Steinbach was in the National Guard, which explained how the General got his hooks into him.

What Polyxena didn't know, because the computer couldn't tell her, was how Steinbach had run into a small legal issue. He liked young girls. Twelve and thirteen were his preferences. Not that he'd ever actually *had* a young girl, he just liked to look and make barely legal ones dress up like they were so much younger. He'd been red-flagged because during a trawl of the deep web sites where that stuff was prevalent. They traced his posts back to a government computer. It was sloppy. It was only words. Fantasies, really. Those perverts sharing what they wanted to do out in the real world, and goading each other on. The MPs had arrested him, but the General stepped in. That was the General's M.O., he was always looking for someone to owe him a favor.

"You know where the phrase if she's old enough to bleed comes from, John? In some cultures, once a girl has her period, she's considered a woman," the General told him, the inference being it was the law, and not Steinbach, who was the problem. "Don't worry, I'll take care of this."

And he did, earning Steinbach's eternal gratitude, and that meant he was forever in the General's debt. Repayment wasn't about money, either. It never was. It was about favors and not being seen to get his hands dirty. The General made it clear that Chiron Black was not to see another birthday. "Handle it, Steinbach."

Steinbach had paid off the two Skulls.

Now it was Polyxena's turn.

Anybody watching the shadows around Steinbach's modest two-bedroom brick home wouldn't have been able to tell her from the darkness. She'd donned a black cat suit and wrap-around black shades. Even her sneakers were black, along with a silencer-equipped 9mm pistol. High bushes grew on either side of Steinbach's front door, offering cover; she waited.

Twenty minutes later, shift over, Steinbach returned from work.

It had been two days since the double homicide in the shower block, and the incident had the whole prison tense, including Steinbach. Especially Steinbach. He had let the General down. The General didn't deal well with disappointment, and while Chiron was still alive the General was going to have to. Steinbach felt guilty and ashamed. He was preoccupied as he approached his darkened front door. He had called the General's phone several times, but the number had been disconnected. That was a bad sign. It felt Steinbach swinging out there on that limb, alone and cut-off.

He felt the cold gun metal kiss up against his neck.

"Don't fuckin' move." It was as though a slice of the night itself had put the cold steel to him.

"Please, I tried," Steinbach blurted out.

Polyxena's whole game plan changed in that single heartbeat; he thought the General had sent her, so she played along.

"Just open the door. Real slow," she instructed him.

Once the door was open, she shoved him inside and shut the door behind her. The whole house was dark. She flipped the light switch on.

"On your knees, cross your feet at the ankles, lace your fingers on top of your head," she told him.

He assumed the position.

"Please, I got the best guys I could—"

"General Priam is very disappointed in you, John. You fucked up, big time, and the General does not like fuck-ups," Polyxena mocked him.

"I know. Whatever I have to do to make it up, I will. I swear to fucking God," he babbled.

"You know Priam doesn't give second chances."

"I know. I know. But you gotta believe me, I will do *anything*," Polyxena's mind spun like a hamster on a wheel, twisting with different possibilities.

"That's good. That's real good you said that. Maybe I can sell it to the General, you're contrite, you want to help, you'll do anything."

"I will. Just name it."

"I want you to do nothing," she told him.

"Nothing?"

"Just wait. I gotta speak to the General. Until then, you sit tight, we clear?"

"Yes, God yes, thank you," he breathed, sounding like a man watching those death row cell doors open after the Governor's reprieve comes through. "I won't mess up, I swear. How do I contact you? I tried to call Dempsey but the number is dead."

Dempsey, she thought, filing the name away.

"That's because Dempsey's been terminated. Your failure was his failure."

"Terminated," he echoed.

She enjoyed the tremor in his voice.

"Yes, you understand how lucky you are?"

"God bless you," he remarked, soulfully.

She had to stifle her laughter. "Just don't let me down, John. And to answer your question, you don't," she answered, opening the door, "I get in touch with you."

"Thank you," he said again.

She wasn't listening. Chiron had wanted Steinbach dead, but Polyxena knew how to use shit to her advantage. She could climb the ladder right to the General himself.

30

The spectacle bordered on a rap concert.

The jumbo screens reminded Paris of the one in basketball arenas.

But then, it was an arena, or more precisely, it was built using the same blueprint. The same architectural company that did construction on the Barclay's Center had built Patricia Randolph's praise house and it was colossal in the most mythic sense of the word. Over five thousand people filled it every Sunday without fail while a million more watched from the comfort of their television sets or streamed the telecast via the Internet.

It was prosperity gospel meets old time religion.

Paris sat back and took it all in, admiring Patricia's face projected from every angle on her own personal jumbotron.

The woman was taking in millions weekly, and with the expansion of her ministry globally, he knew billions weren't far behind.

There was serious money in the God business. There always had been.

I'm in the wrong line of work, he thought to himself as he adjusted the cuffs of his bespoke suit.

Patricia worked the crowd, part motivational speaker style, part down home preacher, part Broadway entertainer style. She was one of the few black female pastors bringing in more money than I.D. Jakes or Pastor Dollar. Her following was enormous, with all their eyes on her.

And her eyes were on Paris.

He was sitting in the front row, several feet from the stage, but watching him and his sexy smile made her feel naked. *Lord, forgive me, but this man makes me tremble*, she gushed in silent prayer as she worked the stage and preached about the essence of life's gift on this Earth.

And Paris is definitely one of them, she laughed inside.

"Let us pray," Patricia entreated the faithful, her voice booming in ten thousand ears, her words warming five thousand hearts.

She always ended with prayer.

It was the moment where all her pastoral skills shone brightest.

By the time she was finished, millions across the country were reaching for the Kleenex with one hand and their credit cards with the other. The only other time that happened was porn.

When she lifted her head, Paris was gone.

The arena erupted with a five thousand voices strong, "Amen."

Patricia's heart fluttered when she didn't see him.

She tried to look out beyond the first few rows, but the stage lights blinded her. The aisles were quickly filled with people making their way to the exits. She scanned the few faces she could see, but he wasn't there. Her fake smile glued to her face, she brushed past praises, air kisses, and other adorations until she reached her dressing room and grabbed her phone.

Why didn't you wait? she texted.

She got no response.

Knowing how crazy his life was, she figured he'd been called away and her heart sank because she'd been looking forward to some of that good lovin'.

She hadn't seen him in three days.

She missed him.

Call me when you can, she texted, and headed up to her office tucked away on the top floor of the arena.

She went there to relax. It was a home away from home. She'd had it decorated like a private apartment, or maybe more like a luxury suite at a five-star hotel. The living room's view looked out over Brooklyn through floor-to-ceiling glass that was tinted from the outside, meaning she could see out but no one could see in. The living room led out to a full bar in one direction and a short hallway in the other. The hallway in turn led to a master bedroom, replete with a four-post bed and a bathroom that boasted a bathtub and a full-size marble Jacuzzi big enough for a holy orgy had those things still been a way of celebrating the gods.

Patricia entered, preoccupied.

She wasn't alone. She felt the other presence right away.

"Are you in here, Consuela?" she called out, assuming it was the woman she paid to be in charge of janitorial service.

"It's possible, but I doubt it."

She snapped her head in the direction of the masculine baritone floating out of the bedroom to see Paris walk up the hallway.

"How did you get in here?" Security at Praise House tighter than a nun's snatch, and gaining access to the exclusive upper floor was harder to get into than said nun's puckered asshole. Paris just smiled and wrapped his arm around her waist to pull her body to his.

"Come on, ma. This is *my* city. You know that. I've got every key," he leaned in to kiss her on the neck.

But it was more than that; Paris was sending her a subtle

message, one that she received loud and clear. There was nowhere and no one that could keep him from her if he so chose. The thought terrified her, knowing what he was capable of, but there was just a trace of excitement to it, too. Like the naïf playing with the devil's fire.

As he tongued her down, Patricia began to take her stage robe off.

Paris broke off the kiss.

"No. Leave it on," he whispered in her ear. "I want you as you were on that stage, imagining what I'm doing to you now." He turned her to face the window, and then made her put her hands against the glass as he pulled her robe and dress up to her waist, exposing her shapely ass in black panties.

She felt the cool breeze of exposure while he caressed her, beginning to tease and rub through the fabric.

She had never been so turned on in all her life. She felt naked pressed up against the window for all of Brooklyn to see if it wasn't for the tinted windows. Meanwhile, five stories below, the city bustled with activity.

"We're almost ready to push the button," he said, breath husky in her ear. "I need us to be absolutely clear."

"I didn't build my empire from a storefront in Bushwick by being opaque. I know what to do. Trust me."

"I do," he said, like he was taking this woman. Later. Not yet.

"Arnold will give me Power of Attorney over this particular deal. He's going to think it's my idea because I don't trust the General, which plays on *his* distrust of the General." Her hands moved, leaving prints on the glass. Her breath misted it. "Once he reaches Liberia, he's going be kidnapped straight from the airport. A ransom will be demanded, I'll pay it, but the Liberian terrorists who see him as an American capitalist pig will still kill him. At that point, the grieving widow will control the 500 million, which I will to transfer to the General in exchange for twenty percent of the net on the subsequent arms deal. Do I get my sugar now?"

Paris chuckled and nodded, slipping her panties aside.

Faith lay back on the bed in the guest bedroom of Paris's apartment and stared at what should've been warm memories, but felt more like a movie she'd never seen before and wasn't particularly enjoying now.

Paris had had all the videotapes that Sugar Ray had taken of them growing up converted to digital files. She watched them on a 50-inch 8k QLED screen trying to connect, but they left her absolutely cold. They were all variations of her up there, her smile, but that was where it ended.

It didn't matter if she was the giggling toddler or baby taken drunken first steps into a stranger's arms. She assumed it was her father, but it could have been the mail man for all the connection she felt, though it did make her smile to see that even as a child she was trying to take giant steps. That felt like a metaphor for tackling life.

"Look at my Achilleía, with the big girl steps," Sugar Ray chuckled proudly.

"Baby, tell me again why you wanted to name her Achilleía," came the same faceless voice she'd heard earlier; Achilleía's mother. Her mother.

Sugar Ray smiled into the camera, "Because she's gonna be the toast of the town."

Faith rewound that part three times.

"Toast of the town."

"Toast of the town."

"Toast of the town."

In the next shot she was maybe eight, wearing a ballerina tutu and spinning around.

"Look Mommy!" she squealed.

Her pirouette was perfect.

She went through scenes of her at Rucker Park, playing

basketball. Her crossover looked like an ankle breaker and her three-pointer was deadly. After that, she began to grow into the woman she was now.

"I just want to say to my future self," Achilleía said to camera, one hand on her young hip, eyes as bright as diamonds. "Even you don't look this good."

Faith burst out laughing at her own audacity.

"I like your style," she told the young woman on the screen.

She saw a young Paris, he maybe twelve in the scene, which made Achilleía eighteen. It was his birthday. He was surrounded by little female admirers and wannabe little thugs, but Achilleía was right beside him, singing the loudest. She could see they were close. Proper brother sister love.

And then she saw him.

Even on screen, his image gave her a chill.

Chiron.

He was dressed in a designer suit and custom-made gator boots.

He tried to kill me, she reminded herself.

Still, it was strange; of all the faces and memories she'd seen, his was the only one that made her feel anything. And it wasn't about looks. She watched them clowning each other in front of the camera, her jumping on his back and him tickling her until squealed.

"To my future self, should I marry this nigguh, or what?" Achilleía questioned the camera, doing her best to look serious.

"To my future self: run!" Chiron yelled over the top of her, attempting to jump off and do just that, but Achilleía put him in a headlock and dragged him to the floor. All Faith could see was their legs, but she could hear them kissing.

"Polyxena, cut the damned camera and get out, I ain't making no sex tape!" Achilleía yelled off camera, then a hand covered the screen amid a lot of laughter. These were just friends having a lot of fun together, being friends above all else.

What had happened to turn this into the bullet in her head?

She touched the scar above her left ear.

It had been there since she was a child according to Hector, but he lied. The more she thought, the more she questioned everything she was. Thinking about him turned to thoughts of Jada. Every day she thought of her daughter, yearned for her and dreaded hearing news reports that she'd lost the fight of her little life. She was too scared to check the Internet, though and the as far as the news on TV was concerned the world had moved on. She was old news.

Faith skipped the digital file ack band replayed it, getting up to the part where Achilleía was singing "Happy Birthday" to a twelve-year-old Paris, then adding with a flourish, "I love you, baby brah!"

"I love you too, big sis," came the reply.

But it wasn't on the screen.

Faith turned around to see him standing in the doorway, leaning against the frame.

"How long have you been there?" Faith questioned, wiping her eyes.

"A few minutes," he replied, coming in and sitting beside her on the bed.

He looked at the screen, at their image, his and Achilleía's, frozen in time.

"You like that? I took all the old home videos and had them edited professionally.

There's plenty because you and Pop loved that damned the camera," he smiled.

"You must've loved," she began, then caught herself and said, "—Achilleía very much."

He looked at her sincerely, and replied, "I did, and I do."

She could tell he was telling the truth. He did love Achilleía, but it was easier to love a dead sister than a live sister he had been forced to compete with. He'd never wanted to kill Achilleía, but she would always side with Chiron, and that meant they both had to go. It was jungle law. Survival.

But now that she was back, it was different, wasn't it? She didn't know who she was. Could he keep her onside? If he could, surely that would bury any chance Chiron had of ever getting out. And, for the streets to see her by his side, he just imagined it, knowing how it would stop all the haters and prove for all to see who was really supposed to run the family.

"What happened to," there was a slight but noticeable hitch before she said, "your mother? You don't talk about her."

Paris hung his head, "She's dead. She died a long time ago. AIDS."

"I'm sorry."

"No, you're not. You hated her, Achie. Really and truly hated. You never forgave her."

"How could I—I mean, how could she not forgive her own mother for something? What crime could be so awful it was beyond forgiveness?"

Paris looked at her and answered, "I can answer that one easily enough, sis, she was the cheating whore who gave it to Daddy." Paris shrugged. "Your words. But unlike you, I don't blame her though, I blame him," he smiled and shook his head. "He was the one who was always fucking around. Different broad every night. Pussy in every state was the running joke, damn near, every county. The ladies loved a bit of Sugar Ray. Don't get me wrong, he loved Mommy, he gave her everything—"

"Except him," Faith cut in.

Paris looked at her, surprised, "That's what you said then, too. Exact same words."

"Because it's true. How can a man love you if he's always fuckin' around?"

"Men love different."

"Bullshit," she spat.

"Maybe. Maybe not. Anyways, Mama got fed up. She wanted

him to see how it felt so she cheated. It was a one-night stand. She never even saw the guy again. But he left her a little something to remember him by until the end of her days. She didn't use protection and he was HIV-positive. Crazy, right? How's your fuckin' luck? Pop fuckin' all over town, but Mama do it once and life's a bitch then you die," he finished bitterly.

Faith let it sink in, "So how could Achilleía not forgive that? I mean, the way you explain it, it's not some huge crime it's a woman crying out for love...."

"Because you was always Sugar Ray's baby girl," he replied. She could hear the jealousy and envy that he tried to hide. "He could do no wrong. He walked on muthafuckin' water."

"It must have been more than that."

Instead of answering, Paris just stared at the screen.

"I wish you could remember. We were happy back then."

"Achilleía?"

Faith and Paris turned to look at the door to find Medea standing there. He face was haunted. Maybe because she was seeing a ghost.

Torn.

That was the best word to describe Medea in the moment.

Torn.

Ever since that conversation with Quadir, she'd been second-guessing her engagement.

Just like Quadir had predicted, Paris had told her, as soon as they got married, there were several accounts he wanted to transfer into her name. Did that make him psychic, really smart, or just someone who knew how the game was being played? Not that she'd argued with Paris. If that was what he needed, she was there for him.

Wasn't this the reward for her loyalty that she felt she deserved?

But now that she had it in her reach, she hesitated.

"I've never let you down before," Quadir had reminded her.

He was right, he hadn't. He was one constant in her life. But the problem was Qua had his own agenda. Medea didn't know if he truly loved her or if he wanted to use her. The same could be said of all the men in her life. At the end of the day, she only wanted to be loved. To be a good woman to a good man and leave all the games behind. Until then, she needed to stay on her toes, play it smart. But she was damn near knocked off her feet seeing Achilleía in the flesh.

She had been there when Quadir got the call that Achilleía was with Paris, but seeing her sitting there next to him, that was just different. It was *real*.

She was in the lion's mouth and she didn't even know it.

"Achilleía?" she had gasped, as they stared at one another.

Medea searched her eyes for *any* sign of recognition, praying that the other woman wouldn't recognize her from the hospital, because that grandmother disguise was hardly foolproof.

She stood up. "My name is Faith."

Medea looked at Paris.

She didn't get it.

Paris's eyes said, *we'll talk later*, but he said, "She doesn't remember us."

Faith didn't say anything, but she was thinking, *oh no, I definitely remember her.* She'd recognized Medea the moment she set foot inside the room. It was her eyes. You could never disguise the soul behind them. Ever. But Medea's presence confused her. She knew Polyxena was with Chiron, but Medea being with Paris didn't make sense, not when the two women were together at the hospital trying to kill her.

Faith kept her mouth shut.

Maybe Paris didn't know, her mind reasoned, but it was thin.

"I'ma let y'all get reacquainted," Paris said, then kissed Faith on the cheek.

"I'll see you later, sis."

He walked out.

Medea and Faith gazed at one another.

Suddenly, Medea's eyes clouded up, then tears began to stream down her cheeks. They were genuine. Which confused her even more. "You just don't know how good it is to see you."

Then she stepped forward and hugged faith.

Faith let her hug her, but didn't return it.

"I'm so sorry, I'm so, so, so sorry."

"For what?" Faith asked, voice absolutely devoid of emotion.

Medea pulled back and looked her in the eyes.

"For all you've been through."

Faith studied her face.

"What's your name? I saw you in the movies."

Medea frowned slightly.

"Movies?" She echoed, then noticed the home video paused on the screen. "Oh yeah, those old films."

Even if she wasn't totally Achilleía, she still had that penetrating gaze that seemed to look clean through to your soul.

Medea went around her, as if she were physically evading the question, and sat on the bed. "I'm Medea. Medea. I uploaded all of these to the cloud." She smiled gently. "Your brother don't know shit about technology. He wanted to put it all on DVDs."

"Are you his girlfriend?"

"Fiancée," Medea smiled, holding up her huge engagement ring.

Faith studied Medea coolly, the silence becoming awkward.

Medea attempted to fill it.

"I still can't believe it's you, girl," she said, shaking her head. "All this time I thought you were dead."

I bet, Faith thought to herself.

"You and Achilleía seemed close. There was someone else with you in the movies, dark skin with incredible the blue eyes?" Faith questioned.

Medea scowled. "Ah, she's a bitch not even worth mentioning.

Polyxena. You were close until she betrayed you and started fuckin' your foul ass husband."

"Chiron?"

"You remember him?"

"No, I saw him on the movies. Why did he try to kill me?"

Medea sighed hard. "Because he wanted to take over the family, but you wouldn't cross Paris and ride with him."

"Take over the family?"

A mischievous smile spread Medea's face. "You don't know who your family is?"

"Only what I read."

"Then you don't know, jack," she said. "Your father, Sugar Ray, ran New York and half the east coast."

"Doing what?"

"You name it. He started with drugs," Medea explained. "Heroin. He invested. He grew. He created an empire, so when he died and wanted to leave it to Paris, Chiron bucked. He felt like you should run the family, which to him meant *he* would run the family. You two were inseparable."

Faith nodded, understanding why Quadir said she was a queen and didn't know it.

"What about the war? Between Paris and Chiron?"

Medea waved the question off dismissively. "No contest. Yeah, Chiron runs the prisons and a few blocks here and there, but with this move we're about to make, we're gonna crush his foul ass."

"Interesting," Faith replied, sounding anything but interested.

Medea caught her vibe and looked at her. "Look, you may not remember me, but you really are like a big sister to me, so since you're back, I thought maybe we can do it for old time's sake."

Faith looked at her strangely.

"Do *what*?"

"What we do best, shop 'til we drop."

31

Quadir took every reasonable precaution to get to the meeting, and quite a few unreasonable ones, too. He was beyond cautious. Risks got you killed.

He didn't even drive to New Jersey.

He took the subway.

His destination was a small town right outside of Newark, named Roselle, a mixed working-class city, last stop before you reached the more affluent townships.

He took a cab from Linden, a city over, and arrived at a small Haitian restaurant on St. George Avenue several hours after setting out.

"Sac pasé," Quadir greeted the old man behind the counter.

"M'ap boulé," the old man replied. "Where is Dez?"

"Downstairs."

Quadir nodded and headed for the back and the narrow wooden stairs down to the basement.

He found his two co-conspirators sitting around a round wooden table.

There was Dez, one of Paris's people, and Tech, one of Chiron's people.

Both men were suffering from the man-next-to-the-man syndrome.

They were high enough to know what power felt like, but not high enough to actually have it.

Quadir knew how to play on people's desires.

He'd promised them power if they gave him betrayal.

They were selling their soul and he was the devil.

"What up baby boy, what up fam, how are you?" he asked, all smiles as he greeted them with firm handshakes and gangsta hugs.

"You already know, my nigguh," Dez replied.

"Loungin' duke, waitin' on the next move," Tech answered.

Quadir sat down across from them, taking his gun out of his waist and placing it on the table.

"What up with shit in the city?" Dez questioned.

Quadir shook his head. "Shit 'bout to get crazy, yo. Paris about to cut off his connect, literally."

"You mean kill 'em?" Tech asked.

"Dead. Reason being, they been fuckin' with Chiron too. He let it ride because there was a bigger picture, but now shit got switched. Once he dead 'em, he can starve Chiron out, and us, too," Quadir explained.

"What you mean?" Tech wanted to know.

"The Afghans want to fuck with me, which would be perfect, but we gotta time this shit right," Quadir replied.

Both Tech and Dez nodded.

"Well, shit's official on my end," Tech assured him.

"All my soldiers waitin' for is the word from me," Dez bragged, finally feeling like a boss.

The plan was simple. Quadir was playing both sides of the fence while Paris thought he was working for him versus Chiron. Chiron thought the same, but in actuality he was working both ends against the middle.

He'd wait until the right moment, then Tech and Dez would have their respective teams move against Paris and Chiron.

And when the smoke finally cleared only those loyal to Quadir would be left standing.

It would be beautiful.

"Then that's what it is," Quadir remarked, loving the fact that the plan was coming together. "Besides," he added, "I just might have found me an ace in the hole."

His ace in the hole was the return of Achilleía, all he needed to do was convince her neither Paris nor Chiron could be trusted, which all things considered shouldn't be impossible, then the streets would definitely bow down seeing Achilleía by his side. A king with his queen.

He was obsessed and drunk on Achilleía.

Always had been.

32

Tillman had a crazy foot fetish and Polyxena had the prettiest damned feet he'd seen in his life.

It was a match made in Hell.

"Polyxena trembled, arching her back as she came.

Gazing down into those faces she pulled, ripped straight out of a porno had Tillman in a zone. Her eyes kept him in a trance, driving him wild.

"I love your pussy," he grunted, close to either a heart attack or orgasm. It was a fifty-fifty shot. Luckily for him, it was his dick that exploded, not his heart.

Polyxena needed to have Tillman primed. The General's sudden interest in Chiron pushed the clock to now or never.

"You gonna be the death of me," he chuckled.

"How would you like to make fifty grand?"

"No," he replied firmly, instantly emerging from the afterglow into the harsh reality of corruption.

"I thought you said you wouldn't let me down?"

Tillman sighed hard.

"You don't make fifty doing anything legal."

She smiled.

"I just need your institutional code."

"My code? Why?"

"To change Walter Marcson's release date," she told him, which wasn't a complete fabrication.

Tillman laughed.

"Fifty grand for that?" he shook his head, not buying it. "That's the dumbest shit I've ever heard. Doesn't that dumbass nigguh know the release date hard copies are kept in a central location, not at the facility itself? It won't do a damned thing, even if he got it changed. Central check the digital records against the hard—"

Polyxena cut him off.

"*You* know that and *I* know that, but *he* doesn't know that. It's his money, and that's why it'll be the easiest twenty-five grand you'll ever make."

"I thought you said fifty?" He questioned.

She leaned down and pecked his lips, "Howdy, partner."

Tillman shook his head and chuckled. "I'm not comfortable with this, Polyxena. But, what the hell, a nigguh and his money are easily parted. When'd you need it?"

"As soon."

"Okay, do it tomorrow," he surmised. "I won't be at work, and if something happens, I want my ass covered."

"Better idea. Why don't you cover mine?"

She turned around, offering herself up to him again.

"Goddamn, Polyxena, you must be a voodoo priestess," he said, because whatever juju she was working had him.

She laughed because he didn't know how right he was.

33

"It's good to be the queen," Faith giggled, unable to hold her tongue.

Never before in her life—not that she could remember—had she spent so much money in a single afternoon.

When Medea had suggested shopping she'd never imagined what came next. She and Hector lived a nice middle-class existence, but it was *nothing* like what Medea did.

They hit Manhattan and shopped at the biggest names and most exclusive boutiques. It was a whirlwind of luxury.

Faith felt like she had won the lottery.

The only scare came when she turned the corner, heading back to the limo, and she locked eyes with a cop. She'd frozen like a deer in headlights. He smiled and walked on. Her entire body exhaled.

Medea saw the whole exchange and grinned, "Girl, believe me, the one place the police never look for fugitives is on Fifth Avenue."

"I used to own a shoe boutique back in Philly," Faith said as they shopped.

"That sounds *just* like you," Medea snickered. "You always

had the meanest shoe game I knew. See anything you like?" Medea asked.

"Everything," Faith laughed.

Medea smirked then turned to the sales girl.

"We'd like them all in a size five and six."

By the time they got back to Paris's apartment, Faith was exhausted. She collapsed on the couch while the driver and the bodyguard came in with bag after bag.

Medea walked in, took one look at her stretched out on the couch and asked, "What are you doing?"

Faith didn't even open her eyes.

"Taking a nap, then I'm going to take a shower and go to bed."

"No."

"No?"

"Come on Achie–I mean–Faith. Why do you think we bought all these clothes? It's time you sat on your throne."

This time, Faith opened her eyes and fixed them on Medea.

"Sat on my throne?"

"Brooklyn awaits."

Faith sat up.

"Let it wait," she replied sourly.

"Don't be like that, mamacita," she winked. "We don't have to paint the whole town red, but we can at least leave a little splash."

Faith grinned. So much has happened and she was under so much stress worrying about Jade, maybe Medea was right and what she needed was to get out and breathe.

But this bitch tried to kill you, how could you party with her?

"Let me take a shower."

From the moment Faith stepped out of the limo and into the lights of the Brooklyn night, she knew what it felt like to be a star.

She was killing it.

The only thing missing was the red carpet and the paparazzi. They went to Paris's cigar bar and the minute they walked through the door, all eyes were on them. It was like Tupac himself was back, and no hologram this time.

"Achilleía!"

"It's a *miracle!*"

"Oh shit, is that *you*?"

And so it went.

Gangstas and gangsta bitches were the only people in attendance, but you would've thought they were at some kind of holy diver revival, with all the tears being shed. Everybody wanted to hug her, kiss her, or just touch her.

It was too much.

Quadir and Paris sat in Paris's dimly lit booth in the back, seeing but not being seen, taking it all in.

Paris admired how much love Achilleía got, but he was jealous too.

No matter what he did he'd never have that "it" factor that Sugar Ray had and his sister clearly had.

"Look at this shit go. They act like the bitch is the second coming," Paris huffed, angrily flicking the ash off his cigar, and adding, "If it wasn't for the General, she'd be at the bottom of the East River by now."

"Yeah, but with her by your side, motherfuckers'll know that shit Chiron been screamin' all these years is bullshit," Quadir pointed out.

"Don't you think I thought of that?" Paris snapped. "Fuck Chiron anyway! It's over for his bitch ass!"

Yours too, Quadir mused, but kept that little bit of wisdom to himself.

By the time Medea and Faith made it to their table, Paris was all smiles and brotherly love. He and Quadir stood, giving them hugs and kisses.

"Damn sis, if you looking this good, I know y'all turned my black card blue," Paris cracked, earning a conspiratorial giggle from the two women.

"I wouldn't say blue, maybe just a little sore," Quadir remarked, eyeing her like she was dessert. "I love the new haircut. It fits you."

Quadir couldn't take his eyes of her and Faith knew it.

Medea saw it, too. She wanted to kick him under the table.

"So," Paris sipped his drink, "Recognize anyone?"

Faith took a casual glance around.

"No. Nobody."

"Well they damn sure recognize *you*. The queen is back," Paris said, with a smile that didn't quite reach his eyes.

"I'll drink to that," Quadir chuckled, holding up his glass.

Faith toasted him.

I bet you will, Medea seethed in her mind, shooting daggers at Quadir.

Faith sat back, taking it all in. She couldn't lie. It felt good to be pampered and treated like royalty. The eyes of the people who lined up to greet her, showed it all: love, envy, lust, and respect. But she saw fear in there, too. It scared her because she *liked* it. She'd never been feared before, and had never imagined there would be a reason for it. But like a new, exotic dish that you taste and instantly adore, the fear sang on her taste buds and it was delicious.

However, there was one woman in there who didn't feel anything at the sight of Faith beyond pure rage.

In her mind, she'd been waiting on the bitch's return for a long time, and now that this miracle had presented itself, she wasn't about to pass it up. The gods didn't do miracles twice.

The bartender was busy at the other end of the bar.

She leaned over and grabbed the razor-sharp knife he used to cut fruit wedges for drinks, and then turned in Faith's direction as she rose to go to the bathroom.

She gripped the knife tightly in her hand and quickened her pace.

Faith turned her head.

Their eyes met.

She raised the knife and aimed for the throat.

She couldn't believe her eyes.

Her fiancé was fucking another bitch in their bed.

He had her bent over, face down and ass up, banging her back out while the nasty bitch tried to stifle her scream by burying her face in the pillow.

She flipped.

"Nigguh, I know you done lost your mind!"

He looked up, but instead of acting like he was busted, he smiled and replied,

"Don't sweat it, baby. You know I got enough to go around."

She snapped and charged at him.

It took her head a minute to clear to realize he'd back-handed her and sent her flying across the room.

"Bitch, who you think you is?" Her fiancé barked, standing over her, with his big dick still dripping with the other bitch's cum.

"I can't believe you did this to me! I thought you loved me!"

Another slap.

"Shut the fuck up!"

And again, harder.

"You want this dick so bad, huh? You want it? Open your goddamn mouth!" he demanded.

The three slaps in quick succession seemed to rattle her brain, he hit her so hard the whole room tilted.

Tears lined her face. She felt so humiliated. She swore if she ever saw that bitch again, she would kill her.

The other bitch's name was Faith.

Or so Hector would have her believe.

"No, no, her name was—"

"Faith, Desire. It was Faith. Picture her face from the shoe store, remember?" Hector said calmly and patiently.

Desire had a mind ripe for memory transplantation; as long as she was under the influence of the drug, it was like a basic computer drive filled with files ready to be written and rewritten. All he had to do was open the right folder.

"Think back. When were you ever so mad, you wanted to kill?"

"My fiancé cheated on me."

Once she'd confessed that much all he had to do was cut and paste across the real memories.

It took a couple of days, but it started to take.

"The shoe store?" Desire echoed, a slight frown creasing her brow above her closed eyes.

Hector smiled.

"Can you see her face?"

"Yes."

"Clearly?"

"Yes."

"Now, you remember her from that day with T," he intoned. It was a statement, not a question.

"I remember."

"Faith fucked T."

Desire's jaw clenched, "Yes."

"And how did it make you feel?"

Tears ran from beneath her closed eyelids like rain drops.

"I was humiliated. She laughed at me."

"And that made you angry."

"Yes."

"Mad enough to kill?"

"Yes."

"What would you do if you ever saw her again?"

"I'd kill that bitch..."

Hector smiled and caressed her cheek.

"Yes, you will."

The hard part accomplished, the rest was easy.

She was a bad bitch, so it was nothing getting a job at the cigar bar. Hector knew, if Achileía was back in Brooklyn, she'd go there. It was the center of their world. Desire got hired the minute she strutted through the door.

"How you know I'm here for a job?" She simpered, because she loved attention.

"If you ain't, you should be, because you a million dollars waitin' to happen!" he explained, adjusting the sudden bulge in his pants.

She had been there almost a week before that night.

"Achilleía?"

"Oh, my God, girl, is that you?!"

Desire didn't know any Achilleía, so she paid the hoopla no mind, until she caught a glimpse of her face. She looked. She looked again. She narrowed her eyes. Recognition went off in her brain like Fourth of July fireworks.

"I knew it! Oh, bitch, it's on!" she huffed to herself.

The haircut threw her off, but they were Faith's eyes. So beautiful, unforgettable, and in this case it was a curse, not a blessing.

Desire gripped the knife tightly in her hand and sped up her pace.

Faith turned her head and their eyes met.

"I have to go to the bathroom."

"I'll go with you," Medea chimed in.

Quadir and Paris got up so the ladies could slide out.

When Faith inched by Quadir, he whispered, "We need to talk soon."

She looked at him, affirmative in her gaze.

Faith turned away.

Her eyes met Desire's. She saw the knife in her hand and the look of naked rage on her face.

"Faith! You dead bitch!" Desire screeched, just as she raised the knife.

The attack caught Faith off guard, but in the instant that Desire aimed for her throat, her features seemed to morph into the face of an angry, bearded Afghan. The club shifted into an

Afghan village, the fearsome peaks of the Hindu Kush in the background, her Ebonic ramblings morphing into Arabic exclamations.

"Allahu Akbar!"

Her tense body uncoiled and went into action.

Desire's arm swooshed in a downward arc.

Faith leaned out of her trajectory, and at the same time, grabbed the other woman's wrist with one hand and wrapped her fingers Desire's grasp on the knife.

It was as easy and deadly as that.

With Faith in control, she used Desire's momentum against her.

Faith spun her around like they were Chicago-stepping, bringing Desire's back to her chest and then guided the knife straight across her throat.

It happened so fast, half the bar didn't even see it and the for the half that did it

looked as though Desire had cut her own throat.

Blood sprayed everywhere in a long, arching pulses, splashing the walls and leaving a red streaks all the way down Faith's outfit.

Desire sunk to her knees, clutching and clawing at her throat before she fell face first to the carpet, flopping like a fish.

Faith looked down at Desire doing her death dance and said, "You fucked up my outfit."

As soon as the words were out of her mouth, her mind gasped, *where did that come from?*

Paris instantly took control of the situation before it became chaos.

"Everybody out! Duke! Bruno! Get 'em out of here now!"

He didn't have to say it twice. Half of the club was heading for the door already anyway.

Paris turned to Quadir, "Qua, get sis outta here!"

Quadir nodded and put his hand on the small of her back.

"Come on, ma."

Paris thought about dumping the body himself, but he decided against it.

Why implicate myself if he didn't have to?

The decision made sense, but little did he know, that one decision would come back to haunt him in the most unexpected way.

"You're not safe here, Faith," Quadir told her, as soon as they got in the car.

"I'm not safe anywhere," she mumbled.

"But of all places, why the fuck did you go to Paris's? I told you he sent me to kill you!"

"Yeah, but you neglected to tell me Chiron is in jail for actually doing the very same thing!" she spat back.

Quadir shook his head.

"He didn't do it."

"Obviously," she retorted.

"No, I mean, he wasn't the one who pulled the trigger."

Faith looked at him.

"Then why did he plead guilty?"

Quadir sighed hard, "It's complicated."

"I bet."

They rode in silence for a block.

"Look, face to face, I wouldn't trust Chiron either," Quadir said, acting as if it was hard for him to say.

"I don't."

"But you can trust *me*," he told her, looking in her eyes.

Her hard gaze softened.

"How do I know that?"

"You don't. But look at the situation. I haven't let you down yet."

Faith nodded. While she might not know anyone else's motives, she understood his. And that knowledge meant she could control him—or at least manipulate him. So tentatively, she began to play her game.

"You're all I got," she confessed, like it was the secret at the center of her universe. The words went straight to his heart and the gas went straight to his head.

"Shit, I'm all you need," he replied.

"She said Faith."

"Huh?"

"That girl with the knife. She called me Faith. Not Achilleía. She knew my name."

Quadir scowled, "Are you sure?"

"Positive"

He thought about that for a second. "You ever seen her before?"

"Maybe. I don't know."

"Well, keep thinking."

"I'm scared."

He looked over at her. The look in his eyes was all about a superhero putting on his cape to play protector.

"Don't worry, ma," he stretched out his hand. "We'll figure this thing out, okay?"

She took his hand and smiled.

"Do you think I'll be safe at Paris's tonight?"

Quadir looked at her, "Naw, I think you'll be safer with me."

Quadir felt like a high school virgin all over again, fumbling his way through the night.

"You-um, want a drink or something?" he asked, trying to slow his speeding heart.

"No," Faith replied, giving him the look that said, *you know what I want.*

She took him by the hand and he led her to the bedroom.

As soon as they entered, she walked into his embrace. She felt him hard against her. Faith reached down, her eyes never leaving his.

"Tell me what you like," she requested.

"Ma, it's all about you," he replied, relinquishing control.

She smiled.

"Then lay back."

Quadir shed his clothes quicker than a snake and laid back on the bed. Faith stood at the foot of the bed and undressed slowly, all about the show.

"Faith, you are fucking beautiful."

"Don't call me that. Tonight, I want to be Achilleía."

He smirked, "Then let me drink you."

She crawled up on the bed like a panther.

"Say my name," she whispered.

"Achilleía."

She leaned in, close. Her kiss was so passionate, Quadir felt himself getting lost in it, until he felt wet tears against his cheeks.

"Ma, what's wrong?"

"I can't do this, Quadir. I'm sorry."

She crawled into his arms and curled up like a baby.

"Don't worry, I got you," he promised, ignoring his desperate arousal. This had to be the long game, not the hard one.

"I don't know what to do."

"Trust me. In a few weeks, we gonna be straight, okay?"

She lifted her head and looked at him, her mascara streaked and making it look like she was crying black tears.

"What do you mean?"

"Nothing. Just know we gonna be good."

She laid her head back on his chest.

"If they don't kill me first."

He pulled her tighter and kissed her forehead.

"No one will get close enough," he swore.

"Just, just hold me."

And he did.

Faith smiled to herself, because she knew she was the best fuck he never had.

34

"Everything a-go?"

"I told you, it was a piece of a cake."

"I don't want no shit out of you."

"I guarantee it'll be smooth sailing. Even the county clerk has him on the docket." "You better hope so," Polyxena warned then hung up.

It was D-Day for Chiron's plan.

She had just gotten off the phone with the computer hacker. When it came to plans, the fewest moving parts the better, and this one was deceptively simple, which, she hoped, meant it was the best. The hacker broke into the computer system of the Essex County courthouse and placed Chiron on the docket to face an armed robbery charge that never took place. He also planted transfer authorization papers in the county jail computer and the prison system using Tillman's institutional code. The stage was then set. All they had to do from there was send in two fake Essex County sheriffs to pick Chiron up at the prison gates.

Simple.

"Okay, we've got the green light. Let's move," Polyxena said, speaking into her walkie-talkie.

"Ten-four," came the reply.

She was sitting in a stolen car in the parking lot of the prison, her hair in one single long braid, and a skully on top of her head, ready to mark up.

In her cap was a fully automatically AK-47. She had several grenades in a duffel bag sitting on the passenger seat.

Her job was the emergency extraction.

If for some reason, the plan didn't carry off, if Chiron made it out of the physical prison, she was to bust him the rest of the way out.

She hoped it wouldn't come to that, but if it did, that she could handle the guards. They had no military training. It was all about their pay check for them. She didn't want to go in hard, but she was psyching herself up, eating packs of instant coffee for the caffeine rush.

"Don't worry baby, mama's here," she sent Chiron a mental message.

She watched the Essex County sheriff's car pull up to the outside prison gate.

She had to smile to herself. If she hadn't known better, the paint job would've fooled her.

Them Mexicans are some bad motherfuckas, she chuckled.

The two fake officers were both white, one male and one female. They were both sexy. One of each sex, so whoever was working the transfer desk would be so busy lusting or flirting, which would smooth the process plenty. The joys of human weakness. Polyxena knew, one slip, and the whole game was blown.

As the outside gate slid open, it was hard to contain her excitement.

She knew getting *into* prison was easy. It was the getting out that was hard.

Chiron stood in the cell, looking out the sliver of a window, with its vision of the yard and endless trees.

It's over, he thought to himself, *it's finally over*.

His bag was packed. He wanted everything to move as routinely as possible. No hitches. He checked his watch. Everything was in motion. Polyxena was his ride-or-die chick. But there was only one woman for him, and that's where he was headed. If she was in Philly, so was he. Chiron knew regardless of outcome, he was getting out that day. Either free or dead.

"I see you all packed. Where the shit you want me to hold until you get back?" Bang asked.

Chiron turned around and went over to his bunk.

He handed him a plastic bag.

"How long you think you gonna be gone?" Bang asked.

Chiron shrugged.

"Couple days, a week maybe."

Bang nodded.

"Ayo Unck, you got like a gazillion dollars, so I'm tryin' to figure it out. When did you have time to rob somebody?"

"Probably just a mistaken identity," Chiron replied, keeping a straight face.

Bang laughed, "Unck, you slick motherfucka! I know you got something under your sleeve."

Chiron smirked.

"Just hold shit down. You the boss now."

They shook hands and hugged.

"I love you, big homie."

"I love you too, lil brah."

Several minutes later, a C.O. walked to the door.

"Black, they want you in receiving. Court trip."

"My lawyer already told me. I'm ready."

Chiron picked up his bag.

"See you when you get back," Bang smirked.

When they got to Receiving, the two county officers were waiting for him. The male sheriff stepped up to him.

"Are you *Black?*" He said, emphasizing the last name.

The white officer laughed, no missing the double meaning.
"Yeah."

"Prison number."

"0-4-0-1-8-9-5," Chiron echoed.

The officer looking at his file, nodded.

"Yeah, you're Black alright."

"Put your bag down and hold out your hands," the female sheriff told him.

Her shirt was struggling to cope with the Baywatch Pamela thing she had going on.

Chiron put down his bag.

She cuffed his hands in front of him.

"These cuffs are too tight," he told her.

She shrugged, "Deal with it."

She was playing her role a little too well; he didn't appreciate it.

He bit back his anger.

She threaded the waist chain through his belt loops then linked it to his handcuff ensuring that his hands were effectively pinned to his waist, then handed him his bag.

"I'm not your fuckin' valet," she growled.

The male sheriff turned to the receiving officer.

"Where do I sign?"

"Wait a sec, there seems to be a problem with the paperwork."

Chiron's whole body went numb.

He could tell the male sheriff was nervous, but he played it off well.

"Shit, I just pick up. I don't write the order."

The receiving officer picked up the phone.

"Who are you calling?" the female sheriff asked.

The receiving officer just looked at her, but before he responded, someone picked up.

"Yeah, this is Davenport in receiving. Why hasn't this inmate's property been inventoried? I don't have the paperwork here."

The officer hung up after reaming out the hapless voice on the other line. He hung up with a muttered, "Fucking morons. Okay, go have your day in court, Black."

"We did it! You're a stone cold genius," Polyxena gushed.

The officers looked like pretty dolls. Their glassy eyes staring at the ceiling, their bodies side by side.

"They teach this in acting class, too?" Chiron quipped.

"Yeah, it's called playing dead," Polyxena snickered.

They were standing over the male and female sheriff. The only difference being the bleeding red dot in the center of both of their foreheads and the pool of brain and blood around their heads that was slowly getting wider.

Chiron took a casual step back as the blood crept to the edge of his shoe.

"Look at you, ain't been out an hour and you already got two bodies chalked up to your name," Polyxena saidd, loving his gangsta.

"That just means ain't shit changed," he smirked, adding, "You already get the goons to burn the car?"

"Of course."

"What about the hacker?"

"He'll be dead within the hour."

"And your boyfriend?" he asked with a straight face.

She punched him in the chest.

"He ain't my boyfriend, nigguh," she said. "And believe me, I've got something special planned for him. Gonna send the right message to the General."

Chiron nodded.

"Yeah, the General... I don't get it. What him come at me after all this time? He could've moved any time in the last five years... why now?"

"The General's a patient man."

"Yeah, but no, something is off," Chiron replied, thinking

about it a moment before adding, "Fuck it. We'll find out soon enough. Let's go."

"Uh oh, Chir, where you think you're going? You got one more bit of business to handle first."

"What?"

"Me," she growled, unzipping her body suit to reveal she had pure chocolate underneath.

He couldn't lie, Polyxena had the best damned body he had ever laid eyes on, and then some. Up until then, he had only seen her fully naked in selfies she sent to his celly. This was live and direct. She had the body of a goddess the way her smooth dark skin curved in all the right places, like the Big Guy had molded her personally.

"Ma, what you doin'? This is a crime scene. It's blood every-where!" he reminded her, amused by her audacity.

She strutted over to him.

"We gonna burn it down anyway. Besides, what can I say? I'm a freak. The smell of blood turns me on," she wrapped her arms around his neck. "And what I'm about to do to you is a crime."

35

Hoffman was nothing if not persistent.

He knew in his gut that Faith Newkirk was in Brooklyn and that something major would happen to put him back on the trail.

"Hey Hoff, I've got something for you," the Special Agent in Charge of the New York said down the long distance line.

"I hope it's something good," Hoffman replied.

"Well, I don't know if you can call a cold-blooded murder good, but it happened in your area of interest so maybe you would."

"Brooklyn?"

"Oh so much better that that, The Cigar Bar itself."

"I'm on my way," Hoffman said, not bothering to wait for the grisly details of the who and what. The where was enough.

He made it from Philly to New York in record time, driving like a man possessed, and headed straight to the FBI offices. The S.A. chuckled as he shook Hoffman's hand, ushering him into his office. It was the usual government chic.

"You know Hoffman, I gotta say, I feel like I'm in one of those cartoons," he said. "You know the one? Where Bugs calls Elmer

Fudd from across the country, then hangs up and walks straight into Elmer's house?"

Hoffman couldn't help but laugh. "You saying I look like Elmer?"

"Well, now you mention it, there is a passing resemblance."

More easy laughter. Cop humor. With the pleasantries out of the way, the Special Agent slid a file across the desk. Hoffman picked it up and opened it.

"You owe NYPD for the heads up."

The first thing Hoffman saw was a color 8x10 of Desire dead on the floor, her throat cut ear-to-ear. "Take a close look."

Hoffman studied every inch of the shot.

It took a couple of seconds to see she had a bloody knife in her hand.

"At first, they thought whoever did it put the knife in her hand. The blood patterns are off. If someone did that, there'd blood to be under her fingers, or at least smudges, right?"

"Right."

"Wrong," the special agent explained. "Forensics says they are certain that the knife was in her hand *when* her throat was cut. The only prints were the bartenders, but they were under the blood. He said it was his knife, and he used it to cut fruit for those frou-frou drinks. Forensics found residue of fruit on the blade, confirming his story."

Hoffman stared at the picture, shaking his head.

"I don't buy it. Look at her. Why would a pretty girl like this cut her own throat in the middle of that club? Fuck... so what we looking at? Bad acid trip? LSD?"

The special agent just sat and looked at Hoffman for a moment.

He was obviously contemplating telling him something else.

"Come on, Bobby, spill it. I know that look."

He sighed and rested his elbows on the desk, pointing a finger at Hoffman.

"Okay, but you're gonna owe *me* big for this. NYPD doesn't even know."

"I'm listening," Hoffman assured him.

"Have you ever heard of Neuritrinol?"

Hoffman frowned.

"Neuro-what?"

"Neuritrinol. It's a mind-altering drug. Army Intel uses it all the time. The shit is so top secret, if you Google it, nothing comes up and the men in black turn up at your door a few hours later."

"Right. So what does this thing do?" Hoffman probed.

"It suppresses consciousness while at the same time can be used to control memories."

"I'm gonna want you to explain that to me like I'm a moron. Control memories?"

"This is military grade shit, remember. So, say you're interrogating a terrorist but you don't want him to know he's being given the third degree, you shoot him full of this shit and he's all yours. But while he's under, not only can you access his memories, you can create false ones."

"Wait, wait, no... that's fucked up. How the hell you do you *create* memories?"

"Suggestion. Think of it like hypnosis. You make a person *think* they remember something that never actually happened. Paint in the detail so they believe it."

"And she had it in her system?"

"She was full of the shit."

"Shit."

"Shit indeed. Now guess where her body is?"

"Where?"

"No, really, guess, because we haven't got a fucking clue. It's gone. It's not in the morgue, it just fucking disappeared."

"And you're thinking what I'm thinking?"

"I'm not thinking," the Special Agent spat. "It's in some messy box plastered with do not open tape courtesy of the U.S. government."

Hoffman had come to the fork in the road.

He knew this investigation could lead to something that could cost him his career, or more likely his life. On the other hand, there was the age-old desire of man: *curiosity*.

He just hoped he wasn't about to become a dead cat.

Hector lit a Marlboro and inhaled deeply.

He thought he'd kicked the habit, but smoking is like riding a bike, you never forget. The first hit of nicotine made him dizzy, not just from the head rush, but from the memories. *The sound of gunfire, metal bullet casings falling like deadly rain. Screams. Explosions. The whistle of a missile right before an explosion.* It all came rushing in with the smoke.

"Cut her own throat, my ass," he grumbled, inhaling his bitterness right along with the cigarette smoke. Only a fucking idiot would believe that, and he was a lot of things, but a fucking idiot wasn't one of them.

He knew in his gut *exactly* what happened had happened.

Achilleía happened.

It was her signature move; when someone tried to attack her in close combat, either with a gun or knife, she was so quick she reversed the attack, and used the attacker's momentum against them.

Hector shook his head and sucked more smoke.

He would always love her but things had gotten too messy.

She had to go.

In country, their mission had failed for one reason. She refused to give up the one truth he'd been assigned to find: *what happened in that cave.*

Pop! Pop!

Chaff flares exploded off the C-17's stubby wings, as the jet itself swung around into a corkscrew. Hector's fist lay tightly balled in his lap. The plane leveled, then a few seconds later, touched the ground, bounced, and grazed the ground again as it shot along the 10,000-foot runway. The brakes and thrust reversers kicked in and the C-17 stopped in one long, smooth motion.

"Welcome to Brigham Air Force Base, thirty miles north of Kabul, Afghanistan. Enjoy your vacation, gentleman," the pilot joked, knowing this trip would be anything other than a vacation.

"*Hoo-ah!*" came the guttural grunt of the 504th Parachute Infantry Regime of the 82nd Airborne.

Hector couldn't help but smile.

He loved every inch of being a soldier, fighting for your country, kicking ass all over the world. The cry came from his gut, but he meant it with all of his heart.

"Hoo-ah!"

It was shorthand for "heard, understood, and acknowledged" and it was their rallying cry as they got off the plane.

As soon as he got settled in, he headed straight back out, looking for Achilleía.

He found her relaxing with Polyxena in the rec room watching a soccer game on the big screen.

He tiptoed up behind the couch and put his hands over her eyes.

"Whoever you are, go away," she replied lazily, matching her slouched demeanor.

"Is that any way to treat a long lost friend?" Hector replied, trying to sound charming. He removed his hands. Achilleía looked over her shoulder at him.

He would never forget the look of cold suspicion on her face. "What are you doing here, David?"

Looking into her eyes in that split second, his mind automatically asked, *does she know? She can't know. There's no way.* But she acted taken aback.

"Hello to you too, Achilleía."

She stood up and rounded the couch.

She grabbed his hand and led him out of the building.

Polyxena watched them leave, expressionless, then turned back to the game.

Outside, Achilleía found a secluded spot then turned to him.

"No seriously, David, not that it's not nice to see you, *why* are you here?"

"The same reason you are, I was assigned," he replied, with a nonchalant shrug as if it were no big deal. But looking into Achilleía's eyes, he knew she could see right through him, so he went with a different lie, the one she expected. "Besides, I missed you."

Achilleía rolled her eyes.

"Bullshit."

"Bullshit? You don't think I missed you?"

"No, bullshit about being assigned," she said. "We already have a military intelligence officer assigned to this mission, we don't need two."

"Well, technically, I'm not here in my official capacity."

"Meaning?"

"Meaning I'm strictly advisory," Hector answered.

Achilleía eyed him.

"I'm just following orders, Achie, just like you," he tried to reach for her. "But I did miss you."

She stepped back.

"Don't do that, David. I told you before we shipped out, it's over."

"Just like that, huh?"

"David, let it go, okay? It was fun while it lasted, but my itch is scratched. You'll have to scratch your own," Achilleía shrugged as if to say *c'est la vie*.

He chuckled to contain the boil of irritation.

"Don't I have a say in this?"

"You knew I was married."

"I'm not asking you to leave him, I'm just asking you not to leave me." It almost sounded reasonable when he said it.

Achilleía allowed herself to soften. She sighed. "David, I'll always have love for you, but that's it. It was just sex, okay? Good sex, sure. But that's it. There's no friendship. No love. It's done."

With that she turned to walk away.

"Achilleía."

She looked back, and before he could speak, she said, "We're from two different worlds, David. Trust me, it would've never worked out even if I did love you."

Shee walked away, leaving the bitter taste of her departure in his mouth.

"Goggles!" Captain Johnson, the commander of the C-Company, hollered.

Hector had been so focused on psyching himself up he was startled by the noise of the Black Hawk starting up. He stuffed in his earplugs and pulled down his goggles as the helicopter's rotors kicked up to full speed, sending dust and pebbles in a whirl along the tarmac.

"Ready?" Johnson yelled.

"Yeah! Hoo-ah!"

Hector's enthusiasm was on one thousand.

He was ready to take on the world, cradling his fully automatic M-16.

The screech of the Black Hawk's 1800 horsepower turbines rendered his earplugs virtually useless.

The ten-ton helicopter bounced slightly off the runway, eager to be back up in the skies where it belonged.

He glanced down the tarmac and watched Special Forces board a second Black Hawk.

He saw Achilleía duck beneath the rotors as she climbed aboard and wished he were with her. He didn't want it to end like this, but it wasn't like he had a say in his own life.

He tried to focus his mind on the mission.

The Black Hawks rose together, banked left, then headed east, being escorted by two Apache attack helicopters. They flew just two hundred feet above the ground, staying low. That altitude made them harder to hit with surface-to-air missiles or rocket-propelled grenades.

Their mission was simple, but extraordinarily important.

The Taliban had kidnapped Hamid Karzai and because of their extremist brand of Islam, he was to be executed live on TV. The world at large hadn't heard of Karzai yet, so it wasn't as though anyone would know how devastating his death would be to America's ultimate goal, uniting the rival tribes to fight the Taliban. But it mattered because one day not too far away Karzai would be lead his people.

Satellite photographs showed that he was being held in a camp deep in the Kunar Valley.

Hector looked out at the massive mountain ranges that seemed to cut Afghanistan off from the rest of the world. He could picture all the interconnected tunnels and caves that had been cut through them for thousands of years. It was like an art form. If you could cut away a cross section and see inside, you would see another world of hundreds, if not thousands, of Taliban soldiers stashing everything from drugs, to money, to guns, and at that moment, the future Afghan president, assuming he wasn't already dead.

"No white flags!" Hector yelled at Johnson, as he looked into the Kunar Valley.

"You were expecting some?" Johnson yelled back.

Hector chuckled, "Then let's help the bastards get their wings!"

"Hoo-ah!"

The Black Hawks pulled back so the Apaches could take the lead.

They were preparing battle space for the insertion—or in layman's terms they were about to blast the camp wide open so the Black Hawks could dead-drop twenty-two Special Forces-trained soldiers to take on the guerillas down there.

The AGM-44N hellfire missiles lit up the predawn sky like Armageddon had come first to Afghanistan, catching Muslims during their morning prayer.

Twenty-pound warheads, filled with fine aluminum powder, were wrapped around the explosives.

They sprayed molten shrapnel in every direction, killing anyone unlucky enough to be within a twenty-five-foot radius.

Hector watched a third missile zip through the air, trailing white exhausts and before it exploded in an orange fireball.

The crew chief held up five fingers signaling that they would reach the landing zone in five minutes.

The soldiers nodded.

They were expressionless.

In the zone. Itching to be inserted onto the battlefield.

The guerillas tried to fire RPGs, but they didn't have the range to do any real damage.

The Black Hawks reached the landing zone.

Hector put on his night vision goggles.

"Let's rock and roll!!" another soldier barked.

Over the LZ, the soldiers leaned forward, prepared to unhook their harnesses and rappel into battle. Side by side, the two copters descended, while on the plateau, guerillas fired AK-47's that bounced harmlessly off the Kevlar mats that insulated the inner cabin.

The Black Hawk gunners returned fire with .50 caliber-mounted guns.

The brass jackets poured like water from the guns, falling to the valley floor. Guerillas fell by the dozens.

"Now!" Johnson screamed. "Now!"

Almost in unison, the soldiers unharnessed and began to repel down from fifty feet in the air. They looked like deadly puppets on vicious strings, dropping rapidly then jumping the last ten feet.

Hector was one of the first to touch ground.

He wasted no time engaging the enemy. His M-16 screamed into action, cutting down four guerillas, blowing one of their heads off clean off their shoulders. He looked around, knowing even as he did it he was looking for Achilleía. Even on the battlefield, his instinct was to protect her. That was the kind of shit that would get both of them killed. Even so, he couldn't help himself. He spotted her. She was more than capable of taking care of herself, as the Taliban were learning to their short-lived regret.

She moved like a dancer; fluid, fast and fatal.

That was the first time he'd seen her in battle.

He watched as a guerilla came off her blindside, wielding a bayonet AK-47.

He wanted to scream out a warning but there was no way she'd hear him over all the cacophony of war. He didn't need to. He saw her react at the last possible second, as though she'd lured her attacker in, only to show him she'd been the attacker the whole time.

Achilleía sidestepped the sharp point like a matador, and grabbed the guerilla's arms as he stumbled by, twisting them until the bayonet was pointed up under his chin. She used his own momentum to stab up clean into his brain.

The guerilla fell to his knees, very dead even before Polyxena put her M-16 in his ear and sent his brains flying so far, it was like his head spat them out.

His body collapsed without so much as a final twitch.

Hector heard it before he felt it; the rasp of a guerilla throwing a grenade his way.

He'd been trained to recognize the signature sounds of different types of grenades. That training was the only thing that saved his life, giving him the split second to throw himself behind cover before the explosion ripped him to shreds.

Even so, the concussive impact lifted him several feet into the air.

When he hit the ground, he broke his leg with a brutal snap.

His shrieks tore across the field of combat.

"Man down! Man down!" a fellow soldier barked, laying down covering fire to shield him and riddling the grenade-throwing guerilla until what was left of his corpse he seemed to explode with blood.

But that was the moment Hector regretted. He saw Polyxena, Achilleía, and two more soldiers enter the cave. They were the extraction team. They were going in to get Karzai. Once she disappeared from view, he blacked out from the pain.

He knew something happened in that cave. Something of monumental consequence because it changed her fundamentally and nothing he could do could prize what happened out of her.

"I guess now we'll never know," he mused to himself, as he chucked the cigarette butt out of the car window.

His only concern now was making sure no one found out what he'd done to her.

He watched Hoffman walk out of the federal building. Hector knew why he was there and what the S.A.C. had told him.

Followed him at a discrete distance, Hector was determined it wouldn't become a game of Chinese whispers. Hoffman wouldn't get to tell anyone else.

36

"Turn it off," the General said.

His voice was calm but his Lieutenant, McDuffy, knew the General was boiling inside. He picked up the remote and zapped the TV, blacking out the image of Steinbach being led in cuffs to a police car.

The General didn't need to see it play out on CNN. He well aware of exactly what happened. Steinbech had murdered Captain Tillman as he came out of his house. Gunned him down right in the driveway. He was apprehended going to work. He didn't bother trying to deny the charges. He claimed, for the entire world to hear, "The General ordered his assassination! I'm only a soldier!"

It hadn't taken the journalists to put the pieces together and realize which General he claimed was the mastermind; the highest-ranking black general in the army.

A media shitstorm ensued.

Steinbech was out of his fucking tree. He claimed all sorts of bullshit, like Tillman was a part of a sleeper cell of Al Qaeda's and had been planning a terrorist attack on US soil, and that was why the General had given the execution order.

"Nutcase," the General mumbled, pouring himself a double scotch.

But he knew Steinbech didn't invent the story out of the blue.

He knew someone had turned Steinbech and planted that insane story in his head.

Polyxena.

It had to be her. He just didn't know *how* she'd pulled it off.

"I taught you well," he mused to himself, swirling the scotch in his glass. While he may not have known how, but sure as hell knew why.

As soon as shit had hit the fan, he recognized his own tactics being used against him; create a smoke screen for the real mission. Tillman was that smoke screen. Now it was obvious that Chiron was the real mission.

"Sir, permit me to offer an analysis," McDuffy requested.

"It's a free country, soldier," the General gruffed, downing his drink.

"If Chiron is on the loose, a jailbreak is the kind of story the media eats up," McDuffy reasoned.

"No. We're not drip feeding it out there. Right now Chiron is ignorant to the fact we're onto him. He's enjoying his first taste of freedom in a long time. Let him enjoy. Hell, no denying he earned it." The General chuckled. "There are two kinds of lies in this world, soldier, and one of them is the truth. We live in a land that prefers to believe the lies. They're less fattening and taste great."

37

Medea woke up to the delicious feeling of sex.

She moaned, her eyes rolling up in her head as she arched her body into his tongue.

She always slept naked.

"I'm... oh God I'm—" she panted, her heart racing and her body trembling. And then she begin to spasm, and cried out his name, "Quaaaa-dir!"

It wasn't Quadir down there.

It was Paris.

Quadir lay back on the bed, smoking a blunt of sour diesel and feeling like a king.

In the background, he listened to the sound of the shower, and smiled to himself, thinking about who was in there, soaping up.

Achilleía.

They hadn't had sex. It didn't matter. He was already imagining the future. *With her by my side,* he told himself, *the streets will burn!* He could already see nigguhs kissing the ring.

The shower went off.

A few minutes later Faith emerged from the bathroom, wrapped in a towel.

"You know scientists say it's better to air dry. Good for your skin," he assured her.

Faith chuckled.

"I'll keep that in mind."

Quadir's phone rang on the nightstand.

He was so mesmerized by Faith's glow, he wanted to ignore it, but it kept vibrating against the cheap fake wood.

"Aren't you going to answer that? It could be important."

"Not as important as you," he said smoothly, and then reached over and checked the caller ID.

His smile disappeared.

"Who is it?"

"Chiron."

Hearing the name made her stiffen reflexively.

"Don't worry, ma. Remember, he locked up."

With that he answered the phone.

"What up Unck, how you?" Quadir greeted, cheerfully.

"You already know, nephew. Can't keep a good man down," Chiron replied.

Then you must not be a good man because you still down, Quadir thought, enjoying the joke.

"What's good on your end? Where you at?"

"Laid back at the crib with a young tender," Quadir replied, while winking at Faith.

She was felt a knot in her stomach. Instincts were telling her something was wrong.

Chiron chuckled in his ear.

"Okay pimpin', I hear you," Chiron said. "But listen, I got somethin' to talk to you about. So, stay right there, I'm sending my peoples to holla."

"No prob, Unck. Like I said, I got my hands full," Quadir chuckled arrogantly.

"Good to know."

The line went dead.

"What did he say?" Faith asked.

Quadir shrugged. "Not much. He sendin' somebody through to holla at me."

"I've got to get dressed. I can't be here when they arrive."

Quadir hopped off the bed. "Ma, really, you good. We good. Plus, we ain't even finish what we started." He stood behind her, massaging her shoulders and kissing her neck.

Faith subtly moved away, just enough for him to notice. It prickled his skin. "I told you, Qua, I need some time."

Quadir did well to keep the frustration out of his tone as he said, "Then, I'll get you a watch, but ma, you know what I need."

They heard a knock on the door.

Faith looked at Quadir, her expression bordering on blind panic.

He found it pretty amusing. "Ma, will you just relax? I told you, we good, I mean goddamn, the nigguh is in a maximum-security prison a million miles from here."

Hearing his words made her feel slightly better.

Maybe she was being paranoid?

Still, there was that feeling in her gut.

"Stay back here. I'ma go see who it is."

She nodded her head, but as soon as he walked out of the room, curiously got the best of her and she followed him out into the living room.

Her footsteps were so light, Quadir didn't even know she was behind him.

He opened the door and froze, rooted to the spot.

Polyxena awoke with a start.

She had the feeling like she was falling. The sensation jolted her from her sleep. What was it they said about hitting the ground in your dreams? She rolled over to cuddle with Chiron, only to find an empty bed.

She sat up, pissed.

Something wasn't right.

She got up, naked, and went to the bathroom.

"Chir?" she called out.

No answer.

She grabbed her phone and hit him on the burn out he was carrying.

He answered on the second ring.

"Yo."

"Don't 'yo' me. Chir, where are you?" she asked.

"Ma, what I tell you about questioning me? I—"

"I earned that right, nigguh, so don't give me that bullshit. I asked you a simple question," Polyxena spat.

A short pause.

"You right, ma. I'm sorry. You my ride-or-die chick for real. I swear. But I gotta handle something'."

"Why you ain't wake me?"

"Because I have to handle this alone."

Polyxena's stomach knotted. There was only one thing he wouldn't want her around to help with.

"You're going to Philly, aren't you? To face Achilleía." Polyxena sucked in her breath to try to fight back the tears.

"Come on, ma. She is my *wife*."

The word stung like a slap and jarred the tears loose.

"*Was* your wife, nigguh, *was*! Past fucking tense," she reminded him. "Or have you forgot she married the white boy she was fuckin' behind your back, had a daughter, and started a new fuckin' life? She left you for dead, Chir!"

Chiron shook his head.

He knew every word of it was the truth, but something inside him told him, in this case, the truth wasn't enough.

There was more and he wanted to know it.

"Polyxena, she lost her mem—"

"Believe that shit if you want to," she huffed. "Just tell me one thing Chiron, do you love her?"

Without hesitation he replied, "Yes, I do."

It was like a knife to the gut.

"Do, do you love me?"

Again, no hesitation.

"Like crazy, ma, like crazy. Believe me this is as confusing for me as it is for you. I just need to know," Chiron explained.

"Just come back to me, Chiron. Promise me you'll come back to me," she hated that she sounded so needy. This wasn't who she was. And yet it was, now. Because of him.

"I promise, baby, I promise. I love you."

He hung up and put the phone down on the passenger seat.

He was about to see the streets ablaze, but before he did, he needed to find Achilleía, look her in the eyes, and finally know the truth.

After he'd spoken to Quadir, he headed straight for his place.

He didn't want anyone to know he was out.

The only thing better than being a fly on the wall was being the surprise at the front door. It wasn't that he didn't trust Quadir, he needed absolute secrecy for what he had planned.

When he got to the building, he took a cautious look around then put on a Yankee fitted and pulled it low. He tucked his .38 snub in his beltline, then got out and entered the building. Taking the stairs, Chiron reached Quadir's floor less than a minute later.

He knocked.

He waited.

He started to knock again.

He heard the locks turning.

The door opened.

He froze.

Faith gasped.

Seeing Chiron up close and personal did something to her that totally fucked up her insides. She wanted to run, but her feet wouldn't move.

Quadir couldn't believe his eyes.

Chiron couldn't believe his.

They were both frozen.

Chiron recovered first. He caught Quadir with a vicious left hook that knocked him out cold before he slid down the wall and his body slumped to the floor.

Chiron was in a rage, seeing his wife clad only in a towel in what was supposed to be his man's apartment. It was too much for his boiling brain to process. Without even thinking, he pulled out his pistol and aimed it at Quadir's head.

"Chiron, please! No! Don't do it!" Faith screamed, only to him it was Achilleía screaming and always would be. Hearing his name come out of her mouth reached through his rage and grabbed his heart.

He looked at her.

"What. The. Fuck. Are. You. Doing. Here?" he seethed.

"I swear, we didn't do anything! I swear! He's been protecting me!" She explained, willing to say anything because Quadir's life was at stake.

Chiron looked down at Quadir's unconscious face.

A part of him was already seeing his brains all over the floor.

The other part was struggling with Achilleía's presence. Her words.

"Get your clothes, you're coming with me," he instructed her.

"No!" she spat, backing away.

When she saw him coming at her, gun in hand, her frazzled mind shrieked: *he's going to finish the job.*

She turned and streaked into the bedroom, slamming the door and locking it behind her.

That flimsy door and its pathetic privacy bolt were no match for Chiron's passion to have her.

He kicked the door off the hinges, one well-placed foot beside the lock plate, splintering the wood, and stepped inside. She grabbed her phone. He slapped it out of her hand and grabbed her arm.

"Get off me!" She grunted, swinging a punch that missed by a full foot.

Then it hit her.

Whenever she had been attacked, what she had come to think of as her "superpowers" kicked in.

Her breathing regulated, her body felt like a tightly coiled cobra, ready to strike.

But now, nothing.

She was fighting like a girl. Chiron flung her on the bed and her towel came loose. Her nakedness glistened like a diamond.

"Achilleía," he groaned.

She was still every bit as beautiful as he remembered.

She snatched up the bed sheet and wrapped it around herself.

"My name is Faith," she spat back at him, denying him.

Her nakedness had quenched his rage like water on a fire and she could see the tenderness in his eyes.

"No ma, you are my Achilleía," he crooned. "I'd recognize you even if I was blind." He came closer.

She kicked him in the shin.

He smacked the shit out of her.

When he was done, he stood over her. "I told you to get your goddamn clothes!"

"If you're going to kill me, kill me! I'm not going anywhere with you!" She screamed.

It hurt Chiron to hear those words come out of her mouth. How could she think he would ever kill her?

But it confirmed what he already knew.

She wasn't herself.

"Forgive me," he said and before she knew it, Chiron drew back and delivered a blow that took her out.

She fell back on the bed.

To be continued...

THANK YOU

We truly hope you enjoyed this title from Kingston Imperial. Our company prides itself on breaking new authors, as well as working with established ones to create incredible reading content to amplify your literary experience. In an effort to keep our movement going, we urge all readers to leave a review (hopefully positive) and let us know what you think. This will not only spread the word to more readers, but it will allow us the opportunity to continue providing you with more titles to read. Thank you for being a part of our journey and for writing a review.

KINGSTON IMPERIAL

Marvis Johnson — Publisher
Kathy Iandoli — Editorial Director
Joshua Wirth — Designer
Bob Newman — Publicist

Contact:
Kingston Imperial
144 North 7th Street #255
Brooklyn, NY 11249
Email: Info@kingstonimperial.com
www.kingstonimperial.com

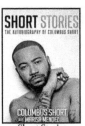

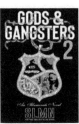

CPSIA information can be obtained
at www.ICGtesting.com
Printed in the USA
LVHW051534270121
677331LV00005B/5